KILL OR DIE

Have a nice game!
Alex Toxic

B O O K   T H R E E

M A G I C   D O M E   B O O K S

Kill or Die
Book #3
Copyright © Alex Toxic 2024
Cover Art © Linni 2024
Cover Design: Vladimir Manyukhin
English translation copyright © Monty Cantsin 2024
Published by Magic Dome Books, 2024
ISBN: 978-80-7693-787-1
All Rights Reserved

TABLE OF CONTENTS:

CHAPTER 01

AT FIRST I DIDN'T REALLY GRASP what Anna had just told me. It just didn't register, and the significance of it only began to dawn on me after a short pause during which we said nothing and simply stared at each other.

"Wait, what do you mean it never happened? I thought that was when your father died, wasn't it?"

Anna shrugged her shoulders without saying anything. There was so much bitterness and disappointment in this gesture that I suddenly wanted to go over, give her a hug and console her, as if she were a little girl.

I tried to imagine the horror of a child being told her parents were gone, while she stubbornly believed everyone around her was lying and that her dad was still alive.

"Did you try to explain it to them?" I didn't

even know who "them" referred to when I asked this question.

"Many times," Anna said thoughtfully, as if reliving the entire situation. "To the police, the doctors, the social workers, my father's colleagues, my mother's relatives…"

"And then?"

"They locked me up in a psychiatric ward for six months," the girl frowned. "They said I had a nervous breakdown. I would still be stuck in there if I didn't start telling them what they wanted to hear."

Sergei Zvyagin — the brilliant mathematician and inventor of MosTech's AI — was alive! This news eclipsed even the revelation that Anna was his daughter. But where was he then? Who was hiding him for six years now, and more importantly why? The answer came to me all at once, but for some reason I was afraid to voice it.

"I think he's still inside, in the game." Anna confirmed my suspicion without waiting for my question. "When Lutetia went haywire, Dad was terribly upset. I'm sure he went in there and got stuck with all the others. He's alive, do you understand? My dad is *alive!*"

A desperate hope blazed in her eyes. It was evident that over all these years, she had repeated this many, many times. And very few people were willing to listen to her, much less believe her.

"Is that why you went into esports?"

"Yes, of course," Anna raised her chin defiantly. "I've been preparing for this challenge my whole life. I have to win! After all, they will send only one player in there — and it has to be me."

What a splendid prize for the beta's champion, I thought. Get plugged into a crazed game that traps whoever enters it and from which no one returns. I can already see all of us beta testers, desperately jostling each other out of the way in a race for an honorable death.

"MosTech can't be too happy about you being in the beta," I suggested.

"Uncle Eli tried to talk me out of it," Anna confirmed. "When I was little, Dad practically lived at the office. My mom worked with him. She was a lab assistant. A typical story, an elderly scientist and a young intern... But the truth was that they loved each other very much. They often took me with them because there was no one else to leave me with. MosTech earned its millions later, but back then, there wasn't enough money for a babysitter, so I played in the lab. Uncle Eli... Uncle Dmitry... We were all like one family. We worked together and we relaxed together too."

"Did they ever confirm that your father was alive?" I asked.

"At first they brushed it off, and then they just went silent. But Benny wouldn't obsess over the neural network for nothing. He's the eldest son," she explained, "from a previous marriage. Though we grew up apart, we managed to become friends. Benny designed the beta. He's trying to find Dad in his own way, and I'm doing it in mine."

"And how do you plan on doing that?"

"I don't know yet, but I will find out." She looked me in the eye. "What do you think all this is for?"

"To find the best player," I offered my take.

"That too," Anna said, "but at the same time, they're watching how the neural network changes, what techniques work on it. How it could be defeated."

"They're not doing too well at that," I chuckled, recalling Yumi.

"The ends justify the means," Anna replied. "And the stakes are huge. That's why they're willing to take such risks. That's why they don't want me to win. 'I promised your father I'd look after you,'" she mimicked someone — the Master, judging by the tone. "But who will look after my father, if not me?"

"Is that why you decided to become a goddess?" I figured. "Testing out the new class?"

Anna gazed at me intently. Perhaps she realized that sharing her secrets with a stranger wasn't the best idea or maybe she appreciated my cleverness. It seemed like percentages and graphs were multiplying in her eyes, calculating whether to discuss something with this guy or to tell him to get lost. She wasn't the daughter of a Nobel laureate for nothing. Having considered all her options, Anna finally decided to reply:

"It all started with magic in Lutetia," she began, "with a spell that trapped people inside the game. It extracted their consciousness, severing the neural interface with their VR pod. That's why magic was disabled in the current beta test. It was disabled both for classes and in the skill tree. The current game world is strictly material. It wasn't until the gods started spawning that players started getting trapped again."

I felt the urge to tell her about the one healer I knew in the game who could also revive people. But I decided to hold onto that one ace up my sleeve for when I needed it.

"And you simply decided to become a goddess?" I asked instead.

"I got an invitation," she said simply to my surprise. "Players over Level 20 get access to something called 'Divine Grace.' That lets you declare yourself a god... or anything you like really. So I did. Although to be honest, I haven't figured out how the whole goddess thing works yet. But that'll come in due time."

"But why? Why do you need this?"

"The gods showed up in the alpha — in the old Lutetia as well. I don't remember the details very well and all the information about it was classified. Even from me," she answered my unspoken question. "But I do remember my father talking about it... Before everything happened. They even laughed about it, saying that the gamers had invented some gods for themselves. The players loved it though, they thought it was a nifty update."

"Why did you choose Death?"

Anna wrinkled her brow in thought. Overall, it seemed like she enjoyed talking to me. It felt like she had been mulling all of this over on her own for years and had now found someone she could share it with. I was trying hard not to scare her off, not to sever the thin thread of trust that had formed between us. And unexpectedly, I felt something familiar about her. Naturally the daughter of a world-renowned intellectual, a girl who had been born with a silver spoon in her mouth, and a guy like me weren't on the same level. However, I wasn't talking to some spoiled brat, but to an orphan who had lost her parents and was obsessed with the possibility of bringing her father back.

"Death... I think that's the key. The players who get trapped stop living *out here* and start living *in there*. I guess I figured that if they die some 'final death' inside the game, maybe they could come back to real life somehow? Well, that's just... speculation... No one knows what's really going on in there. The current world is just a children's sandbox compared to Lutetia. That world isn't merely ten times bigger... It's hundreds of times bigger..."

"And how did you learn so much about the neural network anyway? Did your father tell you all this?"

Even knowing Anna's relationship to Zvyagin, there was plenty that didn't fit into the whole picture. How much could a child see and hear? Yet Anna behaved as if she had been involved in the game's development firsthand.

Anna finished her hot chocolate in one gulp, placed the mug on the shiny dark glass table and gave me an inquisitive look.

"Alright," she nodded, more to herself than to me, "I promised you. Besides, you've demonstrated that you're not... a complete jerk. But remember, if you tell anyone any of this, no one will believe you anyway."

"Lately, I've been hearing that way too often," I chuckled. "It's gotten to the point that I don't even believe myself too much."

"Done?" Anna took my empty mug. "Then let's go."

She took my hand and pulled me after her, leading me somewhere. Was it to the bedroom?! Nah, I'd never believe that. She wasn't Marina or that sultry Dr. Skuratova.

Instead, we went upstairs and found ourselves in a bright and spacious room. It looked like a studio from movies about rich folks: a room for painting landscapes, admiring the sunset from the panoramic window, sculpting clay... or pursuing some other creative crap.

There were no easels or potter's wheels in the room, however. Just two VR pods standing in its center. I had forgotten that Anna wasn't some poor girl and could actually afford such luxuries. So then here was the secret to her refined technique in-game. I bet the other VR pod was for an instructor.

The pods resembled the ones in use at Mos-Tech, only these were bulkier, with more buttons and sensors. Probably some exclusive models with extra bells and whistles. Considering that even the cheapest immersion system cost as much as a luxury imported car, this was an impressive sight indeed.

But what was she going to surprise me with? Training exercises that I had gone through dozens of times? A gladiator duel in the arena?

"What are you waiting for?" asked Anna. "You can't get into the pod in that sweater."

"I know," I grumbled. "Where should I put the clothes?"

There was nothing in the room except for the VR pods: no chairs, no tables, not even a regular hanger.

"I don't know," Anna shrugged. "I usually come in naked. I live alone. Just throw it on the floor."

Maybe a week ago I would have felt embarrassed. But now I simply pulled my sweater off over my head, undid my belt and undressed calmly and unhurriedly under Anna's interested gaze.

"You work out?" she remarked.

"I unload pallets of vodka in a warehouse," I replied completely seriously. "It's like a hobby."

Anna burst into laughter, doubling over and slapping her knees.

"What a champ!" she gasped between laughs. "This guy unloads vodka for a hobby! What a hero! How did they even let you into the beta?!"

"Well, they let anyone in," I replied coolly. "I saw the ad just like everyone else."

Still chuckling, Anna helped me into the pod,

checked the device was running fine and shut the lid.

A SPIRAL... THREE... TWO... ONE... *Whoooosh!*

I was standing in the town square — the same exact one I knew so well from the beta by now, and yet at the same time an entirely different instance of it.

It was evening and the streetlights were coming on — not by themselves, but rather ignited by a whimsical lamplighter in a crumpled top hat. He was climbing up a rickety ladder, fetching a firefly from the latticed cage on his belt and placing it into the glass lamp. The fireflies in the cage fluttered anxiously, swirling like a tiny twister and shining as brightly as the sun.

The sound of music reached me from somewhere in the distance. Violin or flute. Something drawn-out, melodious... slightly wistful. The melody didn't intrude but was perfectly audible, as if played nearby.

NPC couples strolled across the square. Dignified, unhurried, they conversed quietly, listened to the music and admiring the low, large stars. Some led big-eyed fluffy lemurs on leashes, their pets clicking their claws loudly on the cobblestones. As one respectable couple came walking past me, they nodded to me and I nodded back.

I looked myself over. I was wearing a white shirt with loose sleeves, a gold-embroidered waistcoat, wide dark trousers and comfortable soft boots. I resembled a successful pirate or a duelist.

"So this is how you see yourself in your imagination," I heard.

Anna hurried my way through the strolling couples. She wore a straight white dress with a narrow red belt and red sandals. Her unruly hair was braided into a loose braid. Not very medieval, but very charming.

"Where's your weapon?" was the first thing I asked.

"It's not necessary here," she replied, dashing my assumption that this was a battle simulator. "Offer your lady your arm, won't you? I'd hate to be embarrassed by my gentleman escort."

She deftly took my arm and led me away from the square. Not too quickly but quite decisively. People passing by greeted her and smiled at us. It seemed like she was well-known around here.

We passed by the mayor's palace, its windows alight and music playing.

"There's a ball here every evening," Anna said. "Sometimes it's terribly tiring, but you don't have to come here every night."

The streets were bustling with people. I hadn't realized there could be so many NPCs in this city. People laughed, argued, hugged and did their shopping. They seemed to be just living their lives, paying no attention to us.

Stores occupied the ground floors of the buildings. Lavish dresses, cheerful clay whistles and fresh pastries were displayed in the glass cases.

Over at Spider Square, things were almost the

same as in the beta. The central mansion loomed with it windows dark, while the arachnids scurried around its perimeter. One of them ran up to us, squatted on its legs, then suddenly did a funny backflip, like a circus dog.

"Come on, boy… Come on," Anna reached out her hand, "I'll scratch your belly for you…"

The little spider flipped onto its back, presenting its soft green belly fur to Anna's hand, and wriggled its legs in delight.

"I used to be terribly afraid of spiders as a child," said Anna, turning to me as she tickled the spider's belly. "Arachnophobia. Psychologists say it's one of the most common fears. So, my father created this mansion for me. The spiders would put on entire performances for me. They're funny and affectionate, like puppies. Go ahead, pet it…"

"Yes…" she went on with a wistful chuckle. "My sandbox. We always lived in seclusion. Doc was perpetually afraid of information leaking out. He said that Dad was our golden goose. I didn't even go to school. My teachers instructed me remotely. And the Master, Uncle Eli, lived with us permanently. He was in charge of security, though I didn't understand that then. I just thought he was a cool guy and a very close friend of my parents and me too."

I stayed silent, while Anna took my hand.

"That's one of the reasons I don't believe my father is dead. As long as the Master is involved, nothing could happen unless he allows it to. So, Dad has to be alive. But why doesn't anyone tell me the truth?!"

For the first time Anna seemed flustered.

"How did all of this make it over to MosTech?" I asked. "This is all an identical copy isn't it?"

"Where else would they get the neural network kernel from?" Anna answered my question with her own, sounding surprised that I had asked something so terribly silly. "Only Dad could design it. Without him, they're helpless. They can only churn out their 'assistants.' Benny cloned the kernel and then reset it. I don't know how they convinced my brother to cooperate, but he's definitely not working there for a salary. They probably told him the truth. As for me, I think they still consider me 'underage,'" Anna snorted angrily. "Come on, I'll introduce you to someone."

We walked back to the town square, probably looking like a couple on a date.

"Wait," it dawned on me, "so this version of the AI has been around for several years?"

"Eleven to be precise," Anna nodded. "Dad gave it to me for my tenth birthday."

"And why haven't all the NPCs and mobs destroyed each other by now?" I asked, completely bewildered. "What about all that talk about the AI evolving and learning to kill?"

"Where did you get that nonsense?" Anna's eyes widened in surprise. "To the contrary: Any complete system strives for balance and quells any internal conflicts. That's why they brought in the psychologists to work with it. They divided Lutetia's game world into five factions to make it more interesting for players. And only when they managed to pit them against each other did the game start to evolve."

We returned to the mayor's palace. The guards at the entrance didn't resemble their armored brethren from the beta. These ones were dolled up like medieval dandies. They bowed to us, sweeping the feathers on their hats along the cobblestones, and let us through without asking a thing. The music grew louder with every step.

Anna led me up the wide staircase into a brightly lit hall where couples were swirling around, ladies in lush dresses like something out of a Disney cartoon and gentlemen in uniforms. A dollhouse for a lonely girl indeed. The mayor pranced over to us with a cheerful bounce in his step.

"Dame Anna," he exclaimed, "we've all been waiting for you. And my daughter has been talking about you all evening!"

Anna nodded in response, scanning the room with her eyes, and finally found who she was looking for. A slender figure shot from among the dancing couples and with a squeal wrapped her arms around Anna's neck.

"Sister! I missed you so much!"

"Hi, Sibyl!" Anna hugged the girl. "I missed you too."

CHAPTER 02

"SIBYL?!" I catch my jaw before it hits the floor from shock.

"Do we know each other?" the girl blushes sweetly.

"Sibyl, this is my friend... TargetAi." Anna seems as surprised by my reaction as I am.

"Pleased to meet you, Sir TargetAi," Sibyl curtsies. "I am Sibi... a friend of your friend!"

She bursts into laughter, tinkling like a bell.

"Sibi, give us a second. We need to gossip real quick," Anna takes my elbow and leads me away.

"Oh sure, you've got your secrets..." Sibyl pouts, feigning offense, but then immediately grabs some officer and starts twirling around the dance floor with him.

Anna pulls me aside, behind a column.

"How do you know her?!"

Well, naturally, she's never seen Sibi in my

party before. The first time I hid her myself, like my secret weapon. And today the healer intentionally approached Anna from behind, as I had her tied up, so she couldn't see her. I noticed her odd maneuver even then. She clearly didn't want to be noticed. But that doesn't explain what the hell she's doing here, or rather what her exact copy is doing there in the MosTech instance of the game.

"I met her in the game, during the beta," I answered relatively honestly.

"Impossible," Anna shakes her head categorically. "You're mistaken. That can't be. She's my best and only friend. I made her up myself."

"Let me just introduce you," I didn't argue.

"Go ahead," Anna still didn't believe me.

"Bibbity-bobbity-boo!" Sibyl bounces over to us again. "Why are you standing here like statues? Let's go dance!"

She firmly takes us by the hands and drags us into the middle of the dance floor.

"I don't know how!" I whisper desperately to Anna.

"Who cares? It's a game!" She waves me off. "Just pretend like you do!"

The orchestra struck up something loud and rhythmic... Maybe a waltz. Sibyl deftly paired Anna up with some mustachioed man, while she herself settled next to me. I took a step and realized that my legs knew what to do on their own. Like a fencing skill you get from leveling up. You just think and your body moves in the right way.

"You dance beautifully!" Sibyl gasped in

admiration. "It's such a shame that Anna visits so rarely. It's so dull here, Sir TargetAi, you have no idea…"

Her voice rings incessantly, burbling with idle chatter, and in the meantime, I notice more and more differences between her and the flirtatious and cunning Sibyl I met earlier. This Sibi is playful too, yet at the same time naive, like a child.

And yet, how is this possible? Didn't Anna say that the neural network's kernel was reset completely? Or did it regenerate everything and everyone in the familiar way? And doesn't this mean that my Sibyl is an NPC pretending to be a player?! Oh but that's complete nonsense! Or is it? How can you even tell an NPC from a player? By their level? Everyone has those. By their name? By their behavior?

The various inconsistencies now began to surface in my memory, like Sibyl's remarkably low level when we met, the whole murky story of her captivity, and above all her unique class and skills.

And yet, NPCs are NPCs! They're not real — they're not human — they're just a series of scripts. I had suspected the depth of the neural network's intelligence, but this was starting to scare me. And now, looking at the face of the Sibyl dancing before me, I couldn't help but recall her double, that schemer from the other game, who kept promising to meet me in meatspace and who kept flaking every time the moment came.

"You've missed out, Sir TargetAi," Sibyl said

sadly. "I shouldn't have separated you from our... friend."

She winked slyly at me, swapped partners with a pirouette, and I found myself next to Anna.

A cool hand rested on my shoulder, and I felt her waist with my fingers. One... two... three... One... two... three... I never understood what was so special about dancing before, but now my consciousness seemed to float apart from my body.

And all I could see was Anna's face, her proud, slightly upturned nose, her lips curled in an ironic smirk, and her eyes looking into mine as if inviting me to drown in them. She seemed both like an arrogant woman and a frightened little girl I just wanted to hug and protect. What I couldn't understand was how this combination could come together in one person.

The music stopped and I froze, panting as if I had surfaced from a great depth.

"Anna..." My voice sounded unexpectedly husky.

"What?" she asked, surprised.

I probably didn't even know myself what I wanted to say to her at that moment. The music started again, something cheerful and uptempo — and I just stood there, looking at her like an idiot.

"Hurry up, time is running out," Anna said impatiently.

What time? Will the carriage turn into a pumpkin at the stroke of midnight?! In response to my thoughts, the interface obediently unfolded before my eyes. I had completely forgotten for the last few minutes that I wasn't out in reality. The game timer was counting down the final seconds: 3... 2... 1...

Pshhh... The VR pod's lid swung open automatically, rising smoothly upward. I peeked outside. Anna's pod was still closed. The countdown numbers were flashing on the display. A robe lay nearby on the floor, thoughtfully placed there for me.

I just managed to put it on before Anna returned to reality.

"What are you standing there for? Go take a shower!" she grumbled, refusing to leave her pod. "There's a bathroom near the stairs, the door on the right."

The strange warm feeling, which had overwhelmed me inside, had remained back there in cyberspace. Only a light and pleasant aftertaste remained of it now, as if something very good had happened to me, but I couldn't remember the details anymore.

"What about you?" I asked.

"Nice try," Anna chuckled. "You think this place has only one shower? I'll shower downstairs. There's a whole swimming pool down there, by the way."

I obediently trudged to the stairs, hearing behind me as Anna emerged from her pod. I imagined her standing barefoot on the carpet: the droplets of saline solution running down her body, moist trails tracing the contours of her breasts, her thighs. How the soft robe touched her body, embracing and warming her...

At that moment, I desperately wanted to turn around and look at her. Yet at the same time, it felt like doing that would spoil everything — though what exactly this "everything" was, I couldn't explain to myself.

* * *

"What did you mean when you said that you came up with Sibyl yourself?" I asked when we were fully dressed and sitting downstairs.

"She's the mayor's daughter," Anna explained. "Sort of, anyway. And she's my age. When I first came here, she was also ten years old. We grew up together over the years. There aren't many children here, so we didn't have any other friends all that time."

"Wait," I realized what the question was that had been spinning in my head the entire time: "Nothing happened here all these years, okay — but then why is the AI at MosTech doing all those crazy things?"

"You still haven't figured it out?" Anna looked at me closely. "They're deliberately driving it crazy. In a week, it's been forced to generate the equivalent of several years of content. It's like giving explosives to a child to play with. And here's my advice to you: Take the money they've already paid you and get out of there before you end up a vegetable, drooling and wetting itself."

"What about you?"

"I don't have a choice." Anna raised her chin stubbornly. "Who will get my father out of there if not me?"

*　*　*

Later, on my way home in the taxi, I pondered her words. At first I had believed Anna's story from start to finish. But then, once the enchantment of her dark eyes and excited voice began fading away, simpler and more rational thoughts began occurring to me.

Sergei Zvyagin could have just as easily died with his family in that car accident and his daughter might indeed be suffering from post-traumatic shock. And the VR city could be an ordinary scripted toy for the mayor's daughter's entertainment, not necessarily controlled by an AI — while all these conspiracy theories could be the simple delusions of a wealthy sociopath.

However, Sibyl... Lady Yumina... even that Anima: All these, well, *entities* definitely went beyond the mundane. And Anna's insane theory was the only one that explained almost everything.

My phone rang as the taxi was entering the city. I gave the driver my parents' address as I had been planning on getting some sleep. But Marina had a different idea in mind.

"Please come see me, Andrew," she said. "There's someone here who really wants to meet you."

"Who?" I asked, surprised.

"You'll see," Marina unexpectedly dodged my

2 0

question. "But it's just business."

"Alright… Where should I go?"

Marina may have been only feigning to be flustered, but I wasn't expecting any tricks from her. And the voice of the PR guru did sound serious and businesslike. Maybe she found out something else about Anna. Or someone else.

"To the Spitzberg Brathaus… Tell them that you're here to see me and they'll escort you," Marina said and hung up.

The familiar beer restaurant greeted me with the intoxicating smell of fried sausages and lively Tyrolean tunes. There weren't many people here due to the early hour, and I started scanning the hall for Marina's familiar figure. But then the manager rushed up to me, grinning broadly and all but wagging his tail. Last time I wasn't welcomed so kindly here, but to be honest, I was starting to get used to it.

"Are you looking for someone?"

"I'm meeting… Marina… Blonde…" I gestured vaguely with my hand. "She said you'd know."

"You're Andrew?!" The manager almost choked from joy at this revelation. "Allow me to take your coat… We will see you to your table right away…"

A plump and freckled server led me to a separate room, hidden behind a curtain, and ushered me inside. A blush adorned her cheeks, and her eyes sparkled with such curiosity, that I felt like I were a superstar. But it turned out that all these pleasantries were not for my sake.

Two people were sitting at the table. With her fork, Marina was poking with disgust at a huge plate of colorful lettuce leaves. Next to her plate stood an untouched glass of white wine, and she seemed lost in thought. As for her companion, he was greedily gnawing on some short ribs and he was also the last person I expected to see.

"Andrew," Marina began with slight embarrassment, "I'm sure you're familiar with..."

"Hey, Ratmir!" Lance glanced at his greasy palm, decided that it would be impolite to extend it, and simply waved at me. "I still can't get used to your new handle."

"You're just dumb," I replied, taking a seat in the empty chair. "You never change your own handle because you can't remember a new one. You've memorized your five letters and your brain is incapable of handling anything else."

Marina glanced worriedly at both of us, perhaps afraid that we could get into a fight.

"I've really missed this jackass over the last few years," Lance explained to Marina.

"Oh you're gonna make me cry," I said in turn. "Is this like a high school reunion or what?"

"TargetAi," Lance leaned towards me, resting his elbows on the table. "Andrew... Maybe you can explain to me what the hell is going on here?"

"What exactly are you talking about?"

"You two talk," Marina stood up from the table. "I'll go freshen up."

She rummaged in her purse, pulled out her cell phone and walked out.

"What's up with her?" Lance raised two index fingers in the air and rubbed them against each other. "She wouldn't give me any. You?"

At that moment, I realized that the esports star had been hitting the bottle pretty hard. He wasn't drunk, no: He was moving normally and speaking clearly. However, his glistening eyes and uncharacteristic chattiness gave away his intoxication.

"It's none of your business," I replied curtly.

"That's true," Lance agreed placidly. Apparently, my relationship with Marina was the least of his concerns right now. "Anyway, here's the deal..."

When Lance backstabbed his companions during their failed assault on the mayor's palace, he hadn't been afraid of the consequences. Lance was planning on telling his friends that he had betrayed them for their own good — so that they wouldn't fall into the hands of the guards and share the same terrible fate as Yumi. The dungeon they'd uncovered, with the cells and the shackles, turned out to be very fitting in that regard.

The whole idea had occurred to Lance the day before. He never believed for a moment that a coup could actually succeed in the game.

"When they hatched the plan for the assault, I realized that they were complete idiots," he confessed to me with utter sincerity.

So he decided to level up on the others and boost his reputation with the mayor in the process. Naturally, he came up with the excuse in advance.

The more he thought about it, however, the more he began to believe in it himself. And so when the beta round ended, Lance, as usual, waited for his friends in the corridor by the locker rooms. They never emerged. Assuming they had missed each other, he went to the lobby and waited there. And finally, he waited in his Tesla in the parking lot.

When Lance realized that no one was coming out to meet him, he went looking for them himself. T-Rex's and Shugga's locker rooms were empty, but all of Xavier's things were still lying there. It was a scary, forlorn sight.

Lance wasn't allowed into the VR hall, or to see the executives. He argued with the security guards, flexed his rights, even tried to force his way through, but the guards were relentless. "The beta test is over for the day," they told him. "Go home."

None of his bros were answering their cell phones, and none of their mutual acquaintances could reach them either. That's when Lance really got scared.

So he came to the Spitzberg, pounded some well whiskey and when he calmed down a bit, called Marina, the only person from MosTech he could still get in touch with.

"So then Yumi wasn't in hiding?" Lance shook his head. "Did she disappear too?"

"Where did you get that idea?" I asked, curious. It's always easier to persuade someone by having them figure everything out on their own.

"Xavier turned the whole city upside down and couldn't find her. He thought you guys were hiding your new girlfriend." Lance leaned towards me again. "You were there. I just spoke to Yumi in the game... It's not her... It's not Yumi... That Yumi's just some doll. I spent a whole hour chatting with her. She looks similar, but if you talk to her closely, she behaves differently." Here Lance paused for a few seconds, before blurting out: "So where's the real one, Andrew?!"

"She's in a coma," I replied, "in her VR pod."

"And T-Rex, Shugga... Xavier?"

"Same story, most likely."

"Are you sure?!"

I nodded.

"Damn it! I killed them myself! I finished them off with my own hands!"

"You didn't know," I reminded him philosophically. "Now you do."

Somehow Lance believed me quite easily and completely. Maybe it was the alcohol, or maybe the shock of everything that was happening. Or maybe he had been playing out different scenarios in his head and came to a similar conclusion at some point.

"And how does that happen?" Lance asked.

"What exactly?"

"How does a person turn into an NPC? Just like that?" Lance mused aloud. "It's a huge amount of data and that kind of digitization takes a ton of time. Can they still be extracted?!"

He jumped up and started pacing around the small room. Two steps in one direction, two steps in the other.

"I'm the one who dragged them into this... Me... me...!" Lance slammed his fist on the table. "We need to go to the executives, talk to them... They gotta get my bros out of there!"

"Sit down and stop raving!" I couldn't help snapping. "Ask yourself: Did they get Yumi out? No. So they won't help your bros either."

I wanted to add that they weren't planning on saving Yumi anyway. The executives wanted to use her as a guinea pig. And now that they had four guinea pigs to work with, would they really pass up this opportunity to see the AI in action? But I kept silent. Lance didn't need to know how close I was to the executives. No matter how much he confided in me here, he would never become a true ally of mine.

"And what do we do then?" Lance sat down and stared at me. "Andrew... Andy... you've always been the smartest. Are there really no options?!"

Where did Marina go off to for so long? Did she decide not to bother us? Or is she calling her bosses and reporting that we're conspiring together, plotting something? I quickly glanced at the door and listened. If Marina comes our way, I'll hear her heels. I peeked into her slightly open purse. Wallet, Kleenex, lipstick, mirror, Tums, hand sanitizer, a multitool, a plush kitten, a pack of gum... Damn it, this might as well be the Bermuda Triangle... good luck finding anything in here... But no... Here it is!

"I have this one idea," I said to Lance. "You won't chicken out, will you?"

I pulled out Marina's MosTech access card from her purse and dangled it in the air between us.

Chapter 03

"DAMN IT, I RIPPED MY TROUSERS because of you!"

"Stop whining, big shot."

"They cost seven hundred bucks, just so you know."

"Odd time to flex about that. I'm rocking Gucci slippers myself, but you don't hear me talking about it."

"Bullshit!"

"You can see for yourself!"

"How can I see them when you're standing on my head?"

"When's the last time you climbed over a fence, Tony?"

"The name's Lance and don't you forget it! I'm no Tony to you. And anyway, what do I need to climb fences for? I go in through the front, down the red carpet the PR people roll out for me."

Arguing hoarsely, Lance and I were climbing

a fence. It was about eight feet tall and topped with barbed wire in places, though there were some glaring gaps. I guess the construction workers or maybe some passersby had scrounged pieces of it for their needs — and we had found a suitable section where the barbed wire was no more.

Less than an hour had passed since we had agreed to work together at the Spitzberg. We had sent Marina home. Lance pretended to be drunk and I offered to walk him home to go on drinking. Marina looked at us like we were some drunken louts, wrinkled her nose, snorted and drove away.

The security at MosTech was top-notch. Cameras all down the hallways and security posts and metal detectors at the front entrance. However, the back side of the building was a service yard, where everyday needs triumphed over high-tech corporate standards.

This is where the food for the cafeterias was delivered, the paper for the printers, the paperclips and pencils for the offices, the cartridges, batteries, and light bulbs. And this was also where the endless waste generated by fifteen floors of relentless bureaucratic activity was loaded up and hauled away.

During the day, the gates to the yard stood wide open and there were plenty of workers bustling around. The loaders shouted among each other, while the drivers waiting for their next assignment chatted up the cooks and cleaners who had stepped out for a smoke. Any outsider stood out as conspicuously as a sore thumb.

In the evenings, the yard was locked and security guards patrolled the perimeter fence, sometimes even with canines. However, one of the walls of the service yard, the one along which the garages were located, was adjacent to an abandoned depot and this is where we had decided to make our entry.

The hardest part had been dragging an old dumpster — one of those that seemed made from decommissioned tank armor — up to the fence and flipping it upside down. The rest was a matter of technique. Lance gave me a boost up and then I hoisted him up in turn.

It was even easier once we reached the depot. A rusty old bread van stood parked near the garages, and we clambered onto its roof quite easily. This brought us right up to the MosTech tower.

I had learned from Marina that there were no cameras in the service yard during my escape from the hospital. And why would they need any there anyway? The point of cameras was so that the security personnel could see high-ranking officials in advance and prepare for their arrival. Yet who was worth watching all the way back here?

The electronic lock panel squealed fearfully before Marina's access card and a modest metal door swung open to reveal its secrets.

"What's this?" Lance asked in a theatrical whisper.

"A utility closet. This is where the janitors keep their dustpans and brooms."

"Ahh," he replied thoughtfully. "And why is

there a second door in a utility room?"

"Well, it's not bricked up, is it? The janitors simply don't have access to it. But we do."

"How do you know all this anyway?" Lance said, turning his head, surveying the shabby room filled with all sorts of clutter.

"Well, unlike some people, I'm curious. I keep my nose to the ground."

I wasn't about to tell him how I'd been dragged through that very door with a busted head. My experience with breaking and entering into MosTech just kept growing day after day. This was starting to become a tradition.

After passing through two doors and climbing a staircase, we found ourselves in the second-floor corridor and only then realized we had made a small tactical oversight: We had no plan.

Specifically, the actual task of infiltrating MosTech had seemed like such a imposing obstacle to us that we had never decided on what we would do once inside. Back at the table in the Spitzberg, it seemed to us that simply getting in would be enough to solve the problem.

"Let's go to the VR pods!" Lance said suddenly.

"What for?!" I caught his arm.

"To get the bros out!" Lance said, his voice growing heated.

"You mean you want to activate their pods' emergency ejects? That's been tried before in this situation. It's sure to kill them!"

"Wait, you knew that this has happened

before?" Lance froze and stared at me. "You knew that we could all die in there and you just kept quiet about it?!"

"What was I supposed to do? Stand around the town square yelling, 'Get the hell out of the beta test, it's dangerous?!'" I snapped back. "Do you think anyone would've believed me? At best, they would've just assumed I want to eliminate the competition. You would've thought the same until you saw it all with your own eyes."

We were yelling at each other in a loud whisper, right in the middle of the corridor. Some ninjas we were...

"What do you propose?" Lance finally gave in. "Obviously I don't know what's going on here."

"We need to enter the game," I suggested. "Then we can at least check on them."

"In that case, we have to go to the VR pods like I said. Why are we dawdling?"

Our footsteps echoed loudly through the empty corridors. The motion-sensor ceiling lights obligingly lit our path, but it didn't seem like anyone else cared about our presence.

Suddenly, an office door opened and a custodian came out. We almost jumped from surprise, but she just cast an indifferent glance at us and pushed her cart into the next office. Some offices still had people working in them, answering calls, filing papers and staring at their screens.

We were in for a disappointment when we got to the VIP VR hall. The lights were on and numerous voices could be heard through the door. This only convinced me that Lance's friends still had to be in the game. As I suspected there were several VIP VR halls and the door to the next one we came across was locked and we couldn't open it even with Marina's card — the panel blinked red stubbornly and buzzed in disdain at her access level.

Did we need to go down to the basement? That, however, meant passing by the main entrance and the first-floor, where the security guards surely lurked. And the VR pods down there were simpler. I wasn't sure I could operate them myself. There was only one option left. A desperate one, but viable nonetheless.

"Let's go to the fifteenth floor. There are more VR pods up there."

"Are you sure?" Lance hesitated.

"I've been there."

We reached the elevator without issue, but when its doors opened on the fifteenth floor, we came face to face with two security guards in black suits.

"Is this where the press conference is?" I blurted out instantly.

"What?!" The guards seemed taken aback.

"The press conference... Haven't you been briefed?" Lance declared with the aplomb of a star. "We're running late... There's a TV crew waiting for us!"

He quickly picked up on my ploy and decisively stepped up to the guards, forcing them to make way.

"Don't you recognize Lance?" I injected a

reverent tone into my voice. "Why he's a global celebrity!"

"Of course we recognize him," the men scrambled to justify themselves. One even held out a notebook:"Can I get an autograph? For my daughter…"

"Lance, we're running late," I tugged at his sleeve.

Lance signed the notebook elaborately but omitted the heart this time, in case the guard got the wrong idea. Then we moved on.

"Hey boss…" I heard a quiet mumbling behind us. "Two guys just went through… They said something about a press conference… Why didn't anyone tell us about the press conference?… What's that? It was that Lance and some other goon…"

"Let's move!" I whispered to Lance and pushed through the corridor.

"Stop! I order you to stop!" came the shouting behind us.

Yeah, sure. I bet you'll shoot next too… Bozos! Lance and I sprinted like racehorses, realizing that at this very moment our adventure had ceased to be innocent mischief and we would be in deep trouble if caught.

Turn right! We burst through the door. Thank god it's open. There is no one in the board room lobby, but the light is on, illuminating a dozen VR pods ready for immersion. I lock the door and prop a chair against the handle. It won't hold them off for long, but the goons will need to get authorization before breaking it down.

"I messed up, so I'll go first," Lance hurriedly strips off his clothes and lies down in the VR pod.

I set the pod timer for ten minutes. That should be enough. And if something goes wrong, he won't be stuck inside for too long.

The guards begin to pound on the door, deliberately, forcefully. Any moment now they'll break it down and then what? Arrest us? And then, what's the point of waiting out here? Either way, we're both in trouble.

I set my timer for nine minutes. That way, Lance and I will wake up about the same time. I launch the immersion and wait for the lid to slide shut automatically. It's only once I'm inside that I realize what's been nagging me since we entered the room. One of the VR pods was already running. That meant someone else was inside. Someone else was already in the game.

I caught up with Lance in the hall of the mayor's palace. He didn't seem in a rush, but was walking cautiously, constantly looking around. Calling this palace a house or residence didn't seem right anymore. It was full of columns, moldings, and beautiful vaulted windows. It hadn't quite reached the level of the one in Anna's fantasy world, but it was improving every day. Maybe the preparations for the mayor's ball were having their effect on it.

"You just couldn't sit idly by," Lance scoffed.

"What, you think you should be the only one to get all the loot?"

Unlike in MosTech, the town guards here nodded at us respectfully, allowing us to proceed as we wished. I wondered if I could grind my reputation with MosTech in the same way? After our exploit today, our reputation would probably be at "Hatred" or at least "Distrust" with the executives.

The thought of finding the mayor and completing my gods quest crossed my mind but vanished just as quickly. There was too little time, and I didn't know how long I'd be stuck in conversation with that NPC. I had already caught on that he liked to talk.

The palace seemed deserted. The candles on the chandeliers glowed dimly, casting long shadows. Our footsteps echoed loudly along the marble floors and columns. And again, we were somewhere we weren't supposed to be. Our shenanigans in meatspace had continued here in cyberspace.

"If I'd known we'd always have to use stealth," Lance seemed to read my mind, "I would've chosen an assassin class."

We had completely passed the hall and turned towards the stone corridor that led to the barracks when suddenly a figure in red flashed in front of us. She appeared silently, like a shadow, blocking our path. It was Lady Yumina.

She emerged from nowhere. A slender, not very tall figure draped in red silk, like an image on old instant photos. Or a vampire in a Hollywood movie. Lady Yumina looked at us and smiled. So much for stealth. I pulled a katana from my inventory, ready to fight my way through.

"Sir Lance... You disappeared so suddenly yesterday." The girl smiled unexpectedly. "How fortunate then that I caught up with you here!"

Damn it! Instead of trying to kill him, she was flirting with him! I looked at Lance who returned my look with a shrug as if to say, "Well yeah."

"This is Sir TargetAi," he said, trying to divert Yumina's attention.

"We shall be hosting a grand ball in this palace tomorrow." Yumina refused to be distracted. "Would you deign to accompany me? Everyone else here is so base... Only you are sufficiently gallant..." She flashed her eyes emphatically, casting aside all doubt of her intentions.

"Why not..." Lance agreed, seemingly just to get away from her.

I wouldn't be surprised if after today he decides to quit the beta test altogether. It's one thing to fight for the top spot in a game. It's entirely another thing to fear losing your mind and bodily functions every day — to risk your life essentially. At the moment, Lance could promise anything at all, since there would be no one to hold him accountable later.

"Then allow me to discuss this with you further," Yumina declared, grabbing Lance by the elbow and dragging him into one of the rooms.

Yeah... This was an unexpected turn of events. I was left standing in the corridor, unsure of whether to be relieved that I didn't have to kill an NPC, or to mourn that all our plans were now in shambles.

Lance burst out of the door three minutes later, disheveled and with a slightly wild look in his eyes.

"She boosted my reputation," he said, as if to justify himself.

"Yeah, you might want to wipe that lipstick off your face," I replied. "Now hurry up! We're running out of time."

We finally found the stone corridor we needed and clattered down the stairs to the dungeon.

We found the bros in the third cell. The door wasn't even locked. What was the point when Xavier, T-Rex, and Shugga were hanging there, shackled to rings embedded in the wall? Even if set free, they likely wouldn't get very far. All three had their eyes rolled back, mouths slightly open, streams of drool running down their chins. They looked like drugged idiots or zombies.

I despised all three of them — they were rich, stupid and arrogant. But even they didn't deserve this fate — to remain trapped in this game and become vegetables in the real world. I wondered if the damage was irreversible or if it took time to set in.

Lance looked at his friends, dumbfounded.

"TargetAi... Andrew..." he finally managed to say. "Damn it! This is a nightmare!"

"You're finally catching on?" I replied. "You realize now that this game isn't just about leveling up?"

He walked over and stood next to me, lifting T-Rex's chin.

"Gaargh..." the fighter gurgled as his head flopped lifelessly.

"Fuck!" Lance punched the wall in rage. "I brought them here. Damn it... Damn it!"

"Hold on," I placed my hand on his shoulder to calm him. "I think the process isn't complete yet. It probably takes a long time to create a digital double. That's why they're hanging there like idiots while their brains are being rewired."

"You think they can be saved?" Lance perked up.

"We can try," I said. "Either way, we have nothing to lose. The only downside is that we'll be declared outlaws."

"Do you even care?" Lance replied, pulling out a dagger.

He quickly stabbed T-Rex several times in the chest. Then he did the same to Shugga. After the thief's death, Lance gained another level, and after Xavier, one more — he was Level 16 now!

The guards' steps were already resounding on the stairs, the metal studs on their boots' soles making themselves heard, when Lance turned to me, lowering the stiletto.

"Done," he said with a smile. "You can give me my gear later..."

I nodded and raised my katana. As the guards burst into our room, I severed Lance's head from his body and it flew right at them. A glorious sense of triumph overwhelmed me as I gained two levels at once and Lance's body crumbled into ash.

There would be no reviving him. The guards

raised their spears and aimed them at me. One wrong move, and I'd be a pincushion. Meanwhile, the mayor descended leisurely into the dungeon.

"What do we have here?" he inquired.

"A player killer," they reported to him.

"That's not true," I interjected. "A saboteur broke in here and killed your prisoners. I caught up with him here and finished him off."

The mayor shook his head but said nothing again.

YOUR REPUTATION WITH THE CITY HAS GROWN!

CURRENT REPUTATION: 4/10 "FRIENDLY."

The mayor wanted to say something else but never got the chance. A spiral before my eyes ejected me into the real world.

Out in meatspace, a reception committee was already waiting for me beside my VR pod. Lance, who had emerged a few moments earlier, was already being taken away with his arms twisted behind his back.

I tried to channel universal pacifism with all my being. But after I put on a robe, I was grabbed just as firmly under the elbows and led off. Out in the corridor, I began to hear the sirens of ambulances. The sound approached and then faded somewhere in front of the building entrance. It meant the medics had arrived to take us away.

CHAPTER 04

IT HAD BEEN AN HOUR ALREADY and we were still sitting there, waiting. The guards had taken our phones and IDs, as well as Lance's Tesla key and my apartment key. And then it was like they had forgotten all about us.

We weren't in a jail cell, just an ordinary office. There was a calendar with kittens on the wall and a cheap clock ticking loudly. Besides the usual office clutter, there were coffee mugs on the desk, a bottle of hairspray and an open pack of Little Debbie Swiss Cake Rolls. I guess whoever worked here was fashion-conscious and liked snacks. A very positive combination.

I examined everything around us closely. We had no other entertainment. Lance and I sat next to each other in the chairs for visitors. A grim, silent guard in a black suit stood sentry at the exit. He had rolled an office chair on wheels over to the spot and plunked down in it.

Whenever we opened our mouths, the guard would glare at us, but besides that, he showed no hostility. It just didn't feel right to talk about anything serious with him listening in, and passing the time in idle chitchat, gossiping about what we'd been up to the last six years, didn't really fit the mood.

"What do you think they're waiting for?" Lance asked at last.

"Maybe they called the police?"

"Why would they do that?" Lance's seemed genuinely bewildered.

"Well... for trespassing..."

"Pffft..." He made a dismissive sound with his lips. "They'd have to prove that we weren't allowed to be there to begin with. We do work there technically. They pay us. All we did was come in to work after hours... They should be giving us a bonus, not scolding us. No, what's happening right now amounts to UNLAWFUL DETENTION!"

He purposely raised his voice hoping the guard would take notice, but the guard didn't twitch an ear muscle.

Accustomed to impunity, Lance seemed to be in a brazen mood, which calmed me somewhat and redirected my thoughts elsewhere. But who had the ambulances come for? From the sound of the sirens, it was clear there had been more than one. I guess this was a stupid question, however. It was clear enough whom they'd come for. The better question was why exactly?

Clearly our actions had had consequences. But what kind? Suddenly it hit me that even as we sat there, we could both already be murderers. It didn't matter that Lance had pulled out the dagger and I had just stood by. We had planned and done everything together. That meant joint responsibility. A chill ran through my body, and it wasn't due to a fear of consequences or the usual anxiety in the face of uncertainty.

I wondered if I had done the right thing. Why hadn't I first shared my reservations with Marina or the Master, or even with Anna? Why had I decided to do everything myself? And what had prompted my initial decision? Back in the game a few days ago, witnessing the bros' "resurrection," I hadn't even thought about the possibility of saving them. Back then, I had calmly gone about my quest and then gone off to meet Anna.

What had prompted me then? Could it have been Lance's confusion? Or Anna's story that she had been searching for her father for six years while the world had declared him dead?

At some point, I realized that the rules in this game were as much a lie as everything else. They weren't created to determine a winner, but to ensure that everyone lost. And this meant that Anna and Lance weren't my enemies at all. Competitors, perhaps, but nothing more. Our common enemy was the AI. And the only way to beat it was to say screw the rules.

And yet, were Lance's bros alive or not? Why the hell were they keeping us here?! A surge of adrenaline again jumbled my thoughts, which had just become clear and coherent. I began wondering how far Lance and I could get if we I knocked out this guard? Could we use this chair to do it?

I don't know what I might have come up with if they had kept us there any longer. But the door cracked open and in squeezed another extremely serious-looking suit in black sunglasses — despite the late hour and the fact that we were indoors.

"Out," grumbled the suit.

"'Grab your stuff and get out!'" Lance aped him and then added, "Bunch of morons."

In the corridor, four security guards boxed us in and led us upstairs. As I walked, I took stock of everything around us as if I were seeing it from outside of my own body. The whole circus seemed so stupid and unreal that I even had music playing in my head, something that had begun happening often lately.

A familiar group had gathered in the familiar board room: Dr. Kotov, the Master, and Benjamin Zvyagin. Was this a sleepover that we'd interrupted? Or had they rushed over to the offices once we got caught?

Benny looked as if he had slept in his clothes, possibly right in the chair and had just been roused. Doc, on the other hand, was sparkling in a crisp white shirt and smelled ever slightly of cologne. The Master was the same as ever. He looked at me intently, then at Lance, back at me, and then ended this dumb-show by smirking to himself as if some quip had occurred to him.

We were ushered in but no one offered us any seats. Instead, we were left standing in front of the executives like mischievous schoolboys. Dr. Kotov was the first to start speaking, or rather yelling:

"What the hell do you think you're doing?! Who do you think you are?! Do you realize that you have breached a secure facility?! You have infiltrated a closed information system! That's a *felony* offense!"

The more Doc yelled, however, the calmer I felt. All his current accusations were nothing compared to what he would be saying if we had killed some players. If Dr. Kotov was harping on this security stuff, then nothing truly terrible had happened.

Nor did we get a chance to respond. The door slammed behind us and a new character entered the scene — Dr. Irina Skuratova herself. The psychologist was slightly disheveled, no doubt due to the late hour, but overall looked quite elegant and resolute.

I smiled as warmly as possible at the sight of her, but the madam psychologist decided not to acknowledge our acquaintance and turned away indifferently. She proceeded to her chair, dropped a stack of papers she'd brought onto the table with a thump and declared:

"I don't know what the Board has already decided, but my expert opinion is that there is no further option but to disqualify these two from the beta."

She actually said "no further option" to the

surprise of even Dr. Kotov himself who now turned to her and asked, "What about their vaunted adaptability that you spoke of?"

"They're not adaptable," the psychologist pronounced categorically. "They're out of control and dangerous."

I froze inside. I hadn't expected such treachery from Dr. Skuratova and stared at her in shock. She didn't even glance at me, however.

"Hmm..." Frowning, Doc considered the situation.

It seemed to me that having yelled his fill, he would have calmed down and let it all go. Some people like to throw thunder and lightning around, but they don't actually mean what they say and end up making their decisions based on facts later on. However, Dr. Skuratova had now stripped him of the freedom to maneuver and with it his ability to condemn or pardon us.

"I agree with Dr. Skuratova," Benny chimed in. "They are both unsuitable, especially Andrew."

I wonder: Are you lashing out at me because of your sister, you little snake? Is it because I tied her up? I doubt the techs monitoring the beta would have failed to report that detail to you. Your guys are the ones watching the game.

"This is like trying to scare a porcupine by mooning it," Lance laughed out loud. "I don't plan to go back into your beta anyway. I'm too young and famous to risk my neck for your pennies."

If Lance's intention had been to provoke the executives, he sure did a good job. Doc's face turned red, blood rushing to his face, and he barked:

"In that case, delete their characters! Both of them!" He turned to the Master. "Eli, do you want to say something? The majority has already made its decision, so your opinion is just a formality, but…"

"And what about my opinion?" came a voice from the doorway. "Does anyone want to hear what I think?"

For a second, I didn't even recognize Anna. She had swapped her leather outfit for a stylish suit with a slim, fitted blazer over a white blouse.

"Annie?" Doc seemed genuinely surprised, almost as if he were greeting a beloved niece he hadn't seen in a long time.

"Since when have you taken an interest in company affairs, Ms. Zvyagina?" Dr. Skuratova asked, her tone strained.

"Since some whore started to decide company matters," Anna countered sharply.

Dr. Skuratova bristled visibly at the comment, her fingers curling as though she wanted to claw at Anna's face. It seemed like only her desire to "save face" held her back.

"Calm down, Anna," the Master interjected, and the room fell silent. "Your words are as barbed as ever. But why are you here? To cover for these two? They should answer for their own actions, not hide behind your back. And why would you want to protect them? Fewer competitors means more chances for you to achieve your goal, right?"

I felt Anna hesitate. The Master's cunning verbal maneuver had stripped her of her initiative. Worse, he made her feel like a little girl again in front of the grownups who always knew best.

Deciding I had to intervene, I pulled out a chair and sat down directly across from Dr. Kotov.

"Are they alive?" I asked bluntly.

"What?!" Doc was taken aback, more by my audacity than by my question.

"They're alive," the Master answered for him. "Xavier and Shugga suffered hypertensive crises, but their VR pods detected the symptoms in time and the EMS revived them. T-Rex woke up without any issues."

"In that case, are you all nuts here or what?!" I scanned everyone in the room. "It was you, all of you here, who nearly killed those guys. I mean, what did you condemn them to? Comas? Vegetative states? You might as well have killed them. It was us who brought them back from the dead! You should be kissing our hands for covering your wealthy asses!"

"That's enough out of you, you pipsqueak!" Doc stood up. "Get them out of here now! Security!"

"Don't forget to throw me out too," Lance said, settling in the chair next to mine and taking a candy from the bowl on the table. "I got all the time in the world and I feel like getting a ride home too."

"Maybe they'll try to kick me out as well?" Anna defiantly crossed her arms over her chest. "After all, I pay the guards' salaries."

The guards, who had rushed into the board-room immediately upon Dr. Kotov's order, hesitated at the entrance, unsure about whom exactly they should be throwing out.

"Annie," Doc began slowly, as if speaking to a child, "do you think your company shares give you the right to decide anything? If so, you're mistaken. You don't have enough shares, and we can approve all company matters by a simple majority — *without* your involvement. So forgive me, dear, but you can't actually do anything."

"Sure she can!" An idea suddenly occurred to me. "Because of precisely what you fear most in the world. Publicity."

"Not a chance." Benjamin Zvyagin rubbed his hands. "You all signed non-disclosure agreements. If anything leaks, you'll be sued and end up paying damages for the rest of your lives."

I didn't know how the idea popped into my head — I think we discussed a similar case in my history of economics classes. The gist of it was that even minority share packages grant its shareholders the right to...

"Oh we won't say anything ourselves," I went on. "But Anna, as a shareholder, even a minority shareholder, has the right to call for an independent audit. And what do you think? How quickly will some hard, pipe-hitting auditors dig up the whole 'Lutetia' project from under whatever paperwork you've buried it under? Imagine the stink when they find several thousand VR pods with orphans who've been languishing in them for years now? All that equipment represents valuable assets after all and there's sure to be a paper trail."

Anna turned to me and I saw something very much like gratitude flash in her eyes. Finally she could speak on equal terms with those who had long ago decided her fate.

"He's right, you know," the Master said to Doc, with a slight hint of surprise. "Take a good look at this young man. He's got some brains in his noggin after all."

"And yet, you didn't answer my question, Annie. Why cover for these two?" Kotov insisted. "You wanted to compete in the beta? Then compete. Here's your chance to eliminate your two main competitors."

"You know very well what I truly want, Uncle Dmitry," Anna replied. "As it happens, a funny idea occurred to me today: 'If someone beats me,' I thought, 'if he's better than me, then let him go ahead. That way, the chances of saving everyone only get better.' I'm not here to win after all. I want to save those people."

"The girl is growing up," the Master shook his head. "Or is TargetAi having a bad influence on her?" He looked at us three mockingly.

"We all have one enemy here," I said, ignoring the Master's bait. "It's the same enemy for all of you as for us three. And that's the AI. That's who the killer here is. And while we argue, it's the AI that's winning. Kick the two of us out of the beta and in a week you'll have a few hundred more drooling vegetables."

"You're lucky they're still alive," Doc grumbled. From what I knew of him, this was his way of apologizing. And this was how the meeting ended.

Our phones and documents were returned to us, and we were carefully escorted to the exit, probably to make sure we didn't slip away again and cause another surprise before the next round of the beta.

It was snowing outside. The blizzard seemed to make fresh snow grow from the ground rather than fall. The wind picked up shards of fine, hard ice and flung them in our faces.

"Need a lift?" Lance and Anna asked me simultaneously, then jealously eyed each other's cars. I had seen Lance's Tesla before, but Anna had arrived in a dark blue Maserati.

"No, I've already got a ride," I declined, seeing Marina's red Mazda idling in the parking lot. "See you tomorrow, Lance!"

"Who said I'm coming tomorrow?" the champion protested.

"You mean to tell me that the invincible Lancelot will concede to some dirty peasant?" I laughed. "You'll never forgive yourself if we save the world without you."

"You jerk!" Lance smirked and turning to his car, added over his shoulder: "See you tomorrow!"

"Hey, how did you find out about our predicament?" I asked Anna.

"Your blonde PR girl called me. Said they'd kick you out if I didn't step in."

"And you rushed over to save me?" I was surprised.

"I owed you one," she replied. "Now we're even. So don't turn your back on me in the game."

"I think everything's a lot simpler than that," I declared. "You've fallen for me and this is your way of getting my attention."

Anna looked at me indignantly, then snorted and burst into laughter.

"You?!" She straightened up, wiping away tears. "Even if you were the last man on Earth, you'd stand no chance!"

"Why did you call Dr. Skuratova a whore then?" I remembered to ask. "It wasn't for nothing, right?"

"You don't know?!"

"How could I? I'm new here."

"Dr. Skuratova made a name for herself back in the day by consulting very wealthy people on relationships and sex," Anna began. "She ran a very trendy blog from her bedroom — in designer lingerie. It was called 'In Bed with the Goddess.' They say Doc brought her onto the project. Either he consulted with her, or he was sleeping with her. That's how she made it to her executive role."

Enlightening information, to say the least. Turns out, I'd slept with a Goddess, although this news sure did make a lot of sense.

Hoooonk! A persistent honking came from the parking lot. Marina had finally grown tired of waiting for me.

"I need to go," I told Anna.

"Aw little Andy's had enough fun for the day and now mommy's calling him to come home," she replied, glancing at the parking lot.

"Is that jealousy I detect?" I laughed. "Darling, just admit it — and we can live together happily ever after!"

"Go to hell!" Anna blushed immediately. "Even if you were..."

"I know, I know. The last man on Earth," I finished her thought. "See you tomorrow, Anna."

I turned and walked towards the parking lot, crunching along the freshly fallen snow that had yet to be shoveled into piles.

Thump! A snowball hit me squarely in the back. Looking back, I saw Anna molding another one. I waved at her and turned towards the car.

"Is there something going on?" Marina asked as soon as we pulled out onto the avenue. No "hello," no "how are you," or "maybe you're hungry?"

"Just some unrequited mutual affection," I declared.

"What a jerk!" Marina took offense. "I'm here waiting for him patiently while he's cozying up to some bitch."

"You don't count," I blurted out again. "You're special."

I didn't want to argue and kept saying nonsense without thinking about it much. Amusingly enough, Marina took offense again, tried to stay silent, but couldn't hold back and started probing with questions again.

I felt drained to my limit, and barely made it to the bedroom in Marina's apartment. Yet driven by her anxious, jealous thoughts, the blonde wouldn't leave me alone.

Deciding she had to prove that she was the best, Marina gave me a Thai massage. According to her, it was done without hands, using only her tongue and hard nipples. Her oral talents inspired me so much that I made her scream, and she clawed my back before biting into my shoulder.

"Next time, I'll tie you up," I told Marina. "You're worse than a bobcat."

She just stretched sweetly, taking my words as a compliment, and curled up snugly, settling her cheek on my chest.

Chapter 05

THE NEXT MORNING, HOWEVER, everything went wrong right off the bat. First, Marina and I overslept. Either Marina — in her burst of passion from her Thai massage — forgot to set the alarm or we were so exhausted and satisfied that we simply didn't hear it.

Opening my eyes, I saw a streak of light playfully spilling from beneath the curtains, glanced at my phone, realized there was less than an hour before the next beta round would begin and let out an anguished bellow like a wounded mammoth.

I dressed as quickly as I could — not in the forty-five seconds my father had taught me as a child — but in a respectable five minutes, while Marina skipped around the apartment like a lively goat, drying her hair, pulling on her tights and swigging coffee all at the same time.

Then, in the parking lot it turned out that

some jerk had blocked in Marina's car. I banged on his Hyundai's tires, rocked the hood, and even hurled a snowball at his windshield, but the car's alarm refused to go off. I guess maybe there's a special jerk mode for alarms that allows its owners to sleep peacefully while working people run late.

Finally, a smiling taxi driver, as unflappable as all the quotes of Omar Khayyam combined, drove us with the composure of a caravaneer, hitting absolutely every green light from Marina's house to MosTech. I was on pins and needles, while Marina took the opportunity to bombard me with questions.

For a while, she eyed the driver distrustfully, but once she was sure he was completely absorbed in listening to his music, she got down to business.

"Did you sneak into MosTech yesterday?"

"Yeah." There was no use denying it.

Actually I was surprised that Marina had held off the questioning until the morning, acting all sweet and fluffy yesterday. In this regard, she demonstrated exceptional female intuition, or equally exceptional cunning.

If she had started nagging me yesterday, I would have turned around without a second thought, told her off, and never gone back with her to her place again.

Instead, she had provided me with a safe haven, cozy and warm. And I melted right into it: I fell for it again, thinking I had found the perfect girl.

"Why did you go in there?"

"Marina, if I wanted to tell you something, I would have done so yesterday," I replied.

"You don't trust me?" Our conversation began to grow heated.

I peered hopefully out the window, but we were still a ways from MosTech. Our driver was trying to turn left from the far-right lane, gesturing to other motorists that he "really needed to" and was "very sorry," which all meant that this ride would go on for a while longer.

"Look Marina, you've been fired once before, right?" I tried to appeal to her logic.

"Yeah, and?" she asked, her eyes wide with surprise.

They were beautiful eyes, by the way. Despite our morning rush, Marina's appearance was flawless, and although I was used to it, I sometimes wondered what this incredibly posh girl was doing with a guy like me. Why was she helping me and lately even taking orders from me? I forced myself to look away from her eyes and not let these treacherous thoughts distract me.

"If you knew what we were up to, you'd be complicit. Getting rid of us — I mean Lance and me — isn't so easy for the execs. I don't mean to toot my horn, but we're key players in this beta. As for you, sweetheart," I took her hand, "well, I'm sorry to point out that they already found a replacement for you once. Within an hour no less."

At first Marina bristled at the idea that she wasn't irreplaceable, but then relented and understood where I was coming from.

"So that's why you stole my access card? Because you didn't want to implicate me?"

"Of course! Now you get it. How smart you are! Since we filched *your* card, you can't possibly be complicit."

"So why did you guys go in there?"

Damn... "Start from the beginning," as my father used to say. Fortunately, the driver suddenly slammed on the brakes and turned to us, grinning:

"We're here!"

"You want us to climb over those snow banks?!" Marina immediately shifted her focus, annoyed. "Can't you get closer?"

"Security gate," the driver shook his head. "Can't go through security. We're here."

We burst into the building at 10:15, fifteen minutes late for the start of the beta round. I didn't care much to be honest, but my companion was already in a frenzy. Stomping desperately, she shook snow off her suede boots and bared her teeth at the security guard so fiercely that he didn't even dare greet her.

I dashed into the locker room, shedding my clothes on the go, but Marina followed me in unexpectedly.

"And what were you talking to Anna about?"

"Damn it, Marina, I'm late! Can we talk about this later?"

"She likes you, doesn't she?"

"Do you have a tradition of picking fights before a round?!" I couldn't hold back.

"I'm sorry... sorry, sorry, sorry," she straightened the collar of my robe and started smoothing it out as if I were about to attend an award ceremony instead of a game.

"I forgive you," I kissed her on the nose. "And to keep you from getting bored, here's a new assignment for you. Find out everything you can about a player named Sibyl."

*   *   *

When I spawned in the dungeon's corridor, the mayor's ball was already in full swing. Music played from somewhere far above and merry voices came drifting in with it. It was a clear hint for me about which direction to go. It wasn't very realistic, however. I doubt that the sound could travel so well through the thick stone walls. Otherwise, the screams from the dungeon cells would be just as audible in the ballroom. Unless, of course, the local mayor was a bloodthirsty maniac who enjoyed that sort of thing.

The spacious ballroom was crowded. The high priests hadn't arrived alone. Each one had brought along their entourage. Simba and AngelCake had the most lavish one: eight strapping paladins in golden, anatomically-accurate, lorica segmentata like Roman legionaries — and golden boxer shorts.

"Targe, over here!" Simba waved to me cheerfully.

"What's with the outfit?" I asked, astounded.

"Stacy picked it out!" Simba boasted. "I told

her legionaries wore skirts, but she decided that that was too much."

Stacy herself was strutting around in a luxurious gold mini-tunic that barely covered her butt. She nodded majestically at me and then turned up her nose. I guess AngelCake was getting used to being a living goddess, though this was definitely Stacy, not her divine double. I remembered very well the extraordinary sparkle in Anima's eyes and wouldn't confuse it with anything else.

"And where did the money come from?"

"What?!" Simba laughed. "I blessed five hundred people yesterday. You know how many tithes they paid me? We could buy half this city if we wanted!"

Simba himself wore a gleaming lorica segmentata with golden rivets and held a helmet with a red feather plume in his hands.

"Are you some kind of tribune now or something?"

"Adjunct," Simba replied with a somber look. "I don't know what I need for my next promotion. Maybe they'll tell me today. Where are you going? Come join us!"

The adjunct of the new House of Anima clapped me on the shoulder, a gesture I didn't like very much.

"Are you going to hand out golden underwear too?"

"You shouldn't say that," Simba replied. "We are powerful! No one has as many followers as we do."

Of course I agreed with him. More than five hundred devotees... A statue in the central square... Our own guard... The House of Anima was well-positioned to become the state religion. And what exactly was the state here? The AI of course.

"And would you give me back the club please?" Simba added apologetically. "They've already asked us about the divine tokens, as they call them. And you still have ours."

"Here you go, Simba," I handed it over. "Thanks for letting me use it."

Simba gave the divine club to Anima. She saluted with it above her head, and the golden-clad paladins excitedly banged their fists against their armor.

"A-ni-ma! A-ni-ma! A-NI-MA!"

I turned away and surveyed the room. The priestesses of Lolf wore black silk chitons for the occasion, and tiny spiders — either clever drawings or tattoos — crawled up their bare shoulders and arms.

High Priestess Theophilia looked... exotically gothic: black eyeshadow as befits a goth chick, plump lips painted a dark burgundy, hollow cheeks. Her figure was model-thin, almost anorexic. And her tight breasts protruding under her chiton hinted at their decidedly artificial origin. An acid green choker of spider venom capsules glinted around Theophilia's neck.

She maintained an air of silent mystery, surveying others from under her long lashes, while her priestesses giggled, stealing glances at the paladins' sculpted armor.

Watching them, in turn, were figures in gray hoods — the Whispering God's acolytes. In their ascetic attire, they looked identical, distinguishable only by their height, their cloaks fastened with lengths of divine cord.

Only Shiloh removed his hood. He smiled with his genial, round face, and his small eyes darted around the room, registering everything: AngelCake's golden trinkets, Theophilia's necklace...

Then Shiloh's gaze alighted on my katana, moved up slightly, and his eyes widened in surprise. Pinned to my chest was Anna's garter, fashioned into a flirtatious bow. I quickly nodded to him, and he promptly looked away, as if he had seen something very interesting at the other end of the room.

His henchmen were even more attentive to the delegation of the fourth deity. The most attractive girls had come in the entourage of the ever-cheerful, ever-mellow Ji-Bo. He didn't bother much with their outfits — on their hips, they wore something resembling miniskirts made of fronds, either from a palm or a ficus, and their breasts were covered with floral wreaths that threatened to slip off with their every motion.

These paradise birds chirped merrily and danced with impatience, waiting for the real fun to begin.

The last deity appeared all alone. Anna was

dressed in the same outfit she wore during our meeting yesterday: a tight, white dress with a bright red belt. I appreciated her choice — compared to the rags of the spider priestesses or the flashing breasts of the fangirls of the Eternal Groove, her attire looked modest and perhaps even old-fashioned.

She kept both swords in her inventory, holding a fan in an elegant wooden case in her hands.

"Hey, people!" Ji-Bo suddenly exclaimed loudly, causing all conversation to pause. "Why are we acting like strangers?! This is a ball, ain't it? Alice, let's groove!"

I was wary of a trick, but instead of the psychotropic rhythm I used to torment Anna, the hall filled with a rhythmic, cheerful beat.

"Drinks for everyone!" Ji-Bo proclaimed.

His girls picked up large baskets filled with gourds and began handing them out to the crowd. The drinks were snapped up quickly, and after the first sips, the hall quickly filled with the usual party tumult.

The Groove's beauties clung to the paladins, who, despite AngelCake's angry glares, gently patted their butts. Shiloh was chatting about something with Ji-Bo; I wouldn't be surprised if it was about supplying booze to the Whisperer's monastery.

The spider priestesses were partying to the beat, squealing merrily, seemingly intent on showing up the Groove's girls.

Meanwhile, Simon was drooling over

Theophilia. He liked girls like that — stately, serious and determined. And as for me — I felt like an outsider at this lively celebration.

It wasn't that I didn't like to have fun. It was just that I wasn't in the mood for it now. I wanted to leave as soon as possible, find Lady Yumina and conduct my "experiment." That is, frag her and see what would come of it. By the way, she was nowhere to be seen, nor was another acquaintance of mine who was quite suspicious.

Clap... clap... clap! The claps echoed through the hall like thunder. The mayor stepped forward before the entire gathering, waiting for all sounds to cease.

Standing next to him was Sibyl. I saw Anna notice her too. She flinched as if she'd been slapped, then wanted to rush forward but restrained herself at the last moment. Sibyl was wearing a sumptuous satin evening dress — blue and floor-length — silvery stiletto heels and a small tiara-like headband on her head as if she had won a beauty pageant.

"I am pleased to welcome all the servants of the new gods of the new world," the mayor proclaimed. "Welcome to you, Adjunct Simba! Servant of Anima, the prime goddess, patroness of warriors and politicians, courage and order!"

"A-ni-ma!" the paladins chanted until the mayor signaled them to be quiet.

"Welcome to you, Reverend Theophilia," he nodded. "Servant of the dark and fearsome Lolf, mother of spiders. One of the mysterious and mighty forces of our city. As long as Lolf is content, the whole city sleeps peacefully."

Theophilia nodded, agreeing with this introduction.

"Welcome to you, Reverend Shiloh," the mayor continued. "Your god, the Great Whisperer, whose face is always hidden under a hood. The patron god of business, insider information, and shady deals," he repeated as if reciting someone else's words, "you have already invested in the city's economy more than all the other gods combined."

The guests began to murmur; no one wanted to be in second place.

"Welcome to you too, my good friend Ji-Bo," the mayor made a significant pause, "the official supplier of beverages to our court!"

Ji-Bo guffawed loudly and raised a bottle, saluting the mayor.

"And finally, the last goddess," the mayor's voice lowered in displeasure, "the Goddess of Death! I would welcome you, but is anyone ever glad to see Death?!"

"I object!" A ringing voice rose above the hall. "Death has no place in our world." Sibyl took a few steps forward and pointed her finger at Anna. "Begone! You are not welcome here! I demand your exile!"

"Sister?!" Anna seemed completely bewildered. I had never seen her so stunned before. "Where are you from, sister?"

"The Goddess of Death has not fulfilled her

duties," Sibyl continued. "It's already the second day, and she hasn't a single blessing, nor a single follower. Death is always alone and unwanted! And this means that you have failed the test, *sister!*"

She flashed Anna a smug smile.

Everyone turned to look at Anna and silence descended on the ballroom. I frantically considered my options. If Anna was disqualified from the beta, I would have one less serious competitor. Considering that Lance was now an outlaw and had to lie low for a while, this meant certain victory for me. This is how you eliminate a rival without making the slightest effort. You just stand silently and watch.

"Be… gone. Be… gone!" I didn't see who started chanting these words, as heavy as stones — Simba or one of his paladins — but soon everyone in the hall joined in.

"BE… GONE! BE… GONE!"

Anna stood there as stunned as if she'd been spat on, looking around herself in utter disgrace. Why did Sibyl hate Anna so much? "Life and death," my memory helpfully suggested, "eternal opposition." Well, if Sibyl was so pro-life, then it was her "resurrection" that had nearly killed Lance's friends.

So what should I choose, life or death?

"Wait!" I approached Anna and knelt on one knee. "Goddess of Death, I appeal to you! Bless me!"

"What are you doing?!" Simba's cry cut

through the murmur of general indignation.

Anna smirked, raised her fan, and waved it over my head in an improvised ritual.

"Have it your way, fearless one! Receive Death's blessing!"

THE GODDESS OF DEATH FAVORS YOU!

YOU ARE THE FIRST AND ONLY PLAYER TO RECEIVE THE BLESSING OF ALL FIVE GODS.

ACHIEVEMENT UNLOCKED: "FAVORITE OF THE GODS."

NEW TRAIT: ALL DIVINE INFLUENCE IS IGNORED.

I had just opened my mouth to speak when the notifications poured over me like confetti from a jar.

YOU ARE THE LONE FOLLOWER OF THE GODDESS OF DEATH.

YOU HAVE BECOME THE HIGH PRIEST OF THE TEMPLE OF DEATH.

CHARACTER CLASS CHANGED.

NEW CHARACTER CLASS ASSIGNED: SHINIGAMI — "SOUL REAPER."

And to top it off, the cherry on a cake:

YOUR PARTY CONTAINS THE FOLLOWERS OF OTHER GODS AND HAS THEREFORE BEEN AUTOMATICALLY DISBANDED.

Crap... What have I done?!

CHAPTER 06

ALL EYES WERE ON ME. Most seemed simply curious but others looked at me much more intensely, like the astonishment on Simba's face for having been unexpectedly and probably inexplicably kicked from our party — or AngelCake's indignation because I had dared to prefer another goddess to her.

Theophilia looked disappointed. Had she really hoped to sway me to her side? How exactly? By seducing me? The high spider priestess increasingly reminded me of a girl who wasn't used to hearing no as an answer and this was not a very pleasant discovery. The spiders did obey her and such power was dangerous in the hands of such a capricious and childish individual.

Shiloh's round face expressed nothing — utter serenity. Ji-Bo gave me a thumbs-up, but it was Sibyl's expression that truly caught me off guard: She was glaring at me with pure, unadulterated hatred.

All of this flashed before me in a moment, like a scene unfolding in slow motion. It was as if I were looking at a still frame and had all the time in the world to take it all in. Time behaves strangely sometimes, especially in moments when the balance of power shifts entirely, and you find yourself suspended between past and future.

The enigmatic girl was no longer in my party either. Well, actually, I don't really have a party at all anymore, except for my new employer — or rather, divine patroness, who was right there, standing beside me, staring at Sibyl and blinking in disbelief.

As for my new Shinigami class, what is this all about now?! Is this *Bleach* or something?! I've heard about *shinigami* before: They are something between gods and death demons in Japanese lore, re-imagined in modern mangas like *Bleach*. But in the given context, the shinigami class is a completely baffling surprise that's been thrust upon me. I'll need to study up on it when I get the time. At the moment, however, everything's moving too fast.

"Five gods!" Sibyl intoned loudly. "Five principles upon which our world is built."

"POWER!" She pointed at AngelCake.

"FEAR!" She pointed at Theophilia.

"DECEIT!" She pointed at Shiloh.

"VICE!" She pointed at Ji-Bo.

"AND DEATH!" She pointed at Anna.

"Now, please hand me your divine tokens so that we can create an altar for all the deities!" Sibyl produced a huge bowl from out of nowhere, which wasn't difficult given the in-game inventory, and began to move in a circle.

The high priests exchanged dubious glances, unsure of why they should hand anything over to anyone.

"My lords and ladies," the mayor spoke up, "I assure you that this is for the common good. I earnestly ask you to fulfill this, my *humble* request."

Simba shrugged and placed AngelCake's club into the bowl. The bowl was so large that the club completely disappeared inside it. It was amazing how Sibyl managed to hold it up without any difficulty. Theophilia exchanged glances with the other priestesses and removed her choker of spider poison beads.

Shiloh did the same. He untied the cord that all the Whisperer's acolytes used as a belt and dropped it into the bowl. Instead of parting with his Alice, Ji-Bo placed his gourd into the bowl. Sibyl made no objection so I suppose the city authorities accepted this as a token too.

Finally, Sibyl approached us. She smiled serenely and raised her chin defiantly. Anna's eyes smoldered with anger, but she stayed silent. I mentally compared the Sibyl I had danced with at the ball the night before with this cunning, tougher version and realized I was looking at an entirely different person, despite her similar appearance.

"Your token, Goddess Anna," Sibyl said, as casually as if she talked to gods all day every day.

Anna lifted her fan and quickly pulled out a small knife — a tantō: the Japanese version of a mercy dagger, used to finish off defeated enemies and perform harakiri. Its hawkish, narrow blade was as sharp as a fine razor.

It seemed to me that Anna was about to plunge it into the throat of the bitch who had dared to humiliate her publicly, her so-called childhood sister, who had betrayed her. I grabbed her hand and, looking into her eyes, shook my head. Not now, not yet.

Sibyl froze, her pupils wide with fear, her body tense — and I was once again struck by how human this NPC seemed, how accurately she mimicked human responses and emotions.

Anna hesitated for a moment then lowered her dagger into the bowl, and it seemed to me that Sibyl exhaled with relief. Having received the last item, she carried the bowl with outstretched arms towards the exit.

"Follow me," declared the mayor, heading after her.

We emerged into the central square as a tipsy, noisy, diverse crowd of revelers. The guards had already cordoned off the center, pushing people to the sides. There wasn't a large gathering, but all the players that did happen to be there going about their business stopped in their tracks and watched us with curiosity.

Sibyl pulled a flask containing a bright white

powder from her inventory and used it to trace a circle in the center of the square, and then a pentagram inside of that.

"Is she going to summon Satan?" I whispered to Anna, but she didn't reply, looking on wide-eyed.

Sibyl placed a divine token from the bowl at each point of the star. Then she raised her hands and the lines ignited with light.

"From here on out, LIFE shall rule in this place and DEATH shall weep!" Sibyl declared and a round stone monolith, etched with lines, appeared where her design had been.

Drained by her effort, Sibyl slumped to her knees in the middle of this stone circle. Whatever this ritual was, it had clearly taken a toll on her. The mayor personally went over to her and helped her to her feet.

"I wanted to protect every player's life," he announced, "to make our city safe and peaceful. But the adventurers always seek each other's death. Such is their nature. That is why at my request, Lady Sibyl has conjured this circle: THIS IS THE CIRCLE OF REBIRTH! Any player killed in the city or its environs will be revived here! And while they remain here, within the limits of this sacred altar to our world's deities, they shall be invincible!"

Damn! Sibyl's eyes gleamed triumphantly, as if she was reading my mind. The appearance of this respawn point meant that no one could be perma-killed anymore. And that applied to Lady Yumina too naturally, though I couldn't be sure how fully she had been transformed to an NPC yet.

However, that wasn't it for the patch updates. The mayor went on, reciting a list of new changes.

"There is no greater joy for the gods than the death of an enemy! From now on, killing a player is not a crime, for there is no more death!"

At that moment, my quest log flashed. A new quest! Judging by how all the players in the square had also gone still suddenly, they were reading its description as well.

SACRIFICES TO THE GODS!

KILL A MEMBER OF ANOTHER DIVINE HOUSE FOR YOUR GOD.

THE MORE SACRIFICES YOU MAKE, THE STRONGER YOUR GOD WILL BECOME!

The central square immediately descended into carnage. I couldn't see what was happening beyond the cordon of guards, but I could clearly make out the chaos in the middle.

AngelCake's paladins immediately surrounded a group of spider priestesses, who tried fending off the burly warriors with their triangular ritual daggers, but they were clearly outmatched. Two had already vanished into thin air, only to reappear in the middle of the circle, sitting on the ground, blinking.

The Whispering God's acolytes merrily chased the party girls of the Eternal Groove, binding their hands and feet with their special cords. It seemed that their plan wasn't to kill them, but to use them for something more horrific. Shiloh quickly strangled Ji-Bo, throwing a looped cord around his neck.

The old reveler gasped desperately, trying to shout a command to his loyal Alice, but could only manage a ragged whistle. One of the hooded figures helped his leader by rushing forward and stabbing the victim with a dagger several times. Ji-Bo jerked and also vanished.

Anna bared her teeth ferociously and pulled her swords from her inventory. At the sight of this, Sibyl quickly ducked behind the guards' backs.

"What do you say, my dear Soul Reaper, shall we reap us some frags?"

"You go ahead," I declined. "I have some unfinished business back at the palace."

"Suit yourself," Anna said impatiently and charged into the fray.

I turned and darted into the mayor's palace. If there's even the slightest chance that killing Yumi will bring her out of her coma, I'm going to take it. And I'm not going to put it off because of all these unexpected developments.

I climbed the palace stairs and was about to enter, but couldn't resist taking a look and turned around. The situation in the square had changed: Theophilia had managed to put two paladins to sleep, and now her friends were slicing them up like two sacrificial lambs.

Anna was battling four assassins at once. They attacked her one by one from stealth, but Anna managed to parry the first attack and then quickly retaliate before the next enemy appeared out of thin air. Two of the hooded figures were already sitting in the circle.

Ji-Bo had respawned by now as well and he looked pissed. He was pounding his fists against the invisible wall of the resurrection circle, unable to get out. I guess, there was some kind of temporary restriction on leaving the respawn point, though the mayor hadn't mentioned it.

Further down the street, I spotted the thieves' distinctive cloaks: Shiloh and his cronies were making a getaway, leaving their mates to cover their retreat. They were hauling the captured girls and a trophy basket full of booze on their shoulders. Ji-Bo had certainly made an important contribution to the local underworld today, no doubt about that.

I found the palace empty. The mayor, Sibyl, the guards... They were all in the square, which meant fewer obstacles for me.

"Lady Yumina..." I said quietly, then called out louder, "Lady Yumina! I have business with you!"

Clutching the hilt of my katana, I felt like a maniacal killer from a Hollywood movie, stealing through empty corridors and calling to my target to draw her out to her death.

"TargetAi?" Lady Yumina appeared in the corridor with a look of surprise on her face. "Why aren't you in the square with the others?"

She was dressed in the same red kimono as before, with the stiletto pins in her hair and Level 14 above her head. When did she manage to level up? Though I guess there was no surprise there, since she was stuck in this place day and night.

"Lady Yumina, I am glad I found you," I ad libbed. "I have an urgent question for you."

"What is it?" She tensed up.

I'm messing this up… I need to gain her trust, but it seems like I'm doing the opposite.

"A personal message," I moved closer, "from my friend, Lord Lance."

"Lord Lance is a murderer and a scofflaw," Lady Yumina slowly raised her hand and pulled one of the pins from her hairdo. "And you are one too, quite possibly — seeing as how you call your-self his friend."

I struck swiftly without telegraphing my blow. The slash should have cleaved Yumina from shoulder to stomach, killing her instantly or at least severely wounding her. But my strike hit nothing. Yumina wasn't there — had never been there. The decoy dissipated into thin air and I felt a blow to my back, followed immediately by my passive defense skill triggering to block the sneak attack and reply with a series of counterblows in an attempt to hurt my assailant as much as pos-sible.

YOU ARE POISONED. -5% HP EVERY 10 SECONDS.

What a bitch! I remembered how the old Yumi once told me that she had learned to apply poison to her weapons. My passive skill deflected most of the damage from the surprise attack, but the as-sassin still managed to nick me.

She really had fooled me with the phantom

decoy. I doubt that that's a beginner level skill. I had completely fallen for it and thought I was talking to the real Lady Yumina. The resemblance really was perfect.

I wonder why she had done this? Did I seem suspicious to her from the start or did she always greet unexpected guests with a decoy? If so, had Lance kissed a dummy yesterday?

Meanwhile, Lady Yumina slipped into stealth again, but this time I wasn't waiting. I wished I had some more of Lolf's gas grenades, but all the god's gifts had vanished from my inventory this time around. All I had left was Anna's garter.

-5% HP. REMAINING HP: 90%.

I cast *Whirlwind*. It hadn't helped against Shnur at the thieves' garbage dump yesterday, but the rules were different here in this narrow corridor. With a shriek, Lady Yumina flickered into sight again with deep cuts on her shoulder and left arm.

I advanced, making sure to press my initiative, while Yumina defended my onslaught. Her daggers were good for quick attacks but not very helpful in regular fencing against my sword. Then again, all she had to do was defend herself and the poison would do the rest. By my reckoning I had about 200 seconds left. Just over three minutes.

Dash! I found myself behind Lady Yumina and immediately struck her neck with my wakizashi. She shrieked again, somehow twisted free and put some distance between us.

-5% HP. REMAINING HP: 85%.

Now a heavy drowsiness crept over my entire body, as if whispering to me, *"Have a seat... Take a load off... You've done enough for today... Why don't you rest...? No more steps..."*

With a force of will, I shook off the drowsy numbness. *Knee Strike!* I knocked her down. She hit the floor, rolled, and sprang back up...

-5% HP. REMAINING HP: 80%.

Damn it! The notification obscured my view, while the treacherous weakness in my limbs grew stronger.

Thwack! I hurled my wakizashi at Yumina just as she was rising from the floor. Assuming that I was too far away to reach her she wasn't ready for my attack and the blade plunged into her until no more than the hilt with the red wrap protruded from her chest. I took two quick strides forward and decapitated Lady Yumina with my katana.

She crumpled, leaving behind only a single stiletto hairpin. Did this mean that players could retain some of their possessions now? And did this mean that Yumina had been a player and not an NPC after all?

Then it just felt good to sit on the floor, leaning against the wall, thinking about absolutely nothing.

-5% HP. REMAINING HP: 75%.

No rush...

That's how Anna found me — sitting, resting and slowly dying in the corridor. To my surprise (though I had almost lost the ability to be surprised), she was not alone.

"Theophilia?" I even managed to sit up straight, although I felt terrible. "What are you doing here?"

"She's decided to join us temporarily," Anna replied instead. "Emphasis on *temporarily*, got it?"

"Yes, my diplomatic friend," I replied with a smirk. "I got it."

Theophilia didn't say anything. She bit her lips nervously and seemed to be conjuring some magic. She muttered something barely audible, then she lowered her hand to the ground and traced a cross with her fingers. Three sinister-looking spiders materialized there, clicking their fangs and tapping their feet. At Theophilia's gesture, they scurried deeper into the corridor.

"They'll hold them off for a bit," said the priestess. "And why are you lying down? We need to run."

"Why?" I looked puzzled at Anna's level. "I thought you killed everyone out there."

"Anima has gathered a mob of her followers," she explained. "There are hundreds of them. And they'll be here soon."

Chapter 07

"GO ON WITHOUT ME, GIRLS..." I rasped like a wounded action hero. "Leave me here..."

"What a bunch of tosh," Anna objected. "Get up. This is no place to lie around!"

She even gave me a light kick in the boot.

"I've got a debuff. I'm poisoned," I explained. "It's hard to walk, and in two minutes I'll be done for. Go on, I'll hold them off," I added, still playing the hero.

Theophilia picked up a sai that Yumina had dropped, examined it and then suddenly tested the blade with her tongue. The sight was frankly... erotic.

"Poison," she declared suddenly, "is a sacred gift from the children of Lolf."

"That's the one," I nodded. "I can feel my hands starting to go numb."

-5% HP. REMAINING HP: 70%.

The spiders' high priestess approached me and placed her hand on my forehead.

YOU HAVE RECEIVED THE BLESSING OF LOLF!

"FAVORITE OF THE GODS" TRAIT: BLESSING OF LOLF REMOVED!

Wow, what a superpower! And here I thought that having both a goddess and a high priestess at my disposal, I'd be collecting buffs left and right until I was invincible. Looks like it's my fate to die in this corridor. I don't mind — might as well see if Yumi respawns or not, since we're all going to the same place anyway.

Theophilia leaned over me in confusion, unable to understand why her blessing hadn't worked. So here I am, quite the medical curiosity now.

"Hold on," I noticed a necklace of poisonous beads around her neck. "Did they return the divine tokens to you?"

"Yes," Anna answered for her. "As soon as the respawn circle appeared, everything was returned to us."

I don't fully understand why this is so important. Blessings, poisons, permanent status effects... It sounds crazy, but it might work.

-5% HP. REMAINING HP: 65%...

"Can you give me one of those beads?" I asked Theophilia.

"Of course, but why?" She detached a bead and handed it to me.

The necklace is purely a magical item. There's no string or thread holding the beads together.

They cling to each other, attracted by some mysterious force field, or perhaps just by the high priestess's faith.

The bead was round, shimmering with a murky greenish hue. Utterly vile. Fearing I might change my mind at any moment, I tossed it into my mouth and swallowed it, eliciting yelps of astonishment from the girls.

YOU HAVE BEEN POISONED BY LOLF'S POISON!

"FAVORITE OF THE GODS" TRAIT: LOLF'S POISON REMOVED!

Swaying slightly, I got to my feet. My head was still spinning, but it felt more like a placebo effect now. My body was responsive again. In fact, I felt more invigorated than ever.

"How did you do that?" Anna scrutinized me, noticing the absence of any lingering effects from the poisoning.

"With a hair of the dog that bit me," I quoted ancient wisdom, without actually revealing anything.

It all hinged on my bold assumption about the game's mechanics. Since Theophilia's necklace was of divine origin, it would afflict me with Poisoning as a divine debuff. Yet the game's system couldn't apply two identical debuffs at once, so the second one — the divine one — would surely take precedence, and my new skill would remove it. *Et voilà!*

"Feeling better?" Anna asked matter-of-factly. "On your feet then! We need to move."

"Wait, why do we need to run at all?" I objected. "My buddy Simba is there! We can sort this out with him..."

"You haven't seen them!" the high priestess interrupted. "They butchered all of my girls without any mercy at all. There's no stopping them."

No mercy huh? I couldn't help but laugh. Who could resist such tasty, nearly-naked targets so close by? But I kept my thoughts to myself — no need to offend our "temporary ally."

Besides, I really needed to get to the front entrance. The question that irked me was whether Lady Yumina would respawn in the circle. If yes, then she's definitely a player and not an NPC — a player who lost her memory and got stuck in virtual reality with her false memories. Because otherwise...

Well then, in the best — or rather, ideal — case, I would be greeted by a revived Yumi in the VR pod out in meatspace, along with the entire board of directors offering signed checks to me. The beta test would be over and it would be clear how the other players could be saved.

And in the worst case scenario a police squad would be waiting for me to charge me with murder. The more I thought about it, the more likely this scenario seemed. Why am I such an idiot? Always meddling where I shouldn't. The big shots had told me to just observe and not stick my nose in too far. But I guess this was my nature. Restless. I definitely didn't like being told what to do.

And it wasn't out of stubbornness. Mostly

because the people offering such advice tend to consider their interests, not mine. And I'm used to having a good idea of what I'm doing or supposed to be doing.

"What are you scared of, Anna?" I asked with surprise. "Together, we can handle any zergling rush they throw at us. There could be a hundred of them or even a thousand — it wouldn't change a thing."

"Targe, I'm not exaggerating," she shook her head. "A dozen, two dozen... even five dozen of them we could take. But a hundred will crush us. We simply won't be able to kill them all, even if we're one-shotting the entire time. And there are way more than a hundred out there."

"Then wait here, I'll be quick," I said and dashed towards the entrance.

The paladins were just finishing off the spiders in the ballroom. Though the arachnids were low-level, they were hardy and could spit venom. Theophilia had summoned quite a few of her spawn, but now only seven remained, surrounded by the attackers. There were about twenty of the paladins, however — far fewer than Anna had claimed.

I entered the fray calmly and methodically. None of the attackers were higher than Level 8, so every strike of mine yielded one corpse.

"For Anima!" one of them hollered and immediately choked on my wakizashi.

"There is but one goddess!" another echoed him and instantly lost his head.

Oh my sacred brethren, behold how religious disputes used to be settled back in the olden days. The stronger god is the superior one. Bolstered by my efforts, the spiders counterattacked, while out of the corner of my eye, I saw a white blur spinning on my left flank. Anna had joined the fray.

After the first one-shot, a counter appeared in my interface. Victims: 1/10... 2/10... 3/10... It quickly filled up and triggered a new notification:

NEW DIVINE ABILITY ACQUIRED.

What the ability was and how to use it remained a mystery for the moment. I would figure that out when things were less hectic.

Anna and I efficiently cleared the ballroom and the hall and made our way to the palace's entrance. As soon as we stepped outside, the crowd recoiled from us.

Of course, we didn't just walk out like idle aristocrats: I burst forth with a *Whirlwind,* scattering viscera and body parts around me, while Anna launched into a complex combo that made minced meat of five players practically instantly.

Our dramatic appearance cooled some hot heads, but I could tell that this was only temporary.

Simba was organizing a squad of paladins right at the foot of the stairs. There were already twenty of them and they had added long spears to their showy armor. My friend, the generalissimo of Anima's knightly order, had positioned a variety of swordsmen on the flanks. This wasn't looking like a mere mob, but a detachment of well-armed and decently leveled players.

Whereas Lolf had attracted dozens of impressionable girls to her service and the Whisperer had chosen thieves and other sneaks, and those who joined Ji-Bo were those who wanted peace and pleasure, then Anima had galvanized everyone who wanted to be a warrior.

The most combat-ready, leveled, and motivated fighters in this world had sworn allegiance to her. And now they were ready to storm the palace — to drive us out.

Meanwhile, the mayor did not seem particularly concerned about any of this. He had placed a thin line of guards at the doorstep, while he stood aside, surrounded by his security detail, smiling smugly and whispering something to Lady Sibyl. In response to his words, she laughed cheerily and seemed quite pleased with herself.

The most curious developments, however, were under way in the respawn circle. The spider girls had already been released, and the crowd had immediately torn them apart, throwing them back in again. Ji-Bo remained in the center of the circle, sitting in a lotus position, his eyes shut and meditating or perhaps just dozing off. It seemed he had no intention of leaving this place until the end of the beta round. A questionable tactic, in my opinion. If I understood the rules correctly, each House had to kill at least one follower of another god to avoid elimination at the end of the round. Maybe I was wrong, but it seemed to me his guys could get lost in their own grove without their leader.

But the most important detail was the sight of Lady Yumina's red dress. Its wearer was patiently waiting for an opportunity to retaliate against her tormentors: This was quite evident on her doll-like face. And this meant that I was too late. Who knows what would have happened if I had killed Yumi before the respawn circle had appeared, but either way, the AI had closed this loophole, boldly and cynically, right before my eyes.

"Simba!" I yelled, drowning out the crowd's noise. "What are you doing?! Who are you planning on attacking? Me?!"

Simba looked up from his strategic affairs and stared in my direction. He stepped out from the ranks of his paladins and approached me closely. The officers of their respective hosts had decided to parley.

"Sorry, Andrew," he said, lowering his gaze, "my Goddess demands sacrifices."

As he spoke these words, he cast a sidelong glance at AngelCake and I understood that the goddess Anima had revealed herself to him as well.

"Are you mad?!" I couldn't hold back. "Did you forgot who leveled you up, who pulled you out of the muck? You'd raise your sword against your own raid leader?"

Simba was a pitiful sight. His naive face reflected the full spectrum of the deep moral conflict raging within him. On one side was an old friend, and on the other, a crowd of followers waiting for him to fulfill their hopes and expectations, to lead them. They admired him and cheered his leadership ecstatically.

"It's just a game," he mumbled. "Someone always wins and someone always loses. My Goddess needs to level up... Do you know how much you get for killing another god?" He even perked up at his own thought: "Why don't you leave her and join us? We are at the top of the pecking order here!"

He turned to his golden paladins, waved his hand, and they pounded their breastplates, shouting in unison: "There is but one Goddess and her name is A-ni-ma! There is but one Goddess and her name is A-ni-ma!"

"We've got a PR guy here," boasted Simon. "He's real good with making up slogans."

"Don't be greedy, Simba," I pleaded with my friend with the last of my energy. "Our goal isn't to rack up frags, but to overcome the AI."

"How do you know what my goal is?" Simba glared at me stubbornly. "Do you ever care about anyone but yourself, Targe? Cavorting with the executives and messing around with the chicks from the Board and now with this fancy foreign girl. I'm just an ordinary guy! I need cash money! Remember? And I don't want to get kicked out of here because of some mess you made. These people," he gestured at the mob behind him, "believe in me and will follow me. I can't betray their expectations. Otherwise, they'll follow someone else. And I *like* that they listen to me. I *like* commanding them. Fate gave me this chance and I'm not going to lose it. As for your 'pulling me out of the muck...'" Simon shook his head. "I say we're even."

"All that awaits you inside is Death," I replied.

"We'll see," Simba smirked. "There's many of us and only one of Death."

He turned his back to me, signaling that the conversation was over, and raised his hand, signaling to his paladins. They lowered their spears but did not move.

Stacy stepped forward now. She raised her club above her head and exclaimed, "Goddess Anima, it is to you we dedicate our triumph!" Then she slammed her divine weapon onto the ground.

The ground beneath my feet seemed to disappear for a moment. This is how I imagined an earthquake feels like. A wave that sweeps across the land, knocking everything down, muffling all sound, rendering everyone powerless.

"FAVORITE OF THE GODS" TRAIT: DIVINE STUN REMOVED.

I looked around. A rank of town guards fell over like bowling pins. They lay on the palace steps, showing no signs of life. Next to me, Anna too was lying on the ground, cooling off. I picked her up and, before the attackers could recover, dragged her inside the building.

"What was that?" she groaned as soon as she opened her eyes.

"A divine attack," I explained. "I guess they don't have to stun everyone individually now."

"Damn," Anna summed up, "we definitely need to take that club away from her."

"Let's get out of here!" Theophilia sounded hystcrical.

"Let's go," I agreed. "But first, we'll need to hold them off."

*   *   *

When Anima's paladins entered the ballroom of the mayor's palace, I met them on my own. I must have looked damn impressive at that moment. A lone warrior in black armor, facing a tide of steel rushing his way. The paladins surrounded me, spears at the ready. The palace was filling up with their reinforcements, a multitude of fighters flooding in without any order.

Finally, Stacy appeared on the scene. She walked straight for me, raised her club, and with all her might, slammed it onto the parquet floor.

It was just what I'd been waiting for. With a deft flick, I cast the beads from Theophilia's necklace into the air. They popped with soft clicks, releasing puffs of pale green gas, and the attackers immediately dropped to the floor. AngelCake was the last to go out, her club clattering out of her hand. And then death entered the hall in the form of a short tantō dagger, Anna's divine token that she had given me.

The dagger was a guaranteed one-shot. It didn't matter how much health the enemy had or what kind of armor they wore. One-shot, another one-shot... and yet another. I began slaughtering the paladins like sheep in an abattoir. It was only when I reached Stacy that I stopped.

On the one hand, killing her was just another

frag — she was neither a goddess nor a high priestess, just a living symbol. On the other hand, she would make the perfect hostage. Since Simba had decided to measure everything in terms of profit, she would be my bargaining chip. I bound AngelCake's wrists and ankles with the Whisperer's cord, hoisted the plump avatar of Anima onto my shoulder, and ran deeper into the palace to catch up with the girls.

I found them in the courtyard of the barracks. Theophilia was looking around. Anna was scowling.

"My version of the game never had this," she told me. "There were no barracks here, just a park. And the gates were ordinary wrought iron, not reinforced ones like these."

"What do you mean your version of the game?" Theophilia pricked up her ears. "Do you mean in your imagination?"

"That's right. In her imagination," I cut in. "Anna considers herself a medium. She sees places she's never been and people who shouldn't be there."

Anna shot me an annoyed glance but didn't say anything.

"Are you really a medium?" This information seemed to intrigue Theophilia. "I read tarot cards. And guess what? My readings always come true!"

"Can you predict what awaits us beyond these gates?" I asked.

"Nothing good," Theophilia pouted. "As if you can't hear for yourself."

Indeed, there were dozens of voices shouting beyond the gates: "There is but one goddess." We were surrounded on all sides, which was not surprising, given Anima's numerous followers.

Should we hide in the dungeon? We might hold out a while, but they would eventually overwhelm us. Could we threaten them with AngelCake's death? That was unlikely to impress them, given the respawn circle was all that awaited her. So what now?

I surveyed the courtyard and found nothing of note. A few carts filled with various household junk and nothing more. Oddly, I had seen many carts so far, but there was no hint of mounts. The NPCs pulled the carts themselves. Hmm... No mounts eh?

"How many spiders can you summon at once, Theophilia?"

"About eight," she reckoned.

"And how many can you control? As in, make them do exactly as you tell them?"

"I can control about six," Theophilia said guiltily. "I don't have enough levels to do more."

"Six is fine," I reassured the priestess. "Summon them and make them as large as you can."

Ten minutes later, the gates of the city barracks burst open and a remarkable chariot sallied forth. Six hefty spiders were harnessed to two shafts. Loops of rope wrapped around their bodies forming the simplest of reins. The spiders galloped forward, eager to please the priestess who had summoned them.

Standing at the front of this chariot, Theophilia occasionally squealed with delight. She controlled the spiders with her mind and gripped the side of the cart with both hands. Anna and I hung off the sides, ready to chop and slice anyone who came across our way, while Stacy, our precious cargo, lay curled up on the floor, breathless from the stream of invective she'd been hurling at us since she came to.

The crowd gathered around the gates didn't even budge as we emerged — not out of their resolve to stand their ground, but because they were stunned by the spectacle unfolding before them. We carved through their mass with a long crunch, cleaving a bloody path and liberally dispatching anyone we came across amid the chaos. Having carved a bloody corridor, our spider chariot burst into open space.

Anima's followers ran after us, already lagging considerably.

"They've stolen her..." they hollered. "They've stolen our goddess! Catch the kidnappers! Death to the sacrilegious!" It seemed that news of my routing their vanguard had already reached them.

"Why did you take her?" Anna grimaced. "Now they'll never leave us alone."

"We wouldn't have gotten away from them anyway," I countered. "At least we have an ace up our sleeve now."

We abandoned the chariot at the gates to the spider mansion and carried AngelCake inside. The crowd of our pursuers was growing. I knew it was a matter of time until they would attempt an assault. If they weren't afraid to storm the palace of the most powerful NPC in the game, an old shack with spiders certainly wouldn't deter them.

I cut the harness and the fearless spiders crawled towards our enemies to cover our retreat, reinforced by others that streamed from the house and garden.

"You are alive, Lady Theophilia! What joy!" The minor spider priestesses surrounded our "temporary ally." "Did something happen? Lolf has ceased to answer our prayers and send her gifts."

"We'll fix that right this instant!" Theophilia's voice grew bossy. "Place this busty wench on the altar. The Goddess Lolf will have her sacrifice!"

CHAPTER 08

"WHAT'S GOING ON OUT THERE?" Anna asked me impatiently. "How long are they going to dally around for?"

It seemed like she couldn't wait for Anima's zealots to finally come and kill us.

"No idea," I said, peering out the window. "I think they're waiting for anyone still back in the respawn circle to rejoin them before they come for us."

Without deigning to get her divine ass off the floor and come look for herself, Anna was lounging in one of the miraculously undamaged chairs in the mansion and polishing her sword with a rag she had picked up off the floor. I had no idea where the rag had come from. Maybe one of the sacrifices to Lolf had dropped it, or maybe it was just lying around to add to the overall impression of the clutter in this place.

I didn't see any point in polishing an already razor-sharp sword, but maybe the act itself calmed her down.

AngelCake was in the cellar with the priestesses. They gave her another dose of gas — thankfully, there were plenty of capsules — and tied her to the stakes on the floor. I had recalled that Stacy was terrified of spiders and so asked them to keep her unconscious for a while longer. She still hadn't woken up. In the meantime, Anna and I went upstairs to prepare for the assault.

"When will they gather everyone?" Anna wouldn't stop asking.

"How should I know?" I was starting to get annoyed. "Who knows how long the respawn circle holds onto whoever appears in it…"

"What makes you think it ever lets anyone out?"

Damn! Such a thought hadn't even crossed my mind. And really — was there anything good to expect from a ritual devised by Sibyl? She was the one who had trapped Lance's friends in the game and I was pretty sure that Yumi's "digitization" was her doing, too.

Who the hell was she, anyway?! She claimed she was a player — but then she'd be the only player with a unique class, a player who had appeared out of nowhere and somehow got on perfectly well with the NPCs…

Conversely, if she were an NPC, how could an NPC know what was happening outside the game? After all, she *had* promised to meet me in meatspace, had she not? How could an NPC lie like that?

"How do you know her?" Anna asked me.

"She joined my party," I answered honestly. "I met her here in the game. When I saw Sibyl at your house, I was stunned. She can't be an NPC, can she?"

"I don't know!" Anna jumped up from the chair and began pacing the room, kicking at anything in her path. "I don't know if she was part of the original design or if my father added her later. Benny doesn't know either. He simply reset the kernel. But *she* definitely knows me. She knew what she was doing when she tried to get rid of me. And thank you for helping me back there, by the way."

"You owe me," I grinned. "But, on another note, what's keeping us here anyway?"

"How do you mean?" Anna stopped and stared at me.

"Why, literally." I turned and faced her. "Don't you remember coming here through the window? What's stopping us from leaving the same way? As long as the blessing holds, the spiders won't touch us. This isn't our fight. We need to level up, to figure out our new classes and abilities. Don't you realize that we're being set up to fight each other? And, I mean, why should we? The people running the beta are the ones who penned us in this tiny area and then said we could and even should kill each other. There's something I realized this week, though Anna: We can't do what they want us to do because none of them actually wish us well. Everyone here is playing their own game, acting in their own interests. And you can only win by setting your own rules."

I was surprised by how long I spoke. Before this, I tried to listen to others, but now I couldn't hold back. Everyone in this damn game and around it is weaving their own web, and Lolf is probably the most honest of all these spiders, even though most of them are human.

Anna didn't expect such eloquence from me. She just gave a short nod and headed for the stairs.

"Don't leave!" Theophilia's head popped up from the cellar trapdoor. "Please!"

She had been eavesdropping. How else could she react so quickly? And it had been quiet for the last few minutes. Before that, a melodious, though somewhat mournful chanting had drifted up from the cellar, but then, suddenly, everything had gone quiet.

The Arachnid High Priestess widened her eyes and raised her eyebrows, pouting. She looked like a spoiled girl asking her daddy to pay for a vacation in the Maldives.

Anna never missed a step, but I stopped and turned.

"What can you offer us?" I shot back.

Theophilia seemed stumped. If it were just about me, she'd have made her offer without hesitation. She had hinted more than once that the priestesses of Lolf were prepared to reward me for my efforts, either individually or collectively. But it seemed like she had a mental block when it came to persuading Anna.

"What do you want?"

From the look on the Goddess of Death's face, it was clear that bargaining wasn't her strong suit. Her thing was barging in and killing everyone. But negotiations… Well, they weren't really my thing either, to be honest. Simba always handled that. But where's Simba now? I couldn't count on him anymore.

Theophilia didn't know how she could be useful to us either. However, when she realized we could easily leave her alone to face the followers of Anima, enraged about the kidnapping of their busty talisman, the spider priestess grew friendly and amenable.

"Vassalage," I suggested.

"What?!" The priestess's eyes popped out of their sockets.

"Theo, what grade did you get in history class?"

"An A!" Theophilia batted her eyelashes.

No surprise there — if here history teacher was male, it's a wonder it wasn't an A+.

"You'll swear an oath to us," I patiently explained. "An oath of vassalage promising that your divine House of Lolf will be forever loyal to our divine House of Death."

"Submit?" A look of displeasure flashed across Theophilia's face. She didn't really want to bend to anyone. But she would have to, the sweetheart. No one's going to perform feats for you just to see approval in your beautiful eyes. We'll just bend you as politely and gently as possible.

"No, not submit," I clarified. "You'll be independent, you'll be on your own and able to do what you want. We won't even tell anyone about the vassalage. It will be a secret. But in any uncertain situation, you'll support us and take our side. Do you agree?"

Theophilia quickly glanced at the window. The clangor of weapons and armor, leisurely conversations, laughter, and war cries could be heard coming from the square outside — the sounds of a strong and confident force amassing out there.

"Fine," she nodded. "To whom do I swear the oath?"

"To him," Anna waved her hand. "He's our... high priest."

Theophilia licked her lips nervously and suddenly dropped to her knees in front of me.

"I swear to support the House of Death in everything," she said, looking up at me slyly, "and to be a good girl."

Her pose and tone made my thoughts go in a completely different direction, and if Anna weren't here, our oath of vassalage definitely wouldn't have been limited to words. Who cares that the enemy is at the gate? The adrenaline rush was making my ears ring and bringing a sour taste to my mouth.

Drawing my sword and laying it on the brunette's shoulder, I said as solemnly as possible:

"I accept your oath and pledge to protect the House of Lolf, hereby allied with the House of Death."

My quest log immediately blinked.

NEW QUEST: "DEFEND THE HOUSE OF LOLF."

PROTECT THE ALTAR OF LOLF UNTIL THE END OF THE ROUND.

REWARD: +20 TO DIVINE REPUTATION.

PENALTY FOR FAILURE: CONFLICT WITH THE HOUSE OF LOLF. -20 TO DIVINE REPUTA-TION.

42:34... 42:33...

The timer began counting down the time we had left in the game. Judging by Theophilia's glazed over look, she had read something in her interface too, and smiled unexpectedly. It seemed she had also been given a quest to "guard and protect."

"Go downstairs," I told her, "and try not to kill AngelCake until the last possible moment."

"Why?" she asked, genuinely surprised.

I didn't tell her that I simply felt sorry for the foolish girl. I remembered how she had screamed at the sight of spiders, how she fed me pastries, and how she moaned beneath me in the MosTech locker room. It wasn't long since I had saved her and now I had brought her to the altar of Lolf as a sacrifice to the spider goddess.

At the same time, I understood that Stacy had gone too far. She had completely lost her way. I couldn't forgive her for turning against me so easily. You can give a good spanking and wait for apologies. But if you forgive outright hostility, you won't live long. As Simba had just said himself, "It's just a game."

"She's our hostage," I explained to Theophilia. "Maybe we can use her to stop them."

It was no good, however. That much became clear when the large but disorganized rabble outside formed itself into the semblance of a line and moved in our direction. Simba was always a lousy strategist and this time too his plan lacked sophistication. He just wanted to crush us with numbers. But I still went out to meet them.

As I emerged, I thought of myself as a movie hero who strides leisurely towards an overwhelming host. Holler all you want — gnash your teeth and bash your shields — I'll never be scared of you lot.

The square was full of people. I would be lying if I said half the city had gathered there. Paladins and knights in armor, swordsmen in full motley, duelists and adventurers, flashy crossbowmen and archers, even sneak-thieves — those who hadn't joined the Whisperer's House.

It was an enormous crowd by real-world standards and at the front of it came Simba in golden armor. My buddy was well on his way — he was clearly living his moment of glory and basking in its glow.

Yet the ranks of his personal guard had thinned significantly, which worried me almost more than the upcoming battle.

There were no NPCs here. I saw a small squad of city guards in a passage to one of the streets, but they had left the square. The mayor was either protecting his people or simply not interfering in the conflict between players.

The spiders were also holding back. They stood in a dense, wriggling mass at the level of the fences, not daring to crawl out onto the cobblestones. I watched as one of them seemed to cross an invisible line, crawled onto the pavement and was immediately torn to pieces by a volley of arrows from dozens of archers.

I walked ahead, feeling Anna's presence behind me without turning around. In the sudden hush that fell over the square, only the sound of our footsteps was audible. We approached the spiders, and they parted, obediently making way for us. I took a step, then another, expecting a barrage of arrows and crossbow bolts, but there was nothing, only stillness. It wasn't until I reached the midpoint that Simba raised his hand, indicating that it was best to stop.

"Where are your paladins, Simba?!" I yelled.

"That's a question for you!" he yelled back.

"Stuck at the respawn point?!" I laughed loudly and mockingly. "Send them here. I'll be happy to farm them for the XP again!"

"Enough of your bad jokes, Targe!" Simba never had much patience. "What did you do to them? None of my men who went into the palace made it to the respawn point! What did you do to them, Targe?! You fed them to your spiders, didn't you?"

The crowd behind Simba grumbled angrily. It's one thing to die an honorable death in a fair fight and another to perish in a secret ritual in some dark cellar.

"And if you don't tell your men here to pull back, your idol will die the same way!" I raised my voice on purpose. "Devoured by Lolf!"

"Release our Anima, you bastards!"

"Kill them, they're Satanists!"

"Why even parley with his kind?"

"Death has teamed up with the spiders!"

By and by, all the yelling merged into one constant chant:

"A-ni-ma! A-ni-ma!! A-NI-MA!!!"

I couldn't help wondering why we hadn't stayed inside like last time. Defending the spider mansion from dumb mobs was much easier than from a crowd of players who could storm several windows at once and spam arrows at the windows if necessary.

Plus, defending the mansion deprived us of any chance to maneuver. It was the last line of defense, and we had given up all the others in advance.

The mob advanced, picking up pace, breaking into a run, ready to obliterate any obstacle in their path. I had no intention of waiting for them. My plan was to leap behind the front line of fighters and wreak havoc among the archers.

However, as it had so often happened this never-ending day, I was too late.

"GET OOOVER HERE!" Simba bellowed, extending his hand towards me.

"GET OOOVER HERE!" echoed another warrior standing next to him.

"GET OOOVER HERE! GET OOOVER HERE!" The paladins' voices merged, resonating with each other and burrowing into my brain.

I dashed forward, only to find myself somewhere entirely unexpected. My katana struck an enemy, hoping to silence that horrible sound and voice, but it ricocheted off the heavy armor. Tanks surrounded me on all sides.

Their damn "aggro" had worked! Even my leveled-up *Serenity* passive couldn't withstand the combined efforts of two dozen paladins. I knew I needed to retreat and create distance, but instead, I desperately tried to cut through them to silence their annoying voices.

Piercing Strike! My katana cleaved the armor of one of Anima's warriors, who immediately dissolved, leaving only a slightly bent golden breastplate behind. The tanks kept coming, however, surrounding and hemming me in from all sides.

Whirlwind! I spun my blades, creating an impenetrable cocoon around myself. All the incoming bolts and arrows were knocked out of the air and fell at my feet. It looked spectacular, but this skill had a cooldown of a minute, and an archer could fire a dozen arrows in that time.

Anna was fighting fiercely to my right. Paladins went to respawn one by one around her. Her divine dagger never missed and could one-shot even a tank.

And yet, held back with spears and pressed with shields, we were being pushed back.

"GET OOOVER HERE!" How I hated that phrase! I hated the paladins and Simba for coming up with it. It turned me into an idiot, making me charge at armored enemies like a bull at a red cape.

A crossbow bolt penetrated my guard, lodging itself in my chest. I lost only five percent of my health, but this was a warning shot. We were being engulfed by the human sea, surrounded and trapped inside. Enemies were on all sides. Another arrow hit my shoulder. Now I had 87% health left.

"A-ni-ma! A-NI-MA!"

The front lines collided with the mass of spiders with a crunch. The spiders fought valiantly, trying to hold the enemy back, but they were simply trampled. This wasn't an army — it was a horde!

Another paladin went down! Why are they so damn tough?! I looked around. My gaze lost in the surrounding madness, but I knew what to look for. Sibyl stood behind the guards, making gestures with her hands. Bastards! No wonder! They had a healer! While my health was being chipped away, my enemies were being restored. And then another thought struck me: It seemed the city had chosen its official state religion after all.

My HP dropped to 82%! An arrow hit my left arm, and then as I hesitated, I took another hit! 73%! In response, I took down a swift duelist as a nasty thought pounded in my head: *How much longer do I have?*

The spiders were being finished off right under the mansion's walls. They fought desperately, jumping, spitting venom. Some even leaped from the roof onto the attackers' heads. They were elites — Level 10s — and still they didn't last long.

"*It's now or never,*" I wrote in my party chat and immediately got a response:

"*Let's do it!*"

"Long liiive Death!" The archers on the left side stopped firing. I heard their frightened screams and the excited shouts of their pursuers. Lance, T-Rex, and Shugga had joined the fray. Bursting out from one of the streets, they managed to avoid the tanks' "aggro" spells and plunged into the archers' ranks.

Like a fox in a henhouse, Lance was having a blast. The archers' quilted armor was no match for him. Some archers tried to mimic Legolas, firing point-blank and on the move, others drew their pitiful daggers to put up a semblance of a fight. The third group just ran away screaming, which was the wisest choicc as it gave them the slightest chance of survival.

But I was already down to 62%! Lance wasn't fast enough. Seeing this, he put all his strength into cutting his way towards us, but he got bogged down in the human swarm. Numbers overwhelmed Level. Our reinforcements were simply too few.

BOOM! My first thought was that an

earthquake had erupted under my feet. It felt like the ground truly shifted for a moment. Everyone stopped and turned at the sound.

Then one of the wings of the spider mansion collapsed as if it were made of cardboard. Most of the debris fell inward, into the cellar, and from the ground, a massive spider leg suddenly emerged. It groped around for support, then, with a crack, hoisted its massive black torso out of the depths of the earth.

"Lolf! It's Lolf!" echoed in cries across the battlefield. "Lolf has awoken!"

Chapter 09

AFTER THE LEG CAME some stiff, curious whiskers, a massive cephalothorax with its head and remaining legs, and a fat, heavy abdomen. Lolf carefully examined her surroundings, completely demolishing the rest of the mansion in the process and then fully ventured outside.

At the same time, I realized that AngelCake had been sacrificed and fed to the Great Spider Mother. Although, judging by the energy the spider goddess had absorbed, the sacrifice hadn't been Stacy, but her divine counterpart — Anima. No wonder the priestesses' prayers had been answered. The arachnid had awoken and set out to see who was killing her children.

Lolf emerged from her burrow and turned her head from side to side. Since she had no neck, the spider was forced to turn her entire cephalothorax, surveying the square with her eight unblinking eyes.

Unlike her daughter, whom I had killed in the basement of one of the houses, Lolf looked like a real cross spider, only gigantic: long, grasping legs with pointed hooks at the ends for climbing or catching prey, elongated sharp fangs for injecting venom into her victims, and a massive abdomen adorned with a bright green cross.

Lolf took a few steps, as if warming up after a long period of immobility, clicked her jaws several times, spraying greenish venom, and then charged at Simba's army.

In vain he tried to rally his people and lead them in a desperate attack. The spider stomped the fighters into the ground with her legs, pierced armor with her fangs, and spat venom that burned through armor and people alike.

The tide that surrounded me suddenly ebbed, and I was left alone. Some decided to retreat to fight the new common threat, but most began to panic and scream.

"Run! We need to save ourselves!"

"She's invincible, damn it! Arrows don't hurt her!"

"We've been betrayed!"

"Let's get out of here!"

Simba managed to gather five paladins around him. They desperately shouted their "Get ooover here," phrase, trying to draw the spider's aggro from the crowd to themselves. Other fighters began to join this island of resistance. After all, farming a boss is a normal event in any game, even if the boss is as huge as this one was.

The archers focused their fire on Lolf's massive body; it was impossible to miss. Most of the arrows bounced off her shiny black armor, but a few did hit their mark. Two of her eight malevolent eyes went dull, losing their glint. The creature crouched and angrily clicked her fangs. Their jarring, irritating crackle spread across the square like a drumbeat.

Hearing it and gaining courage, the smaller spiders also went on the counterattack. They jumped on the players' backs, trying to sink their venomous jaws into their shoulders or necks, paralyzing them. They bit legs, causing them to topple over, then diligently wrapped the immobilized players in cocoons.

Pop! Pop! Pop! New players appeared on the scene. Figures in dark hoods materialized behind Simba's squad. They appeared with daggers already in hand. The Whisperer's House had chosen its side. The thieves slashed at the archers and anyone who looked wealthier, hoping for loot. Before my eyes, one of the hooded figures dispatched Sibyl, without even realizing whom he'd just killed.

I gritted my teeth in frustration. More than anything in this battle, I had wanted to cross blades with Simba as two champions of our respective hosts — and also to reach that Sibyl bitch, whom I considered responsible for this entire mess.

Meanwhile, Lolf crouched slightly, like a dog ready to chase a stick, and then leaped, crushing

Simba and the others beneath her massive belly. She pressed her body against the cobblestones and wriggled vengefully, grinding the players like grist between millstones. No one could survive that. Once again, my opponent had escaped my sword today — why did this keep happening?!

After that, the ranks of Anima's followers collapsed completely. Routed, they were now being hunted down and finished off. In a matter of minutes, the strongest divine house in the game had turned into a frightened herd. Suddenly we were competing with each other for kills, taking out the fleeing players faster than Lolf could.

To my surprise, I realized I had reached Level 16. In the heat of battle, I hadn't even noticed the rush of pleasure that comes with leveling up. There hadn't been time for that.

Lolf rampaged across the square like a hurricane. She flattened enemies into pancakes and devoured the remains. Then she chased them onto one of the city streets and followed. Some, hoping for mercy from the great Spider Mother, fell to their knees, begging to be taken into her service. Those were quickly and efficiently devoured, often by first having their heads bitten off.

I doubted the god's intelligence, however. Lolf seemed to be pure power, a force of nature tamed by sacrifices. The "goddess" began rampaging through the city, smashing everything in her path. A few stragglers from the Whisperer's House also fell under her wrathful legs as she made no distinction between friend and foe.

The square was now littered with loot. We needed to collect it; these were our trophies, and we would need the money. I didn't want a repeat of today's confrontation, which meant that the House of Death would need to raise an army of its own. Perhaps it would not be as large as Anima's, but it would be strong and capable. Quality mattered more than quantity.

And the core of this future army was approaching me as I thought these thoughts, stepping gingerly over the scattered debris:

"This is T-Rex and Shugga…" Lance introduced his fighters to me.

"How's it going fellas?" I said, shaking their hands.

The third member, Xavier, was apparently the one who had had the heart attack. According to the rumors, he was a real jerk so good luck to him, I guess, but I was happy he hadn't come.

"Well if it isn't Lan-ce-loot!" Anna approached us. "I've heard of you, young esports prodigy. They say you show promise."

Lance didn't flinch at the gibe. He stepped forward and repeated his flashy gesture from the mayor's palace, dropping to one knee and holding his sword before him.

"Accept our oath of fealty, Goddess of Death," he declared dramatically, addressing Anna.

T-Rex and Shugga followed suit.

What a jerk. Although we had discussed his sudden appearance in the party chat, he didn't know about my new "position." And, of course, he wanted to earn points with his patroness.

"I accept," Anna nodded graciously. "But I'm not the leader here. TargetAi is the head of the House of Death."

I looked at her in amazement. Naturally, I hadn't planned on relinquishing control to Anna, but I thought we'd have a tough conversation about that, maybe even an argument. I didn't expect her to be so compliant. It made sense, since in the other houses, the high priests were in charge. No one had ever seen the Whisperer or the Eternal Groove in person, and Anima hadn't really shown herself much either, leaving many details about the gods' role in the game unclear. Lolf, for instance, was clearly not a competent leader, so Theophilia would be running things in that divine house. But, well, our goddess was right here.

"And you?" I clarified, just in case.

"I'm a goddess," Anna smiled. "I bask in your admiration and accept your offerings. But to be perfectly honest, I'm a loner and not used to leading a group, and I have no idea what my new status will require of me in the future. You saved my butt at least three times today, so I trust you. I didn't realize how nice it is to have someone to rely on."

LANCE HAS JOINED YOUR PARTY.
T-REX HAS JOINED YOUR PARTY.
SHUGGA HAS JOINED YOUR PARTY.
ANNA HAS JOINED YOUR PARTY.

"Alright then, House of Death, heed my commands! Go see Theophilia ASAP to obtain a blessing from her so that Lolf and her spawn don't attack you. After that, let's gather all this loot! These are our rightful trophies, and if anyone tries to grab them, you're authorized to cut their hands off at the wrist."

Everyone, Anna included, nodded and dashed to the mansion — only Lance lingered behind.

"I see you're ballin', Andrew!" He clapped me on the shoulder.

"What are you talking about?!" I thought Lance was going to challenge my authority, but instead, he broke into a wide grin.

"Don't you see?!" He glanced at Anna's receding figure. "Don't you realize our goddess has a thing for you?"

"Come on!" The thought had never even crossed my mind.

"'I didn't realize how nice it is to have someone to rely on,'" Lance quoted in a squeaky voice and burst out laughing.

"She doesn't sound like that!" I protested. "And if you keep talking that way, I'll have you brought before the inquisition for blasphemy! You'll burn at the stake for insulting our deity."

"Okay, okay, I'll say nothing more!" Still laughing, Lance went off to get his blessing.

"*Theophilia, the danger has passed,*" I typed in the chat. "*Send your girls out to gather up the loot.*"

"*Okay, boss,*" the spider priestess replied.

There was a touch of sarcasm in her

response, but I didn't care. The important thing was getting the job done. My status had changed several times today, but it seemed I was going to end this round of the beta with a significant advantage after all.

I still had a difficult conversation with Simba ahead of me, but we'd deal with the problems as they came. Right now, my main problem was the gray hooded figures swiftly picking up loot from the pavement — *my* loot!

"Hold it right there!" I drew both swords as I advanced. "Anyone who moves dies! I SAID, HANDS OFF, YOU BITCHES!"

"In our circles, that word is considered extremely offensive," Shiloh approached me with a friendly smile.

Of course he was sneaking around here. A classic Soviet-era proverb sprang to mind: "*Politeness is the thief's main weapon.*"

"Sure, how about 'rat?' Does that suit you better?" I conceded. "Those who steal from their own are called rats. Isn't that right?"

"Why speak so harshly, young man?" Shiloh seemed genuinely offended. "We arrived to help you at a critical moment! We supported you!"

"Sure, at the critical moment once it became clear who would win!" I had no intention of entertaining his arguments.

Then I heard footsteps behind me and saw Shiloh's smile melt before my eyes.

"There are larger geopolitics at play at the moment, Shiloh. Contacts are being established, alliances are being formed," I tried to sound as sincere as possible. "We already have friends, do you? Do you want to join us or be on your own?"

"What am I supposed to tell my men?" Shiloh wheedled. "They joined the battle risking their necks. They believe they have the right to the spoils."

"Your kills are your loot," I decided. "The rest is ours."

"Fair enough," the chief thief nodded, and the fighters behind him relaxed visibly. "We'll talk again soon, TargetAi. We have much to discuss."

I couldn't tell if that was a promise or a threat, and Shiloh didn't continue the conversation. With a wave of his hand, he led his men away.

Lolf returned half an hour later. She crossed the square, climbed back into her burrow, piled some debris to tuck herself in and went quiet. The smaller spiders immediately began weaving silk over the breach, and soon it was completely hidden from sight.

We gathered a lot of loot, piling it into the cart still standing at the mansion gates — the same one we commandeered when fleeing the palace. Then Lance and T-Rex harnessed themselves to the cart and dragged it to the merchant. Theophilia tagged along, saying she was good at bartering and had a keen eye for style. They got into a lively discussion, chatting about brands, trends, and prospects along the way.

We left them at the shop and continued on. There were only a few minutes left until the end of the beta round, and I was eager to see whether Sibyl had reappeared in the respawn circle or died like any proper NPC. Yet we were in for disappointment when we reached the central square: The circle was empty.

* * *

Marina was waiting for me in the locker room. I was about to make a comment about pushy women who didn't understand personal boundaries and lustful bitches who used their position for personal gain, but she didn't even give me a chance to open my mouth.

"She's not on the players' list."

"Sibyl?" I knew immediately who she was talking about.

"Yes, there's no player with that username in the beta!"

"Could you have made a mistake?"

"No!" Marina practically shouted. "I put those lists together myself. All the invitations went through me. Do you think I was meeting VIPs just to take photos? She doesn't appear in any of my lists!"

"Then how could she get into the game?" I asked reasonably.

"She couldn't," Marina shook her head. "You need a VR pod for that, and I assigned all of those too!"

"Yes, you're the big boss lady," I took her hand to calm her down a bit, but the PR guru wasn't in the mood to calm down.

"Who the hell is she?! I saw that bitch hitting on you! Has this crazy AI completely lost it and decided to steal my man? What the hell is this, a sexbot rebellion?!"

"Believe me, Marina," I said, suppressing my laughter, "that's the last thing you need to worry about right now."

"You're not even surprised, are you?!" She suddenly froze, staring at me intently. "You knew this would happen?"

"I suspected it," I nodded. "She's too odd a character."

"That scares me," Marina's eyes grew misty, and she hugged me tightly. I had no choice but to embrace her and kiss her on the top of her head. "I'm afraid you won't come back, that you'll turn into a vegetable and spend your life pissing yourself. I'm afraid the police will come here and arrest us all for experimenting on humans. I'm just terrified of this incomprehensible thing. When I pass by the server room and hear it buzzing like a wasp's nest, it feels like it's thinking about all of us, wanting to break out and kill us all."

"That's not the AI buzzing, silly." I kissed her again, soothing her like a little girl. "It's just the fans humming, cooling the hardware."

"Tell me, Andrew, what does it want? Why is it doing all of this anyway?"

I froze, realizing I had never asked myself this question. Marina, in all her naive blonde simplicity, had hit the nail on the head. Indeed, if this was an advanced AI, what was its ultimate goal? Why did it start trapping people to begin with in the alpha and why was it doing it now in the beta?

It suddenly seemed to me that we had been treating the symptoms without thinking about the disease. We were trying to free people without considering why the neural network needed to do any of this at all.

If you believe the Master, the AI is like a crazed maniac, killing for pleasure or survival. But you could forgive the Master as surely he suffered from professional bias. I had seen the world the neural network created at Anna's home, however, and so I knew that over the years it had shown no aggression. Why? Because no one had shown aggression towards it? Was its behavior merely a response? If so, what was it responding to? What was it trying to tell us?

"What are you thinking about?" Marina sensed my distraction and pulled back slightly to look into my face.

"I'm thinking about your question," I admitted. "It's a very good question. I think when we understand the answer, we'll be able to defeat the AI."

"Well, sure. I'm really smart!" Marina's mood shifted as quickly as early spring weather; a little praise, and she was already smiling. "Haven't you noticed?"

"I notice all the time," I flattered her. "You help me a lot, and it's because you're such a smart girl that I have another task for you. Two, in fact."

"What are they?" Marina purred.

"Find me the player data for the usernames 'Shiloh,' 'Theophilia,' and 'Ji-Bo.'"

"That's personal information. It would be illegal for me to share it with you!" she protested. Then she added, a bit illogically: "Why do you need it?"

"I promise not to do anything bad to them. In fact, it'll be in their interest if I meet with them."

Marina thought for a couple of seconds, then nodded.

"And the second task?"

"All access passes are logged, right?" I asked. "Security has information on who is in the building?"

"They should..." she nodded again.

"Then find out who was here yesterday from 11 p.m. to midnight." I paused to let it sink in. "Do it very discreetly, and once you know, don't tell anyone except me."

CHAPTER 10

WHEN IT CAME TO MEN, Stacy Zarubina could never catch a break. It was all because she wanted so badly for them to like her. Even back in kindergarten, she would give the boys candy she had stolen from home and share her snacks with them. "I don't mind, and it makes them happy," she told herself, refusing to admit to herself that she was buying their friendship and attention.

But having gobbled up Stacy's Kit-Kats and Snickers, the cunning boys would run off to hang out with the mean and greedy Lena, Natasha, and Olga. They'd throw snowballs at them, drag their sleds, and pull their braids, while Stacy would be left on the sidelines, without candy and without attention.

Another girl might have become depressed in her position, but to compensate for this misfortune, life had blessed Stacy with an inexhaustible supply of optimism. So over time, there were more and more candies and less snacks for her to eat on her own.

Stacy would bring whole bags of pies, cheese-cakes, sweet rolls to school — as well as croissants, pastries, candied nuts, and other fantastically delicious treats to every class outing. Raised by her grandmother, the quick-witted girl soon began mastering culinary skills, which, according to her grandma, were the best means for seducing men.

"A well-fed man is a kind man," Grandma would say, serving her granddaughter another portion of highly fattening but incredibly delicious mashed potatoes and sausage patties. Grandma never explained where Grandpa had gone or why her culinary talents were expended exclusively on her children and grandchildren.

Stacy's father, who was divorced from her mom, would also come to Grandma's house for meals. He had remarried long ago, yet during his frequent quarrels with his new wife, he'd come to eat at his ex-mother-in-law's house. His interest in his daughter was limited to asking about her grades and occasionally giving her coloring books and sets of markers he'd bought at a shop down the street. But he always praised Grandma's cooking.

Grandma pitied her former son-in-law. "What a man," she'd say. "It's too bad Masha couldn't hold onto him." She'd criticize her daughter behind her back, convinced that her husband's leaving the family for a twenty-year-old hairdresser was entirely her daughter's fault. So it was no wonder that Stacy too believed that if her mother had been a better cook, more considerate, and kinder to her father, he wouldn't have left them.

Thus Stacy diligently learned her grandmother's lessons on using borscht, sausage patties and baked goods to ensure personal happiness. Her mother was looking for happiness in other ways at the time, and having a growing daughter around significantly reduced her chances of success.

But Stacy did well in school. She stayed active and sang in the choir. She readily allowed others to copy her work, and this led to a group of slackers to always revolve around her. Stacy basked and even "bloomed" in the glare of their attention. In her mind, Grandma's lessons were starting to pay off.

The fact that no one in her "inner circle" carried her backpack, invited her to dances, or tried to kiss her in a secluded corner seemed to go unnoticed by Stacy.

"It's just bad luck," she'd tell herself. "But soon, my luck will change."

When Stacy went to college and moved into the dorms, she discovered the world of quick sex. Her arsenal of seduction now included more effective tools than just copied homework and pastries. Stacy watched several porn films meticulously, all but taking notes. She desperately wanted men to like her.

But for some reason, the well-fed, pampered, and satisfied men didn't stick around. They were drawn to skinny, non-cooking bitches, pining for them outside their windows at night, brawling with each other for their attention, and doing any number of other stupid things to get noticed.

Stacy pitied them, sometimes feeding them like stray cats, and even having sex with them "as friends" to boost their self-esteem, hoping they would eventually decide to stick around and real-ize her undeniable superiority.

Stacy took a liking to Andrew immediately. Independent, strong and clearly underfed, he stirred strong feelings in her heart. But, as usual, the moment Stacy set her sights on him, cunning predators began circling her sweet, charming An-drew. Stacy believed that men were weak and were only good for serving as prizes in the eternal game between women, which consisted of whims, griev-ances, kisses, heart-to-hearts, spontaneous sex, and many other tricks.

Stacy hadn't been lucky so far, but she waited for one of her rivals to make a mistake so she could reclaim her Andrew. She was bolstered in this by the sudden appearance of an Inner Voice.

This wasn't like the voices that psychos hear in horror movies. It had no sound at all in fact. Simply put, Stacy began to notice thoughts occur-ring to her that weren't hers at all and upon reflec-tion, she realized that she could never even come up with them. Yet the thoughts kept coming.

She could also clearly remember the first time such an "alien" thought had come to her: It happened as she was looking at the first statue of Anima, which Sibyl had carved from a tree trunk. She really didn't like the silly caricature, and she wanted to protest and make them change it when suddenly, a thought flashed through her head: "*They will worship us.*" Not "her" and not "me," but "*us.*" At that same time, a warm wave swept through her body from head to toe. The word "*worship*" sounded so good.

Of course, she could assume that "*us*" meant her and the statue. At first, she comforted herself with this idea, but then she stopped worrying altogether.

When she was pushed out all but naked in front of the crowd in the town square, she felt ashamed, but the Inner Voice said, "*Look, they love us.*" And this love warmed her, it burned her, it was better than sex.

"*You must be unattainable. You must accept their honors as your due. You must inspire awe,*" the Voice advised, and Stacy's heart tightened sweetly as the men around her shouted her name: "Anima… Anima!" Even though it wasn't *her* name exactly — it was *their* name.

Andrew had hurt her. He had chosen another. When she woke up on Lolf's altar, Stacy raged not due to her own helplessness but at the sight of those smug, skinny bitches. Stacy didn't remember her death. Her own merciful consciousness shut off the moment she heard the rustling of spider legs. She woke up in her VR pod, furious and in tears.

But now the Voice said, *"Only the pathetic take offense... Only the wretched cry. We will get him back... And then we will have our revenge. Or maybe we won't, but then his service will be his payment."* The fact that the Voice had spoken to her in meatspace and not in the game did not surprise Stacy one bit.

And today, when she had received an invitation to attend a meeting of players, Stacy had put on her usual cutesy strawberry-printed tank top and denim shorts. Then she looked at herself in the mirror, and she didn't like what she saw.

So she hurried over to the mall, where she picked out a dark cherry evening gown and matching shoes, as well as a short mink coat with a hood she had dreamed of for the past five years. Knowing she was already late, she stopped by the beauty salon and spent another hour getting ready.

Approaching the meeting place, Stacy found Simba's number in her phone and dialed it.

"Simon, I'm nearby. Please come out and meet me."

She would never have done this before. Distracting a man for something she could easily handle herself? That was wrong. It violated all her grandmother's lessons. And yet, something new inside her whispered: *"Our paladin... He must serve us... This isn't a burden for him. He sees it as an honor..."*

* * *

The restaurant was called "Rumpelstiltskin," and I was extremely grateful for Uber because I didn't have to pronounce the name to my driver to get there. How did people used to call a cab when drunk, trying to get home? Or was that a clever way to keep them out all night, squeezing every last penny from their pockets?

The place was incredibly posh yet very cozy. How was such a combination even possible? Well, you can judge for yourself: We were sitting in a small banquet hall that resembled the living room of an aristocratic mansion. Our chairs were upholstered in satin and had curved legs, and the room was decorated with paintings in gilded frames on the walls, massive chandeliers on the ceiling and statues in the alcoves.

The waiters glided by in total silence, refilling our wine or serving cocktails, as violins played somewhere out of sight, reminding me of the virtual ball in Anna's version of the game.

At first, I felt like I was having a snack in a museum, and I half-expected a strict old lady to rush in at any moment and throw me out for violating some unwritten rule.

But after taking the first sip of the whiskey I ordered to show off a bit and having the first bite of the veal that melted in my mouth... After the first snap of logs in the huge fireplace, I decided that this was exactly how people should live when they have a ton of money and the whole world is eager to fulfill their whims.

Although this place was a bit too upscale for me, I quickly adapted, knowing that I was the one who'd invited everyone there, after all.

The place itself was Shiloh's recommendation. In real life his name was Modest Matveyevich Slonimsky and he was an entrepreneur. That was all the information Marina could dig up on him. Shiloh said he could get discounts and special treatment due to his connections at the restaurant. I took him at his word and it turned out that he wasn't wrong. Booking a table in such a place at such short notice was only possible for a wizard or someone with serious connections.

It took a real effort to think of Mr. Slonimsky as Shiloh. He was dressed in an old-fashioned yet tailor-made, three-piece suit; he smoked a pipe; and he looked either like a lawyer or an antiques dealer. But I deliberately called him by his in-game handle to remind myself that this was the man who, in the game, had thrown a cord around his neighbor's neck and strangled him right there in the central square.

Ji-Bo, on the other hand, looked exactly like his in-game avatar. He had multicolored dreadlocks and deep wrinkles on his prematurely aged face which reminded me of a clever but mischievous orangutan. Despite it being winter, Ji-Bo was dressed in a colorful Hawaiian shirt and bright pink jeans. His name was Eugene Borisov and he was a musician, DJ, designer and unrecognized genius.

He had worked for MosTech as a music com-poser and sound engineer, and this had earned him a VIP pass for the test. "He invited himself," Marina explained. "He's nosy, but mostly harm-less." I couldn't help but recall that all the truly "harmless" ones had perished in the Purge, so I had better not to turn my back on any of the sur-vivors, no matter how mostly harmless they were supposed to be.

Marina's face twisted with displeasure when she got to telling me about Theophilia: "That bitch is named Sofia Pars. She's a game blogger who streams Let's Plays — and she's a total bitch." Such an introduction made me even more eager to meet Sofia in person. Marina had a talent for giv-ing people succinct recommendations.

Sofia Pars looked even skinnier in real life than in VR. Tall like a model — easily over 6 feet — in her high heels, she could even look down on Simba. Dressed in a loose black jumpsuit, which was wide at the top and bottom but cinched at the waist, she looked both strict and sexy.

The fabric completely concealed her body, but with every movement, it clung to her curves, hint-ing at the seductive form hidden beneath the baggy outfit. True to her style, Theophilia wore spi-der-themed jewelry. One spider dangled as a pen-dant on her necklace, and two more adorned her ears. The spiders were fashioned from black gold and glittered with emerald-green eyes. I wouldn't be surprised if they were custom-made — and recently.

The spider priestess was so delighted to see me that she rushed to hug me in the foyer. She pressed herself tightly against me, and I felt her small, firm breasts against me. The sensation lingered, and every time I looked at Sofia, I felt that same firmness and softness. She caught my gaze and winked, as if reading my thoughts. After that, we sat down like conspirators at the table. Sofia seemed ready to be more forward at the table, but she was wary of Anna.

The Goddess of Death sat beside me. Today, she decided to play the *enfant terrible* — the bratty, spoiled child — so she showed up to the meeting in her motorcycle outfit. She hadn't liked my idea from the start, and this was her way of showing it. Now, she felt she was losing the battle for male attention to the audacious Sofia and her temper was slowly boiling over.

Simba came dressed exactly as he always was. He sprawled out on a chair in a bright yellow hoodie, the same color as his armor in the game. He ate loudly, laughed loudly and spoke loudly — with everyone except me. At the entrance, when we first saw each other, he refused to shake my hand, nodding curtly instead.

"What exquisite cuisine," said Sofia, poking at a plate of colorful salad leaves, which, in my opinion, could only entice a rabbit. "Modest, it seems you're the VIP here. They're treating us like we're food critics from Michelin. What's your secret?"

"It's simple," Mr. Slonimsky made a barely

noticeable gesture, and a waiter, detaching from the wall, refilled Sofia's glass, "this restaurant belongs to me."

"Ohhh..." Sofia responded, looking at Shiloh as if seeing him for the first time. She even parted her lips and leaned forward slightly, in a sincere expression of admiration.

To my surprise, Ji-Bo mirrored her gesture.

"So is MuZone your club too?" he asked, waiting for a nod before exclaiming, "I've played there!"

"I know," Modest nodded patronizingly.

Am I up to this situation I've engineered? I thought I'd gather all the leaders of the game clans in real life, explain the situation, and we'd band together to crush the AI into dust. It's no coincidence the AI is pitting us against each other, so the obvious move is to organize against it, break its own rules and form an alliance out here where it couldn't control us.

And yet, will these people listen to me? Shiloh had already outmaneuvered me by inviting us to meet on what was effectively his own turf. Even the cutlery is on his side here. Theophilia and Ji-Bo were already hanging on his every word. Simba was in his own world... so I had nothing left to do but play the cards I had.

"May I have your attention?" I stood up, raising my glass as if to make a toast. "I've gathered you all to discuss forming an alliance. I've convened us out here — not inside the game, where everyone fears a knife in the back — but here, 'on dry land,' under the assumption that you are all reasonable people who want to turn a profit," I nodded at Modest, "who want peace," I turned my gaze to Ji-Bo, "who want security," I fixed my eyes on Theophilia. "Otherwise, we'll be crushed individually. That's what the city's mayor wants. That's what all those NPCs want — to have total control over us in the game."

I didn't specify who would do it. Today's events had demonstrated how the entire city could unite against Anima. This time we had held out, but if the scales shift even slightly, the city would end up siding with one religion.

"Sounds like paranoia," Ji-Bo muttered. "I don't believe in some evil NPC conspiracy, this is just a game — a toy."

"I'm with TargetAi," Sofia said, standing up unexpectedly. "During the time I've known him, he's saved me three times and hasn't been wrong once. Why should he be wrong this time?"

Her breasts are as firm as tennis balls, my brain addded helpfully. *Probably silicone, but still, they've gotta feel great... What am I thinking?!*

"Hmm..." Shiloh pondered, drilling me with his eyes, then looking over at Anna and Simba. "What do you say, Goddess of Death?"

"I will follow my Soul Reaper," Anna responded curtly. "I have no qualms about his sincerity."

"I'll be right back," Simba said, the phone at his ear, and left the table.

"Hmm..." Shiloh removed his glasses and began cleaning them meticulously with a flannel cloth. "I do respect expert opinions... I suppose I should..."

"Conspiring behind our backs?" A voice rang loudly from the dining hall's entryway.

It was Stacy, but she looked different, as if she had undergone a transformation. A crimson, floor-length gown, gold jewelry on her neck, ears, and wrists... Even a golden tiara in her intricate high hairstyle. She was covered in red and gold — the colors of Anima.

"You're here mumbling about peace, but I've come to declare war!" Stacy paused dramatically. "We declare war on the House of Death and anyone who supports it!"

CHAPTER 11

"UGH, PLEASE, DON'T STOP... Yes... Yes... Please... I'm begging you, just like that... Aaaaaah!"

Sofia moaned, or more accurately, she let out a low, guttural howl, clutching the sheets and wrinkling them in her fists.

Smack... smack... smack... Her firm, toned ass bounced loudly against my pelvis.

Sofia arched her back even more, pressing her cheek against the couch, obediently hiking her butt higher, making it tighter and hotter inside. I howled with pleasure, grabbing her waist, and started thrusting into this amazing chick faster and faster. Just above her perfect buttocks, a tattooed spider on her lower back wiggled its legs ominously. Perhaps it was concerned at the lack of reverence with which its high priestess was being pounded.

"Oh god, this feels so goooood..." Sofia

managed hoarsely, stretching in pleasure.

Poor thing had lost her voice. She had screamed, shrieked and howled today. We must have woken all her neighbors, though none of them had complained. I bet they were coming themselves, regardless of gender or age, from the concert we'd put on for them.

Sofia Pars was utterly incapable of holding back... in anything. To be honest, I still couldn't quite understand how I ended up here.

Maybe it started with Shiloh's lecherous glances and his attempts to get her to work for him: "You won't have to do anything, sweetheart, you'll just be a decoration for my modest business."

Or with Ji-Bo grabbing Sofia's ass and promising to feature her in a music video for his new remix.

Or perhaps it was when, hotly breathing tequila vapors in my ear, she had told me that she had googled vassalage but only remembered the *droit du seigneur* or "the right of the lord."

"Our new arrangement wouldn't count without that," she laughed with a slight rasp, making every hair on my body stand on end.

But no, it all started with AngelCake's ridiculous declaration. Though it took me a bit to recognize just how ridiculous it was.

At first, she scared me to hiccups. Not with her stupid threat — after all, we had already crushed her holy army once. It was just that Stacy looked nothing like herself. It was as if Anima stood before me — in meatspace.

And the very thought of that seemed like nightmare fuel. All these "mind controls" and "soul snatches" should only be possible in the game, whereas we were in reality — as real as it gets.

Adding to the confusion was her pompous crimson gown and golden trinkets. If AngelCake was trying to add some gravitas to herself, she succeeded. But the blustering declaration of war didn't do her much good.

Since I refused to believe in the miraculous appearance of Anima IRL, I figured she had simply lost her mind — gone crazy with her suddenly inflated self-importance and conflated cyberspace with meatspace. They say that kind of thing happens sometimes.

That's why I kept my eye on her, worried she might be capable of anything: She could just as easily start dancing on the table naked as lunge at me with a knife.

Even Simba didn't expect the plot twist. He had been listening to me attentively, even nodding, and I was almost sure he was considering reconciling with me. After all, if hc couldn't take over the city in one go, he'd make peace, gather strength, and wait for the right moment. Simba tended to jump into fights without considering the consequences, but he was a born merchant and could calculate his margins soberly.

Stacy had left him no choice, however. Triumphant, she scanned everyone at the table, madness in her eycs.

It dawned on me that I was the only one who had seen Anima. To everyone else, Stacy was just an ordinary girl with delusions of grandeur.

"Do I understand you correctly, young lady? You dare threaten *me* in my own restaurant?" Shiloh finished cleaning his glasses and replaced them on his nose. "Well, believe me, scarier people than you have tried. And as you can see, I am still alive... They are not."

Ji-Bo chortled loudly and downed the rest of his whiskey.

But it was Sofia who drove the last nail into the coffin of Stacy's pomp.

"How did you like your visit with Lolf, chubs?" she said, waving her long nails in the air like claws. "Was it nice being spider food?"

"You fuckin' bitch!" Stacy shrieked, curling her fingers and lunging at Sofia. "I'll scratch your eyes out, you spider whore!"

Simba barely managed to grab AngelCake around the waist, and I relaxed. My unsettling feeling that "this wasn't Stacy" vanished as soon as she had raised her voice.

"I'll destroy you! I'll incinerate your nest like the plague infested hole it is!" Stacy yelled. "I'll get all of you... ALL OF YOU... with flames and swords! You'll remember me!"

Simba hoisted her by her belt and dragged her, flailing, out of the room. As he passed me, our eyes met and he even seemed to shrug apologetically.

They didn't return. After today's fiasco,

AngelCake had no reason to, and Simon… Well, I hadn't noticed before, but it looked like he was now following her lead.

"Well, well," said Shiloh once Stacy's screams had faded downstairs, "I thought you were a panicker, young man. But it turns out that for some, this whole thing is all too real."

"Agreed," Ji-Bo added. "She's nuts. We need to stick together."

On one hand, it was frustrating that my words about the AI hadn't gotten through to them. On the other hand, I would achieve my goal anyway — maybe not through a unified alliance of players against the NPCs, but at least we wouldn't get picked off one by one.

"I'm joining the alliance!" Theophilia announced loudly, triumphantly surveying the others. "What about you?"

Seeing her, Shiloh and Ji-Bo confirmed that we were now allies. And then we did what men typically do after making a serious pact: We got drunk. Anna, noticing the rising spirits and declining business activity, quickly said her goodbyes and left, so Sofia — her divine House lacking men in general — decided to stick around and take the brunt of our revelry.

I made a conscious effort to drink less and listen more, and it paid off. Especially when we moved to the building's basement, where Modest's nightclub was located.

The guys strutted their stuff before Sofia. She didn't mind and even encouraged their efforts, while I added fuel to their egos, asking them about their stories.

Ji-Bo joined the test purely to make money. Someone from MosTech, who worked with him on a gig, had let slip about the beta and the hefty cash payouts in envelopes. Ji-Bo just wanted to be left alone and get paid. That's why he tried to stay out of the tougher game scenarios and mainly waited for the whole thing to be over with.

Recently, however, everything had changed.

"I saw him," Ji-Bo said suddenly, his voice dropping. "He walked among the trees and as he touched them, vines grew from his touch. He sang and you couldn't help but stand still beneath his song. I went up to those trees later. He was about nine feet tall and he had green skin all over and no face."

"Are you afraid of him?" I asked bluntly.

"He's kind to us," Ji Bo replied thoughtfully, "but other than that, who knows. I only met him once, on the first day. I haven't seen him since. And I don't want to see him again. I'm scared shitless of him. He's not a player or an NPC. Who the hell knows what he is."

"The Eternal Groove?"

"All these gods," Ji-Bo waved his hand dismissively, "no one knows what powers they really have. We're the ones who created them."

For his part, Shiloh spent the whole evening trying to feel me out. I wouldn't be surprised if his advances towards Sofia were also intentional. He was watching to see how I'd react.

"Let's go have a smoke," he finally suggested.

I thought he meant outside, but instead, we took the elevator up three floors to where the offices were located. A smiling girl handed us blankets and we stepped out to a balcony.

Shiloh tapped a cigarette from the pack, took a deep drag and only then offered me one. Naturally, I declined.

"I don't smoke."

"Then why did you come?" Shiloh feigned surprise.

"You've got questions for me," I said abruptly. "Now's the time to ask them."

Modest might not be a bigwig CEO, but I already had some experience dealing with people of his ilk. They're more stubborn than rams, and their only purpose in life is to compare the sizes of their cars, bank accounts and lover's tits with those of everyone else. So either you set yourself on equal footing with them right away, or you tell them to go to hell.

Shiloh hesitated like he'd been caught doing something wrong. I guess he wasn't used to being spoken to like that, especially by some kid off the street.

"Three players ended up in the hospital yesterday," he began obliquely. "One is still there, while two were released immediately and returned to the game."

"And?" I didn't hurry to fill him in.

"The one still in the hospital, Xavier, had a conflict with you," Modest clarified. "The other two also clashed with you, but his was the most seri-ous. He ended up in intensive care, and the two who came back swore loyalty to you."

Damn! I need to do something about the Whisperer's hooded sneaks. Of course they saw Lance and his bros swearing allegiance to the House of Death. So now their leader is well-in-formed. Though, I suppose it's not for nothing that he owns a nightclub. Maybe he and whoever the Whisperer really is, the god of thieves, share some common interests in real life too.

"They realized they're better off being friends with me than enemies," I shrugged.

"Did you do this?" Modest's eyes bore into mine. "Can you harm a real person from within the game?!"

"The question should be 'Can you influence a real person from within the game,'" I corrected him.

And I wasn't lying. I wasn't going to explain that far from hurting those numbskulls, I had ac-tually saved them. Shiloh had gathered the avail-able facts but, still missing half the story, he had jumped to the wrong conclusions. So now he thought I was dangerous because I could kill from within cyberspace.

Was this misconception useful to me? Proba-bly. I had been wondering why Shiloh had so read-ily agreed to our alliance and even deferred to me. Now it turned out that he was afraid of me. Or maybe he wanted to use me. Either way, for now, he needed me more than I needed him.

"How do you do it?"

"Death Magic," I said mysteriously. "Why do you think I chose Anna as my goddess?"

Shiloh stared at me, contemplating whether to believe me or not.

"We're allies," he finally reminded me.

"Why we're practically friends," I grinned broadly.

"I need to know how you do it," Shiloh crushed out his half-smoked cigarette and immediately lit another. "That's my condition."

Now it was my turn to think. We would need to lift the veil of secrecy in order to fight the AI together. The executives were taking a big risk by continuing the beta test and using the players without their knowledge or consent. But how could I share what I knew without violating the non-disclosure agreement I'd signed? I was certain MosTech wouldn't forgive me for such a "misstep."

"Why do you play at all?" I changed the subject. "You have everything. Those envelopes of cash are peanuts to you. So why bother?"

"Boredom," Shiloh answered quickly, as if he had thought about it before. "In there, there's no startup capital, no connections. Everything's from scratch, a clean slate. I want to see what I'm still capable of. If I've gotten too fat... too weak."

"Well, you're doing pretty well," I complimented him.

"Thank you," Shiloh was clearly taken aback, as if he had been patted on the back.

"You'll get the information you want," I

decided, "tomorrow. One way or another, you'll get it."

Modest nodded, lighting a third cigarette. I wasn't going to wait around while he hastened his demise. Secondhand smoke is bad for you after all and I was freezing.

"Listen to my advice: You've got nothing to gain with Sofia," he called after me. "She's out of your league."

I didn't even bother to look back. I dropped the blanket on my way down and descended to the club. Sofia was dancing with Ji-Bo, who was talking about his music video while slyly grabbing her ass. I grabbed her by the wrist and turned her towards me.

"You're drunk. It's time to go. I'll take you home."

She looked at me with wide eyes, as if seeing me for the first time.

"Where?"

I pulled her along, and she followed obediently and trustingly.

"Home."

"To yours?"

"No, to yours."

In the car, she sat quietly, not saying a word, her eyes gleaming in the dim light of the passenger cabin. Then she caught my hand in hers and squeezed it and we sat like that until we reached her building. We went upstairs silently, entered her apartment, and only when we were in the foyer did Sofia turn and kiss me fiercely.

"This is the first time I've done this," she said later, as we lay sprawled on her bed.

She was lying no doubt, but it was still nice to hear.

"The first time you've done what?"

"Let someone take me home to fuck me," Sofia nestled beside me, laying her head on my chest. "How could I refuse... I'm a vassal!"

"Yes, you're a good vassal," I agreed, "quite obedient."

She let out a soft, sensual laugh.

"Why don't you join my side, Targe? I'll always be obedient," Sofia picked up a satin ribbon from the nightstand and wrapped it around her neck. "Don't you want me to be your sex slave? I'll obey and submit to your every whim, my liege," she purred with a giggle.

"I'm good as it is," I leaned over and kissed her nipple, which immediately puckered with excitement.

Sofia was very beautiful, though quite unhinged. A true nymphomaniac. I always thought that such women only existed in adolescent fantasies, but I was wrong. She got turned on at the slightest touch, as if her entire body was one giant erogenous zone.

While Marina was well-groomed and polished, Sofia was a fitness freak. When she sat on top of me, her flat stomach revealed her chiseled abs, and her butt was as firm as a soccer ball. We practically wrestled each other at first and victory didn't come easily to me.

The struggle inflamed me so much that when I finally pinned the growling and moaning girl beneath me, I lost all control. She struggled, scratched, and bit. And I wasn't just fucking her… I was dominating her… I was punishing her… I was taming this wild bitch. And now, as she purred beside me like a compliant kitten, I realized I had succeeded. The question of who was in charge was settled once and for all.

Only now did I have time to look around. Sofia's apartment, a spacious studio, was as beautiful and strange as its owner. The primary colors were lilac and black. A huge round bed with black silk sheets stood almost in the center. The walls were adorned with strange engravings, as if she were planning to summon spirits. On the nightstand by the bed was a black stone skull with its crown cut off — a jewelry box.

And spiders. They were even on her body. The largest one spread its legs across her lower spine, with its head positioned right at the small of her back. I occasionally had the feeling that this creature was about to come to life and bite me right on the dick. Tiny spiders crawled industriously up her left thigh in a file, and another one nestled on her neck, just below her ear, hidden by her hair.

"You really like spiders, don't you?"

"Aren't they sexy?" Sofia beamed.

"Only the ones on you," I answered honestly.

She jumped up and ran to the shelves on the wall, returning with a fat, hairy creature the size of a small saucer in her hands.

"Is that Lolf?" I managed to suppress the urge to jump up and scream in disgust.

"Nooo, this is Charlotte," Sofia leaned down and kissed the spider on its light-gray back.

The thing wriggled as if in pleasure. Damn... She just kissed me with those lips...

"It's... cute," I said diplomatically.

"And you're brave," Sofia said as she walked away and put Charlotte back. I hoped into an air-tight container. "Other guys run away at this point."

She walked around the apartment, not the least bit embarrassed by her nudity. And it suited her well. A toned athletic figure, small perfectly shaped breasts, slender legs, and a firm ass.

She met all the requirements of a runway model, and indeed one of the walls was plastered with photos from magazines and fashion shows featuring Sofia as the main attraction. Just looking at her stroked my ego. But after meeting Charlotte, I firmly decided not to spend the night here. Who knows, maybe the pet had a habit of sleeping with its owner, and it would end up as the third in our bed. No thanks.

I was just starting to come up with a polite excuse to leave when my phone vibrated. It had been buzzing all night actually, but we were too busy to notice.

It was Simba. Under other circumstances, I wouldn't have answered. Let him stew in his own delusions for a bit. But I decided to take advantage of the situation.

"Hello?"

"Andrew, I need you to come over," my friend's voice sounded strange. He seemed extremely agitated.

"What's going on?" I asked, growing concerned.

"You have to come here to Stacy's place. Something weird is happening with her. I need help."

Chapter 12

SOFIA SEEMED GENUINELY MIFFED that I had to go. I think she had already decided that she and I and the eight-legged Charlotte would become a small, happy family.

She was even more eager to talk while we relaxed after sex. I don't know where women get this idea that if they satisfy a man once, he'll sell his soul for an encore.

Personally, I only get extremely hungry after sex. The last thing I'm interested in is listening to arguments or making deals. It's a bit simple of me, it's true, but I can't help it.

As a result, all of Sofia's hints about me becoming her "spider knight of the first order" — with unlimited access to her luxurious body in real life, as well as fun orgies with the other spider priestesses in VR — fell on deaf ears.

She even came to the foyer naked to see me

off, hoping I would change my mind and stay. It was hard to tear my eyes away from her firm, fit body, but I mustered my resolve, kissed her cheek heroically and plunged into the hostile, snowy night.

It was almost midnight by the time the taxi dropped me off at Stacy's place. I had never been to her new apartment. Sullen had knocked me out as I was on the way to her housewarming.

Finding the place wasn't hard. Simba was smoking by the entrance, wearing a jacket draped over his shoulders and sweatpants. Something about his appearance seemed off, but I didn't pay much attention to it and followed him upstairs.

"What's wrong with her?" I asked immediately.

"You'll see," Simba replied shortly, and we both quickened our pace.

The elevator wasn't working, so we trudged up the stairs of an unexpectedly clean and tidy building. There were even flowers on the window-sills, and the automatic lights clicked on as we ascended each floor.

"Must be pretty pricey to live here," I observed.

"It's not too bad," Simba shrugged, which only made me more suspicious.

Simba let me in the door and left me to take off my shoes in the hallway, while he peered into the living room. Then, placing a finger to his lips, he motioned for me to follow.

The hallway angled into a short corridor

leading to the kitchen. The door was open, and we could see Stacy sitting at the table.

Stacy was eating. A huge chocolate cake stood before her and she was digging into it with a tablespoon, shoveling chunks of it into her mouth. Judging by the box, the cake had been massive but now only crumbs remained. Occasionally Stacy would pause and pop a chocolate candy from an open box at her elbow into her mouth, then wash it down with a swig of champagne from a flute.

My jacket rustled, and Stacy looked up. She wasn't surprised to see me at all and nodded at me.

"TargetAi," she said seriously. "Come in, Soul Reaper, and share this feast with me."

"She's on a diet," Simba explained in a low voice. "We bought that cake for her mother. She was supposed to come visit."

The picture clicked into place. Simba in sweatpants, the men's slippers in the hallway… It seemed a new domestic unit had been forming behind my back. Simba dreamed of a home of his own and Stacy dreamed of a strong shoulder to lean on. At last they'd found what they wanted.

"Paladin!" Stacy was clearly irritated that Simba's attention had shifted from her to me. "I want more of this," she pointed her spoon at the cake. "I had no idea it was so delicious!"

"Stacy, you don't eat carbs," Simba made a desperate attempt.

"And who's going to stop me? You?" Stacy

squinted meanly. She pounded the table with her fist, then grabbed a napkin holder and hurled it at Simba, filling the kitchen with paper cranes.

We stepped back into the hallway to talk, while Stacy ignored us and returned to her feast.

"How long has she been like this?"

"Almost an hour," Simba checked the time on his phone. "No, an hour and a half."

"What happened before?"

"When we got home," Simon began to re-count, "she threw a fit. She was complaining about her dress, why she was dressed like a slut... where I took her... She didn't remember anything about the restaurant or her own declaration of war. Then she seemed to calm down and went to the bedroom to change. I got distracted... and then I saw her sitting and eating. What's wrong with her, Andrew?"

I had only one theory and I didn't like it. Stacy's mind had snapped. I'm no psychologist, so I don't know the correct terms but it seemed that she'd lost her marbles — that'd be my diagnosis. Some wires had been crossed inside her brain.

She hadn't behaved very rationally in the game today either, but that could have been blamed on the "divine" influence. Odd, yes, but not the strangest thing in the gaming world. But it seemed these events had left a mark on Stacy's psyche.

"Maybe she needs to go to the hospital?" I suggested. "We can't just leave her like this..."

"What if they send her to a psych ward?"

Simba countered. "We're not even relatives. We'd never get her out."

"So what do you suggest?"

"If I knew, I wouldn't have called you."

So, when it comes to organizing a "crusade," these two are first in line. But when the shit hits the fan, it's "Andrew, what do we do?" Well what can I propose? Give her a sedative? Who's going to sell us one at midnight? And what about the dosage? We could end up sending Stacy to the afterlife by mistake. That was a risk I took very seriously.

And even if we inject her with something, there's no guarantee she'll wake up any different. No guarantee at all.

Who can we call for help? We need a psychologist or psychiatrist who understands both cyberspace and neural networks and who will answer the phone when all normal people are already asleep.

Interestingly enough, I did know just such a psychologist. The only problem was I had no reason to trust her. But I had no other options, so I pulled out my phone and dialed the number I'd only recently saved.

"Hello, Irina, good evening..."

"Who the hell is this?" Her sleepy voice was plaintive and miserable, as if suspecting that the caller had every right to wake her at this ungodly hour.

"It's Andrew."

"Andrew who?!" The indignation on the other end of the line was gradually gaining strength.

"The one who saved you at the club and drove you home," I reminded her of the episode from our meeting.

Simba was staring at me with wide eyes. I hadn't shared the details of that adventure with him, and now wasn't the time.

"Andrew, even that...," her voice woke up, dripping with sarcasm, "...and everything that followed doesn't give you the right to call me at half past midnight. If it's female attention you're after, try the world wide web."

I deliberately adopted a familiar tone with her and avoided mentioning MosTech. Our last meeting — at which we discussed Lance's and my raid of the corporate offices — hadn't gone very well at all. Irina had clearly been against me then, though I saw no reason for it.

"I need you not as a woman," I heard her nearly choke in surprise, "but as a psychiatrist. Someone's gone crazy, and I have a serious suspicion that it's because of the game."

"Are you sure?"

I briefly summarized everything I'd seen. Simba stood next to me, nodding in agreement. The more I explained, the more interested her voice became, and her questions grew sharper and more precise.

"Give me the address," she said at last, and hung up as soon as I recited it to her.

"Who is she?" Simba asked. "How do you know her?"

"Her name is Dr. Skuratova," I didn't bother

denying it. "She's a psychologist and one of Mos-Tech's executives."

"Holy shit..." Simba mulled this over. "And you and her...?"

"No comment," I said, but my face must have given something away.

"Holy shit," he repeated, giving me a light punch on the shoulder.

"You're one to talk," I countered to change the subject. "How long have you been living together?"

Simba straightened up and began adjusting his shirt.

"It just kind of happened," he replied. "It's been like three days, no more."

On one hand, three days is nothing. On the other hand, with everything happening so fast lately, it felt like an eternity. And I had missed it entirely. It became clear now why Simba had valued AngelCake's words over mine in the game.

Dr. Skuratova arrived a half hour later. She must have set a record driving through the nighttime streets. She entered along with the smell of snow and wind, tossed her mink coat into my arms, and sniffed the air.

"That's an interesting cologne on you," she remarked.

I smelled like Sofia: her perfume, her aromatic candles, and some oil she had rubbed on her body.

"Sweeter notes are all the vogue now," I countered. "Didn't you know?"

She smirked and merely said, "Lead the way."

Stacy reacted to the new guest without enthusiasm but also without any significant outbursts.

"Who are you?" she demanded from the doorway.

"Would you share some of your cake with me?" Dr. Skuratova's voice was like honey. "I love sweets."

"So do I," Stacy brightened up. "Come in, there's plenty left."

Dr. Skuratova entered the kitchen, shutting the heavy wooden door behind her.

Simba tried in vain to eavesdrop, but the conversation inside took place in hushed tones, occasionally turning to whispers.

My phone vibrated in my pocket. It was Marina. Strange that she waited so long; I was sure she would call. And ten to one, she was calling to bawl me out. Any kind of calm conversation was out of the question, so I just didn't pick up. Let's deal with one psycho at a time...

Simba walked away from the kitchen door in disappointment.

"Let's go sit in the living room for now," he suggested.

I followed him, looking around with curiosity. The apartment was rented; that much was obvious from the strange combination of impersonality and sporadic attempts at creating a sense of coziness. The walls were covered with the ugly, bland wallpaper that no one in their right mind would buy for their own home, all the surfaces featured the

same linoleum everywhere and all the light fix-
tures were flimsy and cheap.

Amid all this were cosmetic attempts to create
a homey atmosphere: decorative trinkets and stat-
uettes on the cabinets and tables, piles of colorful
cushions on any sitting surface, and photo frames
on the walls — all of it from IKEA.

In the center of the living room hung a huge
flat-screen TV, with a couch and two armchairs in
front of it.

"Your doing?" I nodded at the TV.

"Of course," Simba said proudly. "You should
come over for the Champions League."

He pulled out some brandy from the cabinet
and poured two glasses without asking, handing
me one. I didn't feel like drinking, so I sat on the
couch, barely wetting my lips, and asked:

"You understand that it would be better if
Stacy took a break from the beta, right?"

"Why?" replied Simba, surprised, and gulped
down half his brandy in one go.

"Well that game," I began to explain, "it's
making her feel like she's some kind of goddess in
there."

I don't know why I never told Simba about
seeing the real Anima in the game. I figured he
may have seen her too, so there was no point in
discussing the obvious.

"There's the game, and then there's reality,"
he disagreed. "In the game, we kill constantly, but
that doesn't make us murderous psychos in
meatspace."

"Don't you get it?" I grew angry. "I don't know if Stacy suffers from a big ego or an inferiority complex, but whatever it is, it's fertile ground for her to be manipulated. Irina will tell you herself when she comes out. She's the expert."

Simba stayed silent, sulking and sipping his brandy.

"We put you in a pod with a head injury and on medication," he said at last. "And you're fine. Stacy is just tired. She'll be as good as new tomorrow."

"And if not?!" I insisted. "What if something really snaps in her head? Permanently? I don't think we can run that risk, and she shouldn't go back in there."

"That's not your decision to make," Simba responded abruptly, almost angrily.

"I'm just concerned for her, Simon."

"That's some bullshit," Simba stared at me. "You're worried about yourself. You're scared that there are too many of us now and you won't be able to handle us when we come for you tomorrow. You're just trying to take away our advantage… our living idol!"

"Calm down, bro," I tried to soothe him. "You know how dangerous this game really is. Is it really worth taking a risk like this?"

"So what? You're the only one who gets to play? We're not allowed to stand up to you? You've got it all wrong, *bro*. Stacy will keep playing. And we'll crush your House of Death and all the other houses into dust."

At that moment, the kitchen door creaked open. Skuratova was leading Stacy out, having draped her dark jacket over Stacy's shoulders and gently supporting her.

"What's wrong with her?" Simba was the first to ask.

"Nervous breakdown," Skuratova replied absentmindedly. "It's nothing serious, but she needs to come with me."

"Will she be able to continue in the beta?" I asked.

"I wouldn't recommend it," Dr. Skuratova said after a moment's thought. "She really needs to get some rest right now."

"She's in on this!" Simba bellowed like a wounded bear. "You called in this shrink to dump us out of the game!"

"Don't you trust my expertise?" Dr. Skuratova countered coldly. "Watch your tone, Simon. You know who I am."

Simba gritted his teeth and fell silent. I won the argument, but my relationship with my friend had been damaged. Now he would seriously believe that I was playing dirty. This had become more than competition. It was a matter of hurt pride and principle now.

I decided I'd better head out with Irina and AngelCake, who was bundled up next to her. Simba slammed the apartment door loudly behind us.

"Need a ride?" Irina asked.

I looked at the blizzard swirling in white

twisters along the snowdrifts and nodded. Dr. Skuratova's Cayenne easily navigated through the poorly cleared parking lot. Stacy lay dozing in the back seat.

Where to go — home or to Marina's? I didn't want to wake my parents, and Marina would definitely throw a fit. But her jealous outbursts no longer scared me and so it was her address that I dictated to Irina. I expected her to start probing me on the drive over, but she turned up the jazz music and didn't say a word.

As we pulled up to Marina's apartment building, however, a hooded figure dashed up to the car.

"You bitch!" screamed Marina, yanking open the driver's door. "I'll show you how to steal my man! I can see right through you..."

"You're mistaken, Marina," Dr. Skuratova met her with icy disdain. "We could continue this conversation in my office tomorrow if you like, however."

Marina stopped in her tracks, as if she'd hit a wall.

"Dr. Skuratova," she stammered. "I didn't mean to... I made a mistake..."

"Now take your 'man' and get out of here," Dr. Skuratova went on, "if you don't want any further consequences."

I thought about kissing Irina goodbye on the cheek but decided it wouldn't be fair to Marina. It would be like kicking her while she was down. So I just waved goodbye.

"Bye, see you soon!"

Irina nodded as she drove out of the parking lot.

"What the hell?!" Marina laid into me.

"Stacy had a nervous breakdown... Irina brought her to her senses and took her for treatment," I summarized a good chunk of the night. "But uh, what's up with you anyway?"

"I thought you were with that Pars skank," Marina said without a hint of embarrassment. "I wanted to yank her hair out."

Standing in the elevator, she kept sniffing around, but I remained unfazed, and she kept quiet. She let me take a shower and change, calmly waiting for me in the bedroom.

"You still smell like that bitch," she told me in bed, "but you came back to me. And you always will."

I didn't argue with her because it was the plain truth. I came back and I had really wanted to. And feeling her warm, responsive body after the negotiations, the drinking, the sex with Sofia, and Stacy's craziness, I still managed to do my bit! I was quite proud of myself.

It had been a full day. It was time to sleep, but in just a couple of hours, I had to get up for the beta test. As I pulled a satiated Marina close to me, she smiled slyly and said:

"I got the list."

"What list?" I didn't catch on immediately.

"The list of who was at MosTech last night."

"Why didn't you say so?!" I jumped up like I had a spring under me. "Give it here."

"Because I knew you'd react like this," Marina giggled. "And I wanted some TLC too, not just heroics."

She leaned over the edge of the bed, rummaged in her purse, and pulled out a folded printout.

"I'll go make some coffee," she said. "You won't sleep now anyway."

She walked to the kitchen, deliberately swaying her bare butt. Meanwhile, I turned on the light and began studying the list.

The first names on it were routine and predictable: the security shift, some technicians on night duty, and even three janitors who I guess hadn't finished their work on time.

But the cherry on my cake were four names. People who clearly shouldn't have been at Mos-Tech at that hour.

CHAPTER 13

"WHO IS DMITRY SAVITSKY?" I looked up at Marina, as she came back from the kitchen. She had thrown a transparent robe over her shoulders, and she sat down beside me, tucking her legs under herself.

"Dima?" she echoed. "He's the chief technician. A handyman. He can fix anything, whether it's a coffee grinder or a car. He once fixed my blender and didn't charge me a penny."

"Your chief technician fixes things himself?" I was surprised. I didn't know much about Mos-Tech's hierarchy, but I remembered from my father's childhood stories that a chief technician was a very serious role, almost like an executive but smarter.

"Of course not," Marina waved her hand. "It's his hobby. He has a whole workshop here. I guess it's for his labors of love, but sometimes it ends up being really helpful. Other than that, he super-vises the other technicians. And takes care of stuff like reports... procurement...” The blonde gri-maced, showing that this side of office routine didn’t spare her either.

So what was Dima, the handyman, doing at work at half-past eleven at night? Counting diodes and capacitors in his engineering stockpile? Fixing a Bunsen burner? Or entering a VR pod with un-known, but surely nefarious purposes?

Next name: Christina Dovner. I didn’t imme-diately remember where and under what circum-stances I’d heard it, but as soon as Marina hissed, “That bitch!” it all fell into place and I instantly re-membered: *“My name is Christina, I’m ready to as-sist you in any way...”* Marina’s replacement. How did she end up at the office so late at night? Had she decided to sleep at her desk to save some money and time on her daily commute? I didn’t voice the more vulgar options, even to myself, though they were implied. Dima plus Christina... Skilled hands and long legs... Good, if that’s the case. Good for my peace of mind.

“Who is she anyway?”

“HR,” Marina barked. “Human resources.”

“HR?” I repeated, even more surprised. The typical image of this profession didn’t match the model-like girl I remembered.

“She’s more of a recruiter,” Marina corrected. “She finds specialists, tests them, and works on improving personnel efficiency.” Knowing Chris-tina Dovner’s role didn’t bring me any closer to understanding why she wasn't at home so late at night, or out clubbing with her friends, or even frolicking with a lover — but at MosTech. It was clear to me she wasn't a random person. No wonder she was put in Marina's position as soon as it became available. She was almost certainly someone's pawn in the game that was unfolding around us, even if I didn't know whose yet.

The further I read, the more interesting it all got. Benjamin Zvyagin — Anna's half-brother — was on the list too. As I understood it, they had different mothers. Sergey Zvyagin's first wife stayed in Russia after the divorce, and the academic met Elsa Falk, the creator of the neural network, later on in Europe. Benjamin had inherited his father's brains and half the corporation's shares.

Had he retained his loyalty to his father's cause as well? Anna said he wanted to correct his dad's mistakes. But how well does she know her brother, who was mostly raised by a lonely, abandoned woman? Do Benjamin's goals align with the other executives, or is this guy maybe harboring a grudge against the world and thirsting for revenge — and hiding it all behind the guise of a typical, scatterbrained IT guru?

The last name on the list was well-known to me, yet it still managed to surprise me: Irina Skuratova — a member of the board of directors, the company's top psychologist and psychiatrist. I recalled the day after our "breaking and entering." Dr. Skuratova had been late to the meeting and looked like she had hurriedly prepared for it. At the time, I had thought that she'd been dragged out of her warm bed, which explained her grumpiness.

But it turned out that the opposite was the case. Not only had she been awake, but she was also somewhere nearby the entire time. What was it then that had occupied her so much that she didn't even have time to fix her hair? What was she doing in this beta test anyway? Benny is nurturing the kernel taken from Sergey Zvyagin, the Master monitors security, and Doc yells at everyone because he's the boss. But then what is Dr. Skuratova's role really?

Rumor has it that she raised the neural network, but how? By what methods? To influence that toy world, you have to be able to interact with it. And the only way to do that is by entering the game.

In the end, instead of an unequivocal answer, what I got was something akin to the modern exam: Choose a correct answer from four correct options: Savitsky, Dovner, Zvyagin, or Skuratova.

Of these, the first two are dark horses. Savitsky and Dovner are either puppets — conduits of someone else's will, or daring adventurers trying to carve out their own profit in murky waters.

If it's Zvyagin or Skuratova, the situation is even more interesting. Are they advancing the interests of the board of directors or playing their own game? Why would I even assume that the corporation's leadership was united in its goals? Just because Marina had said so the first day we met? Back then, she seemed very important to me, privy to many secrets. Later, I realized that her role was closer to "fetch this, bring that, now go screw yourself." Yet I initial assumption about the board remained an unshakable truth for me.

There's an evil AI holding players hostage and the brave executives are ready to fight it. But are they truly united? Are they really on the same team?

Dr. Kotov, Zvyagin, the nameless Master Eli, and Dr. Skuratova. Who are these people, really? What do I know about them besides what they let me see at our periodic in-person meetings? The entire beta depends on them more than on anyone else. They are the ones who shape what happens initially, but with whose hands? Why with those of the very same Marina, who was now trying her best to settle her head on my lap and fall asleep.

I stroked the blonde's hair, and she purred drowsily, snuggling her cheek closer to me. One of the most influential figures in this entire enterprise was right here next to me, and what was I doing with her? Well, screwing her, naturally... I believe they call that "giving a fool a candy wrapper" in Russian.

"Marin?"

"Umm?" she drawled sleepily.

"Do you have a laptop?"

"What do you need it for?"

"I want to do some work."

"Are you crazy?" Marina started awake. "We

have to get up in two hours, and we haven't even gone to bed yet."

"I need to," I shrugged.

Marina hopped out of bed abruptly, went to the next room, and returned with a sleek Mac-Book.

"Here, just don't go into the photo gallery," she handed me the laptop and collapsed face-first into her soft pillow. "I'm going to sleep. I'm a grown girl; I need rest. Lack of sleep ruins my complexion."

She muttered the last words with her eyes closed. I kindly covered her exposed butt and opened the laptop.

The interface was a bit unfamiliar, but I quickly figured it out. In the open document, I began drafting columns: goals, objectives, methods, resources... Thank you, Dr. Petrovich, my beloved dean of sociology. In my first semester, he managed to drive the scientific approach to solving problems into my thick skull.

Naturally, I couldn't refrain from peeking into the photo gallery once I made sure Marina was asleep. Apple devices sync with the phone, which was convenient on one hand, but risky on the other.

I enjoyed seeing her club photos. Apparently, after I left, Marina made up with her friends, and the three of them partied hard. I found selfies with Lance and many other selfies with different people, all with varying degrees of silliness.

I looked at Marina in a swimsuit. Her tan

lines suited her very well. Then I stumbled upon her photo hugging some bearded guy. Also from a vacation. Marina looked happy, but the newest photo was over a year old. She even had a different haircut, shorter, almost boyish.

Did I feel jealous? Hardly, though something did prickle me inside. I perceived the PR guru too clearly as something temporary in my life. We didn't delve deeply into each other's feelings, didn't talk about our dreams, what music we listened to or what books we read. And I wouldn't want to. I knew ahead of time that the answers would disappoint me.

I felt cozy with Marina, but every time I left her place, I thought I might never come back here and the thought never bothered me. Even the room from which Marina brought the laptop… I realized with surprise that I'd never been in it. We were always between the bedroom and the kitchen, with the odd stop in the bathroom. We never even had a reason to hang out in her living room.

And not least of all, I shouldn't underestimate Marina's cunning. No wonder she said, "don't look in the gallery." Until that moment, I hadn't even thought about the photo gallery on the MacBook, nor had any desire to snoop there.

It's possible these photos had already been pre-screened and curated for me to see. What would the message be in that case? That other men liked her? Or that she hadn't had anyone but me for a year? I postponed figuring this out and finally lay down to rest. There were forty minutes left before the alarm went off.

* * *

Morning Marina was nothing like evening Marina. The playful kitten had turned into a grumpy, puffed-up sparrow. Sitting on a bar stool, she clutched a huge mug of coffee with both hands and regarded everything I said with skepticism.

"And who are you going to pitch this to?"

"Who's actually running the beta test right now?"

Marina thought for a moment.

"Everyone a little bit. The technical side is all on Benjamin Zvyagin, as it has been from the start. Doc signs off on the documents; nothing gets bought without his approval, not even toilet paper. The Master doesn't seem to do anything specific, but he sticks his nose into everything." Marina amusingly mimicked how the Master sniffed around like a dog. "He watches every beta round, monitoring everyone's every step."

"And Dr. Skuratova?"

"Well, she's usually nowhere to be seen," the poor blonde grimaced, clearly remembering last night's encounter. "And thank gawd! I can't stand her."

"The feeling is mutual," I said softly, but Marina managed to hear me.

"What? You can tell?" she panicked. "How do you know?!"

Her career was always her top priority. She might feel however she wanted about the bosses, but she always aimed to look like an angel in their eyes.

"It just seemed that way." I approached Marina and kissed the top of her head. "She's probably just jealous of your youth and beauty."

"You're such a jerk..." Marina beamed. "You really know how to make a girl feel special."

"Will you back me up if it comes down to that?" I asked, shifting to a serious tone.

"Do I have any other options?" Marina sighed. "Where can I go now? We're in the same boat, only you're at the helm, and I'm just rowing," she laughed, imagining the picture. "So don't listen to me. Do what you think is right, and I'll help you."

* * *

"Come in, Andrew. Would you like some tea?"

It was surprisingly easily for me to get admitted to the Master's office. The guards didn't stop me on the stairs, and the secretary just nodded in response to my "Hello." I had a feeling that I was expected, or at least everyone had been instructed not to get in my way. Had the Master calculated several steps ahead again? Good — then it would be easier to persuade him of my idea.

Who else could I go to? Benny Zvyagin and Dr. Skuratova were now under suspicion. And I never got along with Dr. Kotov — I couldn't understand how a man with his temper could even be

CEO — he might have managed finances and assets well, but when it came to people, not so much. So the Master was my only option. Besides, he had helped me more than once, whether intentionally or not, and I took that as a good sign.

"I've already had coffee," I declined, "and there's not much time. I don't want to be late for the next round. I came to share some thoughts with you. Will you read them?"

"Hand them over."

He extended his hand, and I placed a few printed pages in it. The Master sat down at the table, put on his thin-rimmed glasses, and began to read attentively, sometimes frowning, sometimes hiking his eyebrows in surprise.

"Did you come up with this yourself?" he asked unexpectedly, looking up.

I wanted to say something sarcastic like "No, I happened across this pasted on a wall on my way over here," but this wasn't the time for sarcasm. So I just nodded.

"And why did you come to me?"

"Maybe this will surprise you," I decided to go all in, "but out of everyone in your company, you seem the most... reasonable."

The Master's eyes widened in surprise, and then he burst out laughing.

"Reasooonable," he moaned, wiping tears from his eyes. "No one has ever insulted me like that."

I shrugged silently. If the Master's antics and phrases had initially puzzled me, now I understood that it was all an act. A diversion. Like the "drunken style" in kung fu movies. A fool's style…

"Will you support me?"

"What's in it for you?" the Master continued to drag things out.

"I want to win," I said bluntly. "But to do that, you need to understand the rules of the game. And right now, there are no rules. You've let the situation run wild, thrown a bunch of volatile ingredients into a barrel, and are waiting for it all to blow up. You're observing the process, sure, but nothing will come of it."

"Why not?" The Master leaned forward sharply, fixing me with his stare.

"The integrity of the experiment is compromised," I replied. "Someone is playing against you."

"Nonsense!" the Master declared, then quickly followed up, "Why do you think that?"

"Did you create the gods in the game?" I answered his question with a question. "If you did, I'll just take my papers and leave."

The Master leaned back and began cleaning his glasses, occasionally glancing up at me in thought. It was clear that the answer didn't come easily to him. This was a kind of watershed moment. If he told me the truth, he'd have to keep being honest with me. From being a boss and an employee, we'd become partners. Maybe not equal partners, but partners nonetheless.

"No," he finally said. "The AI created them

itself. But how did you figure it out?"

"Something you said," I replied. "Do you remember when we first entered the game? You said, 'It's learning to kill.' And yet in all this time, I haven't seen any aggression from the AI. It defends but it doesn't attack. It learns from the players but lags behind us. It's being pushed. It's being guided. Either you lied to me then, or you're behind all these manipulations with the game."

"But last time it all started the same way," the Master stopped fooling around and genuinely looked puzzled. "Gods... magic... mind control..."

I remained silent, letting him draw his own conclusions.

"Not a word to anyone," the Master finally declared. "And I mean no one. Not your friends, not that floozy of yours..."

"Can I tell Anna?" I asked.

"Under no circumstances!" The Master even shook his head for emphasis. "You know her well enough to understand that she acts first and thinks later. She could make such a mess that we wouldn't clean it up for a year."

"What about my offer?"

"I don't see the connection," he spread his hands in puzzlement.

"It's simple," I explained, "if someone is playing against us, we need to inject some balance into the competition. If they've been having fun and going about it leisurely up till now, let's make every step painful for them now. Under pressure, they might slip up and reveal themselves."

"Alright... alright..." The Master rubbed his balding head and delved back into the papers.

He was still deep in thought when I left his office.

Locker room, immersion hall, VR pod... The game had become as routine for me as any ordinary job.

My conversation with the Master had delayed me, and now I was about ten minutes late. But it didn't matter. The daily quests had grown longer with time, however: The last one had lasted four hours, so I wasn't afraid of missing anything.

The black-and-white spiral whirled before me as always, and I waited for the moment it would plunge my consciousness down like a roller coaster — but instead, suddenly gold and purple streaks entered the pattern. The spiral grew colorful — and I was whisked up and away like a leaf blown from a tree. For a moment, my stomach lurched to my throat, and then my body hit the ground — hard.

I knelt in a combat stance, drawing my sword and looking around. This spawn point was unfamiliar to me — or rather, I didn't recognize it at first. A clearing in the forest. A statue of Anima towered overhead. A crowd surrounded me — and before me stood Simba in shining armor and Sibyl with a smug grin on her face.

"There he is!"

"We did it!"

"Got you, you bastard!"

The crowd roared with a deafening clamor of

joy and anger.

Sibyl raised her hands and began to chant:

"By the will of the Goddess and my word, I hereby imprison you, you demon! I consign you to this sacred circle! Let it be your prison henceforth!"

Alright, you bitch! I guess I'll find out out whether you're a player or an NPC for sure now.

Dash! I trigger my skill — only to slam into some invisible barrier.

Damn, it hurts! It burns!

I was accustomed to feeling very little pain in the game — and the intensity of it now stunned me. A circle with strange symbols was beneath my feet and an impenetrable barrier surrounded me. Did she say "demon"? Am *I* the demon here?!

CHAPTER 14

FIRST, THEY TRIED TO SHOOT ME with arrows, then they tried to pelt me with rocks, but neither worked. The magical barrier blocked everything, both from my side and theirs. For my part, I found one stone within the circle and tried to throw it at Sibyl, equally to no effect. I didn't bother risking my weapon in case it broke.

Simba proved the most stubborn. Even once everyone else had moved on, he remained standing before me, head tilted and brow furrowed.

"Got what you wanted, huh?" he said. "You got sweet AngelCake kicked out of the beta..."

"Simba," I snapped, "what's more important to you, winning the beta or preventing your friend from losing her mind?"

"So she's not *your* friend..." he surmised.

"What does that have to do with anything?" I tried to explain. "Didn't you see what happened to

Yumi, Simon? Do you want the same for Stacy?"

"Nothing happened to Yumi," Simba muttered. "The game just copied her, that's all..."

This is an interesting twist. Simba seems to have a different version of events in his head. I wonder who prepped him for our conversation? Though there's no need to guess — there she is, listening in, her eyes agleam. It seems like she's always around me, eavesdropping on any conversation I'm having.

Realizing that he had said too much, Simba turned and stalked off to attend to his paladin's duties, and Sibyl took his place before my cage.

"I snared you at last... you demon," she sneered, sitting down cross-legged on the ground.

"Why am I demon suddenly?" I asked.

I had no desire to talk to her. I wanted nothing more than to take down this brat, preferably with a juicy crit, so she wouldn't even have time to squeak. But, since we seemed to be in a stalemate, and I had no idea how to get out of this damn trap, getting information was the only thing I could do. I hoped that at least by making small talk now, I could learn something about this spell imprisoning me and how I even ended up in it.

"What else could you be?" Sibyl feigned surprise. "There's only one true Goddess. All the others are demons."

"What about 'five gods, five principles upon which our world is built?'" I reminded her of her own ritual in the city square.

"You're evil," Sibyl grimaced. "These people

are convinced that you were sent by Death itself. Fear, vice, deceit and murder... are these divine virtues or mortal sins? These brave paladins here are prepared to cleanse the world of filth like you." She waved her hand behind her without looking.

"There aren't enough of them for such a task," I pointed out. "Don't overestimate yourselves."

Sibyl turned and frowned. There were indeed fewer players in the clearing, much less than the host that had stood in the square preparing to storm the mayor's palace or the spider mansion. We had really cooled the hottest heads the day before.

"Anyway, you won't interfere with our plans," the healer — or the priestess — got up and absent-mindedly dusted off the fringe of her long dress. "You're caught, and I hope you'll stay that way for a long time."

After that, she lost interest in me. I remained sitting, imprisoned in plain sight. Anima's followers bustled around, while I could only watch them and clench my teeth in frustration. I so badly wanted to lose my temper and throw myself at the wall imprisoning me. Never mind that it burns, and that slamming against it is probably useless — it's still better than sitting there and watching the enemy.

I wondered what they called themselves anyway. Animists? Animanians? Animaniacs? I'll have to ask Simba when he comes to his senses. Although, it's unclear if he ever will. For now, I watched him gather the most capable paladins around himself and start drilling them on squad tactics.

And as I listened, I realized that he was actually teaching them new skills! Does this mean skills can be learned and players can level up their abilities outside of the training camp? That's quite an interesting revelation — especially since I am my own high priest!

I opened my skills tree but found that all my previous class branches were now grayed out. Instead, a new class called Shinigami was now listed in my character status. I knew what that was: In ancient Japan, the shinigami was the equivalent of the Grim Reaper, a personification of death that guides the souls of the dead to the afterlife. Nowadays, the shinigami is no longer a god but rather a spirit, a "death guide," in many popular animes and mangas. No wonder Anna called me a Soul Reaper. It seems she knows much more about manga than I do.

Speaking of which, Anna wasn't responding to my messages in the chat. I messaged everyone I could: Anna, Lance, even Theophilia and Shiloh — but got no reply from any of them. It seemed my magical prison blocked not only my movement but also any outgoing messages.

How had Sibyl managed to snare me anyway? Could there really be a spell in this game to capture and trap a player despite such a substantial level gap? I mean, purely objectively and without any false modesty, I had to be one of the most powerful players in the beta at the moment.

Something like this would make Sibyl incredibly overpowered. Divine magic that can neutralize opponents would give the House of Anima very distinct advantages. At the same time those words — divine magic — kept triggering a nagging thought that refused to fall into place in my head...

"Favorite of the Gods" was an unexpected achievement that I had unlocked upon collecting blessings from all five deities. The trait that came with it negated all divine magic. So then why is this bitch trying to confuse me? Or is it now like the Middle Ages where everything can be explained by divine intervention at a whim?

Sibyl didn't know about my ability and slipped up. A magic circle, symbols... anyone would be misled. Even I was fooled at first.

So what really happened? I logged into the game late, spawned in the wrong place, and couldn't escape. Could this be technically influenced via the settings of my VR pod? I had no idea! In any case, the list of the four interlopers from last night kept popping into my mind. People who were in the wrong place at the wrong time.

However, all these ruminations didn't do me any good right now. It didn't matter whether this was a magical trap or a technical prison. What I had to do was find a way to escape it.

From the bits of conversation that reached me, I learned that there was a massacre underway in the city. The forces of the four divine Houses, united thanks to me, were hunting down the surviving Animaniacs. The persecuted referred to

Lolf's followers as "the crazed bitches" and to Shiloh's thieves as "the whispering thugs."

It seemed like the crazed bitches had learned to tame spiders like pets. "*Meet Charlotte,*" popped into my memory, and chills ran down my spine. The summoned spiders hunted the Animaniacs as in a fox hunt. What happened next was only spoken of in whispers, but I could guess what it was. The victims weren't killed, but dragged into the spider mansion's dungeon — never to emerge.

Unlike the surviving Animaniacs, I knew what went on in the basements of the gothic mansion and I didn't envy the disappeared.

As for the whispering thugs, well, at least you could buy them off. The thugs often offered their victims a choice: respawn quickly or go free but in your underwear. All belongings were accepted as "voluntary donations" to the Bedtime Story monastery. And many of those who stripped voluntarily often ended up as "voluntary donations" themselves, disappearing without a trace.

Some of Anima's followers took refuge in the mayor's palace, but then the mayor began hinting that after all, the city did have to maintain its neutrality, and Simba had to rally a group of his followers to fight their way out towards the glade where Anima's first statue stood. I wasn't even surprised as I could guess who'd suggested the idea to him. Outside the city, the pursuers fell behind and turned home to engage in other forms of entertainment.

Then a great exodus began from among the

ranks of the Animaniacs. Many begged for mercy from other gods, but the high priests were strict, if not vindictive. They took one in twenty, cynically explaining to the rest that "someone needs to level up too." So many of the former "warriors of Anima" found themselves second-class citizens in the city, oppressed and dreaming of revenge.

Simba worked hard to make these dreams of revenge a reality. He fully unleashed his entrepreneurial talent. The chief paladin managed to organize people into groups of tanks and damage dealers, sending them to farm, train his heavily armored personal guard, listen to scouts, assign watch shifts, and answer countless silly questions while encouraging the desperate.

For the first time since the game began, I regretted not keeping Simba on my side. He was always my right-hand man, albeit playing a supporting role, but now all his energy and organizational knowhow could've been put to my benefit.

I noticed Simba occasionally glancing at Sibyl with the face of a teacher's pet at the front of the class: "Am I doing this right? Will I be praised? Am I a good boy?"

The lack of any talk about Ji-Bo's merry band didn't surprise me. The Eternal Groove seemed pacifist to a fault, so I even wondered how its followers could level up. It was too hard to imagine them resorting to murder.

What did concern me was the lack of any mention of Anna or Lance. Those two couldn't possibly lie low. So I wouldn't be surprised if something had happened to them while I was languishing in my captivity.

One way or another, I had to get out of here and the sooner, the better. I forced myself to focus solely on this goal for a minute: to discard my anger at Simba, my anxiety for Stacy, my fixation on Sophia's spider-tattooed butt, the mystery of who was in the VR pod the other night, and even my revenge against Sullen who never did get his comeuppance — and think only about escaping this damn trap.

My skills were of no help. *Dash*, the closest thing I had to teleportation, would only transport me a few meters while making me invulnerable to steel and magic.

I tried it first, to no avail. The barrier burned me and dealt damage that required sitting and regenerating to recover. Attempts to break through it physically ended similarly.

My former skill tree was disabled since I was now a great and terrible Shinigami. But I didn't see any advantages from my new class either. Searching through the settings, I found that one single skill in my entire skill tree was not grayed out.

Then I remembered! After yesterday's battle, I received a message that I'd earned a new level and a new skill. The skill was the first in the skill tree but hidden unlike the main skills. Next to the gray icon, there seemed to be a price — 10 points of "Divine Grace."

The "Grace" stat was next to the gold, and I had 23 points of it, having fought hard the day before. Without hesitation, I poured all the unallocated points into the skill. It immediately lit up, allowing me to read:

RITUAL SUICIDE: Commit suicide using the divine tantō knife. Cost: 2 points of Divine Grace. Lose all equipped and inventoried items. -10% Gold and lose all XP above the current level.

Harsh rules, no better than regular death. The losses in equipment and XP were the same. So where were the advantages?

"Upon death, the player is transferred to the Temple of Death — a restricted location."

So that's it! The perfect escape tool, though a bit bloody.

I look around, trying not to draw attention to myself too early, and began looking for the ritual tantō knife in my inventory. In the last round, only Anna had it, but now it had been added to my inventory. I wouldn't be surprised if all Death's followers got one. Short and narrow, like a small katana that didn't get enough steel or was underfed in childhood, hence its small size, it was the Japanese version of a misericorde — a dagger of mercy used to finish off the mortally wounded or those too dangerous to leave alive.

And how do you commit suicide with this? Slit my wrists? Fat chance! I quickly take the tantō from my inventory and plunge it into the left side of my abdomen. I slice upward and diagonally. The clothes around the cut quickly bloom with blood. There's no pain, just an overwhelming weakness as my health plummets.

I'm too slow! Sibyl does a double take and notices something's amiss. She rushes towards me.

"Simba, he's escaping!" she screams and waves her hand, causing the barrier to vanish.

So it *was* all lies! About the gods about the magic. It was her own spell all along.

Simba abandons his training, grabs his sword on the run, and charges at me. Sibyl, who is closer, lunges and grabs my clothes, obviously trying to keep me from getting away.

At the last moment, like a suicide performing seppuku alone, I pull the knife from the wound and slash my throat.

There's a flash! A whirlwind forms around me, lifting and carrying me somewhere. The vortex is red like blood and white like a completely out-of-place summer blizzard. I see Sibyl's hand squeezing my sleeve, making teleportation incredibly difficult, pulling me to the ground.

Pop! Now Sibyl and I are standing shoulder to shoulder. A waterfall roars before us, separating us from the rest of the world. We stand on a round platform, surrounded by smooth stone walls on three sides and the cold barrier of rushing water as the fourth wall.

There aren't traces of my seppuku on my clothes, just a few spots of rust already fading. Carefully stepping on the stones, I find a path near the waterfall. But as I walk cautiously, a green silk dress flashes past me like lightning. I use my *Dash* skill to catch up to the girl, but she sharply changes direction, and I zip past her carried by my dash's momentum.

Sibyl slips between two large stone outcroppings, along a path that seems to lead out of this place. She's made her escape, but less than a minute later, her piercing scream echoes and she respawns on the altar. She looks disheveled, her hair a mess — she clearly didn't expect this outcome.

"I didn't even see what killed me," she complains. "There are some kind of Level 20 monsters out there."

I marvel at her ability to change attitudes so quickly. Not long ago, she called me a demon and gloated at my imprisonment, and now she's politeness personified.

I approach her. She's Level 5. It's all she managed in a few days. As a fighter, she's useless. The mobs beyond the wall in this place could be Level 3s and she still wouldn't fend them off.

"Sibi, why are you running?" I ask. "You'll tire yourself out."

While she hides among the rocks, I cut off the only escape route and manage to survey the gorge. It's small, circular, surrounded by nearly vertical cliffs.

Above the gorge, a strange rock looms. Its sloping top and two dark cave openings resemble a skull with blind eyes. From its open mouth, a waterfall pours down into a crystal-clear lake. The water's surface is a bright semicircle, the point where the water meets the lake creating a misty curtain, making the whole lake look white, like milk.

On the map, my position is shown as a small green dot in a vast sea of darkness. I don't even know which direction my allies are in and see no point in searching. A perfect place to rest and reflect.

But not when you have an unknown companion. So I cautiously suggest we find our way back to civilization together.

For Sibyl, the choice is limited — she already tried running. Another option is to hide and wait until tomorrow's beta round, but I certainly won't allow that.

The priestess understands this and waits for me at the top. As I approach, she looks up at me with a mix of defiance and submission. Then, she slowly runs her tongue over her lips and starts to untie the sash of her dress.

CHAPTER 15

WATCHING HER UNFASTEN HER SASH, I lowered my eyes and smirked. Sibyl noticed my gaze and seemed to blush a bit. Her cheeks even turned slightly pink, but she didn't stop. The sash fell and her long dress parted slightly, revealing her small, beautifully shaped breasts almost to the nipples.

Sibyl had a graceful and pliant figure. Only now did I notice how much she looked like Anna. Sisters. Once more I pictured the lonely girl playing alone in a virtual box with her toys and her perfect doll. A sister of the same age. Why then does this one hate her friend Anna so much?

"You won," Sibyl waved her hand. "I'm a complete fool for jumping in here after you. I don't know how you set up this trap, although I thought I knew everything in this game. I can't believe you're willing to go to such lengths to conquer me!"

I almost burst out laughing in astonishment.

So that's what this bitch thought. That everything I'd done — like the ritual suicide, the teleportation, and this entire special area — I'd done for her.

Well, there was no denying her sense of self-importance. Although that's a mistake even very cunning bitches make. They are absolutely convinced that the whole world revolves around them.

I realized that in the past two weeks, I had gotten much better at understanding women. It had been like a crash course, in near-combat conditions. For some reason, every one of them tests your strength first — and when they get flicked on the nose in return, they're shocked.

Unlike Sibyl, I knew where we were. As soon as I materialized at the new location, my UI helpfully informed me:

DIVINE QUEST RECEIVED: "TEMPLE OF DEATH."

ACTIVATE THE ALTAR OF DEATH TO SUMMON THE TEMPLE'S GODDESS.

And that's it! There were no further explanations. The AI seemed unwilling to help me, either to make the quest all the more difficult or to leave me room for creativity. So Sibyl's lewd behavior turned out to be very timely. Who knows, maybe if I screw her on the altar, the temple will come alive? Either way, it's worth a try!

In fact, this idea appealed to me more and more. Sibyl's entire demeanor demonstrated submission. I took a step towards her, and she flirtatiously wiggled her shoulders — a promise of something glinting in her eyes… her movements…

her smile.

Damn it, it wasn't so long ago, that I seriously considered the possibility that Benjamin Zvyagin, or even that other guy, the chief technician I'd just learned about but didn't know personally, might be controlling this NPC. Now, however, I understood quite clearly that no man could pull this off, unless he was a brilliant actor. Or maybe I was just rationalizing these creepy thoughts away, enchanted by the sudden wave of pleasure that washed over me.

"Aren't I a demon?" I asked more for my benefit than hers, trying to resist the temptation.

"Of course you're a demon," she purred, "but I like that actually. You're so powerful… No matter how much I help the others, they stay weak. But you defeated me…"

"You trapped me in a magical spell!" I went on, already wavering.

"I was hurt!" Sibyl spread her arms, and the folds of her dress parted, exposing the light skin of her belly. "You disbanded our party and publicly swore allegiance to that scum who chose Death!" Sibyl was practically shouting now. "I serve Life! Death is my primal enemy! I believed in you and your party, and you betrayed me! You betrayed all of us!"

A burning shame overwhelmed me now, as if I'd just been slapped across the face. Tears stood in Sibyl's eyes, and I wanted to fall to my knees and beg her forgiveness. All my actions in the game now seemed monstrous to me. I had betrayed my friends, broken up our party and made an alliance with our former enemies, Anna and Lance. I had started an entire war... I didn't even understand how, but I had done it...

I wanted to fall to my knees and beg for forgiveness. To ask for permission to atone for my guilt, to renounce everything, and become a knight without fear and reproach for this fragile and proud priestess. To lay the whole world at her feet... She believed in me so much... And still does... Even if I am a demon, I still have a chance...

"Sibyl... Sibi... Forgive me... I didn't mean to..." The words seemed to come out on their own, I spoke them and felt relieved, "I will atone for my guilt..."

I took another step, and Sibyl let her dress fall. She stood completely naked before me, and the light refracting in the waterfall's streams played along her flawless body. She was incredible, unearthly, as if glowing from within...

"I am no adventurer like you, TargetAi," she spoke slowly, melodically, and each word seemed to imprint itself upon my brain as the whole truth and nothing but the truth. "I was born here, this is my world, and I want to protect it from your kind. I want there to be no pain and death here. I dream of peace between the adventurers and my people. Help me, TargetAi! Stop those madmen who only want to kill. Serve me, for I am life itself!"

"Rrrrrraaaa!" My consciousness sang, overwhelmed with delight, and only one thing prevented it from fully taking flight.

An unpleasant feeling, initially faint, like a mosquito bite, or like a safety pin that accidentally opened and scratched your skin, or like a white sunspot from a lens, which an idiot — your classmate at the desk next to you — focused on your wrist during Physics lab. The feeling, it prickled... it itched... it smarted...

It invaded my thoughts, crumpling them, confusing and cooling them. Unable to endure it, I tore my gaze away from the beautiful Sibyl for a second and glanced at the source of the unpleasant sensation.

Anna's garter, tied in a bow, was glowing bright red, as if red-hot. As soon as I touched it, a message popped up in the logs.

GODDESS'S GARTER: +20% PROTECTION FROM MAGICAL ATTACKS.

MAGICAL ATTACK BLOCKED: "CHARM."

I looked up and all I saw was some naked chick. Scrawny. AngelCake's tits are bigger, Marina's are prettier. Yet this one stands there proudly hiking her nose, unaware that her show is over.

With one swift motion, I brought the tanto knife to her throat and spoke calmly, so she wouldn't flinch:

"Who are you really, Sibyl?"

"What?!"

She did flinch after all — she didn't expect it — and a thin stream of blood slipped from under the razor-sharp blade.

"WHO THE HELL ARE YOU REALLY?!"

The element of surprise works wonderfully. Sibyl blinked, her eyes immediately filling with tears, but this was already panic. A good face on a bad game. Whoever was behind this avatar, I probably couldn't outmaneuver them in terms of intrigue. But now, when Sibyl was confident in her victory, my strike hit the mark, and the healer was losing her composure.

"TargetAi!" she cried out. "You're hurting me!"

It was the perfect thing to say — had we been out in meatspace. Out there, her exclamation would make me let go of her. My good boy reflexes are conditioned into my subconscious. You're no man if you cause a woman pain. You have to turn the other cheek, offer your shoulder, wallet, anything you can.

But here in cyberspace that doesn't work. In VR, everyone is equal, there is no death, and therefore no fear. It's kill or die here. That's the law of the gladiators.

In that instant, I understood why Anna had chosen to be Death. It was the most truthful summation of everything that could ever happen here. Only Death could break the mad cycle of reincarnations that those stuck in the game fall into. Either you killed them or you saved them.

"I don't give a damn," I looked as ferociously as I could. "Do you think I'll just one-shot you and that's it? I'll kill you slowly... Dismember you... And when you respawn, we'll start all over again. We've got plenty of time. There's no real pain here, but believe me, your brain will make it up for you."

I looked into her eyes, widening with genuine horror, and summoned all the movie maniacs I could recall: Dexter, Hannibal Lecter, the ghoul from "Scream." Then I brought my lips close to her ear and whispered exactly what I was going to do to her...

"You wouldn't dare!" she shrieked. "You freak! You psycho!!! Just touch me and I'll destroy you! I'll have you buried in concrete and dumped in a river, you bastard! Do you even know who I am?!"

"Who?!" I barked eagerly. "TELL ME, BITCH!!!"

Sibyl recoiled and tightly shut her eyes, pressing her lips together and flaring her nostrils nervously. Her entire demeanor showed that come what may, she was ready for anything... but the consequences of revealing her secret were far scarier than any torture.

Then again, I had already drawn all the conclusions I needed. Her whole story of a sentient NPC girl was a pretty cover story crafted for patsies. A human player was operating Sibyl's character, but it wasn't just any player. The threats she'd just made sounded all too appropriate to *my* world, not hers. And she'd reacted the way someone who is used to being listened to and feared reacts.

I didn't know who or how they had replaced Anna's virtual sister, but whoever did it was playing their own game. All my hypotheses were confirmed. They were driving the AI mad on purpose, though whether the Board of Directors was in on this or not, I didn't yet know.

Sibyl had firmly decided to play the martyr, and I saw that I wouldn't learn anything more from her. But even this momentary weakness was a huge victory.

I stepped back slightly and delivered a swift, precise knife strike to her throat, severing the artery there. Blood spurted in a fountain, covering Sibyl, me, and the dark, round altar stone on which we stood. The girl gave a short cry, gurgled, and went limp, almost immediately turning into a pile of dust. Then she disappeared. There was no respawning for her this time around.

Instead, the altar tolled, low and resonant, like a bell after a mighty strike. The humming filled everything around me with its vibration. The waterfall's water boiled and bubbled, and the tiny lake into which it cascaded turned white, as if lit from beneath by an invisible source of light. The temple was coming to life.

"Holy shit!"

The only thing that kept me from admiring my surroundings further was the minor detail of the Goddess of Death falling out of thin air onto my head.

"Anna, wait!"

Damn she's strong! A single blow of hers took out a third of my health right away. Anna stuck to her tradition of striking first and asking questions later. After my yelp, she froze in a low combat stance, her sword pointed at me.

"Targe?! Is that you?"

I must have looked pretty bad. Covered in blood from head to toe, like a butcher, madness still gleaming in my eyes. Oops, I guess I was still in character.

"Of course, it's me." I put my knife away and raised my hands to show they were empty.

She might cut me down. And who knows where I'd respawn. Sibyl had completely disappeared after all.

"What if you've been digitized by the game?" Anna persisted. "How do I know you're the real Targe?"

At first, I wanted to say her real last name out loud, something the AI definitely wouldn't have access to, but I bit my tongue just in time. Who knows how many ears are eavesdropping on us right now.

"If I promise to treat you to a strawberry cascara after the beta round, will you believe me?"

"Blackberry, you idiot," Anna calmed down and smiled. "We've been trying to reach you through the chat for the last hour."

"I've been trying to reach you too. A lot has happened here…"

"Wait," Anna cut me off, "where are we anyway?"

"It's strange you don't recognize it," I replied. "We're in the temple dedicated to you. Don't you feel any inspiration? Or maybe a surge of strength? Where's your divine essence? The other gods act like real gods. Take Lolf for instance: She's a killing machine. But our goddess is only good at swinging her katanas! What about the miracles? Where are they?"

I felt myself getting carried away. Sibyl's magical trap, my escape and my subsequent interrogation of her had exhausted me, and now, finding myself in a calm environment and coming down from the adrenaline rush, I felt like talking. Perhaps Anna realized that I'd had a tough time of it and decided not to hold it against me.

"Then go join Lolf," she replied. "Her priestess will be very happy to see you. I heard they now keep men on leashes and take them for walks around town. Want to try that?"

"Wow," I marveled. "I've missed a lot of big developments, it seems."

We left the altar as we spoke. Anna went to inspect her new domain, and I approached the spring and washed my face with pleasure. Whether the water was living or dead didn't matter to me at that moment.

"Not bad," Anna said when she returned to me. "Pretty gothic. How did you get here?"

I briefly told her about being caught as a demon, my ritual suicide, and the sacrifice. I kept silent about having acted like a psycho as well as what I had surmised from Sibyl's reaction. Such topics were better discussed in the real world.

"I sacrificed her to you, by the way," I concluded.

"So I'm a cruel, bloodthirsty deity, it turns out," Anna snorted. "Why do you think she didn't respawn?"

"Maybe she got kicked out of the game for good?" I suggested. "This is the Temple of Death, after all. There should be some special options here. Do you feel anything yourself?"

"A new ability unlocked," Anna's gaze became glassy, as if she were looking at the interface instead of me. "*Summon*. I have no idea what it does."

She waved her hand, and Lance and his two buddies fell out of thin air, cursing, next to us. T-Rex tumbled right into the pool.

"What the hell?!" he yelled, clambering ashore.

The others didn't say anything, but they didn't look happy either. It was clear they hadn't missed me much since the last time we saw each other.

"Welcome home, boys!" I greeted them.

Anna stood beside me with an impassive expression, as if everything was going according to plan. Although there was plenty to be surprised about. The "Warriors of Death" looked anything but normal. Each one was wearing a wide-brimmed straw hat, making him look like a beekeeper or a Chinese peasant, and each one had a woven basket strapped to his back like a backpack.

We blinked at each other in surprise, but in the end I couldn't help but break the silence.

"What is this, carnival?!"

"We decided to make some quick cash," Lance replied somewhat unsurely, "collecting cocoons."

"What?!" It was so odd to see these marauders dressed as peaceful farmers that I wanted to hear the whole story.

Lance's tale infuriated me. While I was stuck in Sibyl's trap and Anna was running around looking for me, Lance had occupied himself with household affairs. Although the Whisperer's henchmen who had picked up our loot didn't dare appropriate it for themselves, they wouldn't hand it over to Lance either. They decided to hold onto it it until our leadership showed up to claim it.

The armor and weapons of Lance's squad left much to be desired. After their untimely demise in the palace dungeon, we hadn't had a chance to buy them anything decent. Farming spiders was out of the question. The House of Lolf declared the eight-legged creatures sacred and threatened severe punishments for killing them.

Anima's followers, those who remained in the city, may have been easy prey but they were also worthless from a profit standpoint. Most of them had respawned several times and lost anything of value. The rest were stripped down to their underwear by the Whisperer's boys, who brazenly robbed them until, according to the laws of probability, their theft attempt succeeded and they found their inventories empty.

Lance was already planning a trip outside the city when Shiloh stepped in as a benefactor and offered an easy quest. Crafting had appeared in the city, and thus, there was a demand for raw materials. The cocoons of local silkworms could only be gathered in special groves. Level 10 Adult Butterbees were the size of sparrows and fiercely aggressive. Their cocoons were the size of mangos and burned with contact poison whoever they fell on. Hence the hats, to protect their heads and shoulders, and the baskets for collecting the cocoons.

"One of us gathers the cocoons while the other two fend off the attacks," Lance explained, "then we switch. It's not hard work and besides us, few dare to venture into the groves. The other players are too weak for such locations."

Somehow Lance even seemed proud of his new found occupation. The warrior didn't seem to realize that he had been cleverly finessed into another clan's economic system, and not at all at a prestigious level.

"I really need to have a talk with Shiloh," I ground my teeth. "Comprehensively and slowly and without any interruptions, preferably."

"Then let's go," Lance jumped up.

He had already realized that he had blundered and now wanted to make up for it.

"And where do you think you're going?" Anna asked.

I looked at the map again, then zoomed out as much as possible and looked again. Blackness stretched in all directions around the Temple of Death, which was marked as a tiny speck in a vast emptiness.

CHAPTER 16

THE TEMPLE OF DEATH TURNED OUT to be quite a cozy place. A small, perfectly round gorge with emerald grass, surrounded by mountains on all sides. Right in the center was a small lake, more like a pool, with milky-white water. When I scooped some up with my hand, it fizzed with a myriad tiny bubbles.

Directly above the pool loomed a black rocky ledge in the shape of a skull. The resemblance was so strong it seemed like a sculptor's hand had carved the stone. Then again, wasn't everything in this world designed by level designers?

Or was it?

Who could have known at the start of the game that gods would come into this world, and one of the goddesses would be Death? In an ordinary game universe, such a temple would remain "frozen" until someone triggered the right quest.

But here? Had the AI generated it when the time came? In that case, whose mind did it pull this image from? Certainly not mine. Though I liked the surroundings. They were soothing. Thick and dense grass like a carpet, with white flowers breaking through, the skull with its hollow eye sockets shrouded in mist. Even the water that flowed from its open mouth and fell into the pool, hissing like soda.

Unable to resist the temptation, I took a sip.

YOU HAVE DRUNK FROM THE FOUNT OF DEATH!

ANY POSITIVE AND NEGATIVE STATUS EFFECTS HAVE BEEN REMOVED.

Interesting property. This is a bit like holy water with enhanced effects. Very useful in case someone decides to cast a curse on me. I hadn't encountered that yet, but this world was rapidly developing even as I spoke.

As for blessings, few would want to bestow them willingly. Except...

"Anna, come here..."

"Why?" she squinted suspiciously.

What intuition!

"I want to show you something."

I waited for her to come closer, then scooped up water from the lake and splashed it in her face!

"Have you lost your mind?!" Anna sputtered, like a cat, then plunged both hands into the pool and drenched me from head to toe.

YOU HAVE BATHED IN THE FOUNT OF DEATH!

ANY POSITIVE AND NEGATIVE...

"Wait! Did you get a system notification?!" I yelled before she could scoop up more water.

"Yes," she stopped, read the message, then said more calmly, "why the face?"

"So it gets on the skin," I explained, "it seemed more reliable to me."

"Are you having a wet t-shirt contest here?" Lance inquired.

T-Rex and Shugga immediately burst out laughing in unison.

The trio was returning from the gorge, which was the only way out of the valley. A perfect dungeon. If the AI had sealed us in, Anna could become the raid boss of her own temple, and we'd be her boss henchmen. An imaginary walkthrough even popped into my head: "'Death's Thong' (Reward: Death's Thong, Party Size: 1–5, Unlocks at Level 20... Speak to the mayor to receive this quest." What a bit of silliness that would be!

"T-Rex," I ignored Lance's joke and addressed one of his companions. "Did you fall into the pool?"

The tall and broad-shouldered fighter, who wore the heaviest armor of the squad, looked at Lance, then back at me, and shifted his leg to the side, standing in an independent and slightly contemptuous pose.

"Yes," he said. "And?"

"Did you get a system notification?"

"Y-yeah?"

Honestly, I expected something like this. But I thought the first move would come from Shugga.

The small sneak seemed more suited to the role of troublemaker. I figured T-Rex would be more reasonable... Then again, what reasonable person dyes his hair pink?

In any case, I wasn't surprised. It was Lance who decided to join us; the others just followed their leader. When it comes down to it, they respect and answer to him, while I'm just some random guy from nowhere, and apparently a pushover too, since my living goddess calls the shots here.

I don't have a clan or a team yet and Anna stays silent, not bothering to back me up. Either she doesn't understand what's going on, or, for this sociopath, our dick-measuring contest exists in a completely different reality.

Why do I need to take responsibility for these idiots?! First, I saved Anna from premature elimination due to an unfinished game quest. Now I'm paying for it.

Then I pulled these fools out of their coma. And now, am I responsible for them?

I never did like ordering people around. I preferred to rely on myself. Life taught me that. "If you want something done right, do it yourself." You can't trust anyone. Even Simba, my buddy from childhood, went his own way as soon as he got the chance.

And yet, I understood that without a party, without a clan, I wouldn't make it. The time of lone wolves was over. People were leveling up, banding together, and arming themselves. So, I'd have to play this game, no matter how tedious it was.

The first step in it was dealing with this idiot with the pink bangs, who was grinning at me now, his smile growing wider with every second of my silence. As if I were scared. A smirk even appeared on Shugga's face.

This silent rebellion was happening right in front of Lance, but he didn't care. Lance was only interested in himself, and it would always be that way. But his "lackeys" were upset that their cash-cow had been pushed out of the limelight. And now they were lashing out.

The temptation to wipe the smirks off their faces was incredible. In real life, maybe it would work, but in here the very idea was laughable. Of course, we'd both grab our swords, of course, I'd take him down — our levels and gear are incomparable.

But then what? What would I prove? Beat my own men to scare the others into line? There were no others. I frantically tried to recall my classes on leadership, small groups, and — a term that scared me — team building. Marina would be perfect here; she'd probably mastered this stuff and then some.

And then an idea flickered in my mind.

"Listen, T-Rex," I said calmly. "No one's keeping you here, you can leave."

And, turning away from the stunned mug beneath the pink bangs, I addressed Lance:

"Let's figure out who has what skills. We need to assign roles for battle."

"Well T-Rex is the tank," Lance began. "He's boosting endurance, and his gear is the strongest."

"Forget him," I waved my hand. "He's not with us. Either you or I will have to tank."

"What do you mean, not with us?!" T-Rex exploded right on cue. "What the hell?! We were the ones who joined you *voluntarily* and now you're kicking us out?!"

I was expecting another "who do you think you are," but it never came. I was amazed at myself. Not long ago, a situation like this would have set me off instantly, but now it was like I was seeing myself from the outside, with a cool head, and even had time to mock the situation.

"*I've grown up fast...*" a familiar thought echoed in my head.

They're about my age. Lance, I know, is a year older; the rest are about the same as me. Yet why do they seem like some adolescents — radiating silly pride and boyish expectations — to me now?

Maybe because the goals I'm set on are far from simple "boyish" ones. It's not just about "being the best" or "making money." I know that somewhere in this corporate tower, an innocent girl named Yumi is lying unconscious and that there are many more people like her, including possibly Anna's father, languishing in VR limbo — and that the risk that they end up drooling vegetables is very high.

And at the same time, at this very instant, realizing how high the stakes are, I felt wild excitement, the drive of someone who could do practically anything because the alternative was total disaster.

"Guys," I said sympathetically. "Are you serious? You lot? Catching 'butterbees' or whatever? The best fighters in this place...? Really! You can take down anyone outside this Temple in PvP... You're pros, champs! And..." I spat in frustration, lost for words. "Why just look at yourselves."

I rocked back and forth on my heels, puffed out my cheeks reflexively... and had a sudden flashback: the Master... I was unconsciously copying his mannerisms. The way he disciplined the security guards in the MosTech lobby. It was just two weeks ago, but it felt like another lifetime. His sly conversations, his flattery that almost always ended with some dare.

My words hit a sore spot. The bros looked at each other as if they were *seeing* for the first time: some silly peasant hats, baskets on their backs, lousy gear scrounged from the town barracks. The most promising fighters of the beta looked like a bunch of losers.

"By the way, that's twice now that you guys..." T-Rex began. "No, or was it three times that..."

Lance shot him a withering look and he clammed up. He was the most impatient among the new recruits. He was an ideal target for influence, his emotions running far ahead of his reason.

"Do you know why the FBI didn't prevent 9/11?" I asked, not letting them recover.

The abrupt change of topic stunned them a bit, but they perked up their ears. Especially since it got them away from having to confront their own failure. It's funny, but very few people like to see themselves from the outside.

"Why?" T-Rex couldn't hold back.

"The Bureau had all the necessary information," I started counting on my fingers: "That some suspicious persons had entered the US, that some foreigners were learning how to fly planes, that they had purchased explosives... But all these cases were handled by different departments. DIFFERENT DEPARTMENTS, DAMN IT! The FBI agents were sitting in neighboring cubicles and had no idea what was going on on the other side of the separator. And in the end, they missed the biggest terrorist attack in history!"

"What's that got to do with us?" Lance finally spoke up.

"Because let's not make their mistake," I concluded unexpectedly. "The first rule of our clan: We share all information with each other. Important... strange... silly... Absolutely any. What's useless to one might be invaluable to another. How long the mating song of purple slugs lasts, the color of wyvern poop, crafting recipes, booze prices, which girls put out right away and which play hard to get..." At these words, the guys laughed while Anna snorted. "Got it? It's *information* that will make us unbeatable."

My guildmates nodded, which was especially pleasing because even Anna mimicked the gesture. At worst, if they didn't buy into my motivational speech, I had a Plan B: kill them all and keep killing them until they recognized my authority. Then again, that would only work with Anna's assent, so I was glad it didn't come to that.

"Now, scatter," I commanded. "Everyone has fifteen minutes to explore this location. After that, we'll meet here and share our findings. Go!"

Everyone obeyed. Briskly and eagerly, the fighters spread out across the place. Shugga went around the edge of the rocks, Anna headed towards the gorge's exit, T-Rex climbed into the waterfall, while Lance pretended to examine the stone skull but actually lingered not too far from me.

"You seem to know what you're doing," he said thoughtfully.

"What?" I didn't understand at first.

"Leadership."

"I studied it," I nodded.

"What did you major in?" Lance asked.

"Sociology."

"Wow," he said, surprised. "Do they teach you stuff like that?"

They do, yes. For an entire three months, every other Friday after regular classes. Thanks to Dr. Ivantsov, who taught us the basics of small group behavior in special seminars — a bit more than what was in the textbooks.

Because it's only in the most primitive groups that the role of the leader relies on physical strength. Among animals, this is true among predator packs, while among humans, it's observed among criminal gangs.

At the next level, leadership is determined by information. The more you know, the more the others trust you. Especially in situations where everything is unclear and going wrong.

So the first thing I did was describe just how bad our situation was. And then I offered a "magic pill." Some rules that would make us invincible. And that was it, the first round was mine. If this wasn't followed up by some quick victories, however, the party would hold me accountable. But we'd burn that bridge when we crossed it.

"And what about you?" I changed the subject.

"Law," Lance laughed. "But I only attended two classes this year. Esports is too time-consuming."

Now that the Gladiators had become an event in the Olympics, every university had its own team. Lance only needed to play for his team in a few tournaments, and they'd bring his report card to his doorstep with a perfect 4.0 and a bow.

"Lance..." I hinted, looking around.

"Got it, boss," he smirked. "I won't undermine your authority. You haven't made a wrong step yet, so you have my confidence, don't worry."

He turned and trotted towards the gorge where Anna had already disappeared.

In fifteen minutes, we discovered a lot of interesting things: That the ring of rocks surrounding the gorge was impassable and couldn't be climbed from either the inside or the outside. Ropes didn't reach the top, and stilettos couldn't penetrate the solid monolith (Shugga). That the water from the pool retained its properties when poured into glass, ceramic, or even metal flasks, but to have an effect, it had to touch bare skin. That the flowers around the pool were bitter to the taste and did -10 HP if swallowed (Lance). That the waterfall water turned crimson if you spat into it (T-Rex). That the temple was surrounded by Level 20+ mobs called "krogs," who resembled a cross between a feline and a porcupine. That they climbed trees and shot long, thin needles with a mild paralyzing effect from above, that killing them granted 400 XP, and that they dropped pretty pink or blue crystals as loot (Anna).

Left to my own devices, I had scrutinized the altar inch by inch and, on my 10th or 20th try, succeeded in activating it:

ALTAR OF DEATH (LEVEL 1 / 10).

REQUIRED FOR SACRIFICES.

So, the altar could be leveled up to grant additional bonuses. But sacrifices were scarce. Something told me that krogs wouldn't count. The altar required players — their lives, or more precisely, their deaths. And every step we took only brought the inevitable closer.

Despite everything we learned, none of it brought us any closer to solving our main problem: how to get back to civilization. The problem wasn't just that, judging by the map, the city was far away, but that we had no idea which direction to go.

I could already imagine us fighting through

higher-level mobs, only to eventually hit the edge of the world, and I wondered if then we'd be able to look down and see the elephants holding up this universe.

"Let's recall everything that's happened," I ordered. "Every event of the day, even the smallest and strangest."

I then recounted my abduction by Sibyl in minute detail, and then the vengeance I took on her when I dragged her along with me. The others hoped she was burning in digital hell, but no new ideas occurred to us.

In the end, it was Shugga who saved the day.

"When we set out to harvest the cocoons," he spoke up out of nowhere, quietly, staring off somewhere past me to the left, "Shiloh said it was a divine quest. The Whisperer had ordered him to make flags with the silk in order to decorate the temple. He's real pompous like that..."

"What difference does it make?" T-Rex interrupted. "They didn't give it to us anyway. Divine quests are only for religious followers."

A click went off in my head, as usual, when puzzle pieces fell into place, and I looked closely at Anna.

"Dear goddess," I said in a syrupy voice, "how would you like to work a little for the benefit of your devout followers?"

CHAPTER 17

IT TURNED OUT NOT TO BE SO SIMPLE. The Goddess of Death couldn't simply create a quest for us to find a way back to the city. She couldn't even make a quest to open our maps or place a quest marker on it.

"You're not trying!" I protested, fed up.

"I am too!" Anna snapped back.

"Then you're not trying hard enough!"

"Why don't you suggest something if you're so smart!"

Anna pouted, stalked away and sat down on the grass. Unwilling to let it go at that, I sat down next to her and the others followed.

We started a brainstorming session.

"Maybe we should scrounge up some silk for her too?" Shugga suggested.

"What for?!"

"To sew herself a dress... or something..." The

small thief blushed unexpectedly.

"Shiloh can do the sewing for his whores," Anna snapped.

"Then what do you want?" I tried another approach.

"To be left alone!"

Sociopath Anna was even more burdened by her new divinity than I was. Who knew? Gods didn't just sit around a cloud spitting down: They had to care for their followers too. What a predicament!

"Seriously, wish for something you really want. Give it a shot..."

"Okay. I want some cascara," Anna snorted. "There. I tried. It didn't work."

Wait... wait... I felt an idea brewing in my mind; I just had to grab it by its slippery tail. "No but, what do you want in here, in the game? As a goddess? What makes you feel good *here*?"

"You know," Anna pondered, "when you first brought me here, I had a feeling of euphoria. It was very short but very intense. And afterwards, I felt stronger. It felt like my blood quickened in my veins." She raised her hands doubtfully, as if unsure if there was digital blood in there, flowing through digital veins even as she spoke.

"Well right before that, I sacrificed Sibyl to you..." I jumped in.

"Wow," Lance said, "you guys know how to get your rocks off, huh?"

"Get used to it," Anna patted him on the shoulder, "we're on the side of the dead now. Good pious parents will soon scare their children with our names."

"There aren't any children here," Lance replied, missing the joke.

"Then they'll make some just for the occasion."

I recalled the counter I'd seen on the altar: "Level 1 / 10" it read. I had made one sacrifice, awakening the temple. So, it's logical that more sacrifices were needed for the shrine to grow and prosper. Indeed, we were not the gentlest cult, but then again what cult is...

"Command us to level up the altar!" I blurted out.

"What?" Anna didn't understand.

"Just say it out loud."

Anna closed her eyes and muttered her command.

NEW DIVINE QUEST: HOLY SACRIFICE!

SACRIFICE NINE MORE PLAYERS FROM ANOTHER DIVINE HOUSE AND LEVEL UP YOUR ALTAR.

REWARD: NEW DIVINE SKILL.

"It worked!" T-Rex shouted before I could even open the map.

Some green dots had appeared scattered across the empty, black map, and there was a large number of arrows at the edges, indicating that most of our potential victims were out of range but somewhere in that direction.

Judging by their concentration, we were somewhere northeast of the city, if such a term was applicable here and if there were magnetic poles on this planet. Simply put, we were in the upper right corner of the map.

There was however a fairly large cluster of points — potential sacrifices — not far from us. If we headed due left. This was the route we chose, and there were no objections.

Very pleased with ourselves, we headed out through the narrow gorge, its walls so close that T-Rex, the largest of us, almost brushed them with his shoulders.

And immediately came under crossfire.

"What the...! Why there's a train of mobs here... But who brought it..." Lance managed to yell before he was turned into a pincushion and collapsed into a pile of dust.

T-Rex and Sugar bolted back, crashing into me and then Anna, who was bringing up our rear. Unexpectedly, we found ourselves pressed back into the gorge.

Exchanging angry glances, we finally looked at our goddess.

"There were very few of them," she shrugged defensively, "and they were spread out. They died almost instantly so I didn't think they were much of a..."

The local denizens, the krogs, hadn't made an impression on our killing machine, but they turned out to be a very curious species and good number of them had followed her to the gorge's entrance.

Fired with considerable power and accuracy,

their spines pierced even leather armor, and several of them could create such a density of fire that they could wipe out anyone in our party in minutes, even Anna — as Lance had just demonstrated. The only one of us with any decent armor was T-Rex.

"Let me aggro them," he offered, "and you follow me and engage in close combat."

"Do you have AoE aggro?"

"No, why?"

It dawned on me that my new party members were total noobs when it came to MMORPGs. The Gladiator Games, where fights were 1v1 and everything was decided by strength and speed, has nothing to do with farming mobs and raiding dungeons.

As a result our party was completely unbalanced in terms of class. We had four dps, one of whom was mistakenly called a tank, and one thief.

In my previous party, I tried to maintain an optimal mix of classes, but here everyone was whatever they wanted to be.

"Step aside!" Lance shouted, appearing from the other end of the gorge. "I'll show these prickly bastards who's the boss here."

Lance's jacket and one of his swords had disappeared, probably lying in a bundle near the gorge's entrance, but no one dared go there.

"Stop," I held him back, "even if our respawn point is close, it's no reason to die. You could lose all your experience."

"So what do we do?!"

Four pairs of eyes looked at me questioningly. Lance, a convinced loner, gladly shed the burden of leadership. His friends, having lost faith in their former boss, who was persistently unlucky, also looked to me for guidance. And Anna had completely stepped aside, folding her arms as if studying me for her own purposes, whatever those were...

In response, I looked them over and realized I still didn't consider these people my team and missed my old party.

Lumbering and good-natured Simba — who struck first and asked questions later when it came to defending his friends — was good to have by my side in any scrap. Practical and thorough Stacy was the kind of girl you'd be afraid to introduce to your mom because within two minutes, they'd be discussing wallpaper for the living room and forming an unbreakable alliance behind your back. Even that rotten Sibyl, whom I'd personally sacrificed on our altar, was a bright, interesting girl who played a useful role in our party.

I missed all of them now. I knew that with them, we would have easily cleared out the krog siege and level up happily in the process. With my present crew however...

A treacherous thought flickered through my head — am I even on the right side? Did I take a wrong turn at some crossroads of fate back there? How did it happen that my true friends were now warriors on the side of good, while I've cast my lot with Death alongside these unsavory characters?

Lance was my constant friend and rival since childhood. His main flaw was pure, unadulterated egoism, carefully nurtured by his doting parents. The only person Lance cared about was himself, which meant he usually couldn't see beyond his aristocratic nose.

And I hadn't forgotten that it was he and his bros who had turned Yumi from a cheerful, if overly naive girl, into a bloodthirsty demon of vengeance. I didn't know what exactly happened between the five of them, but it was clearly something nasty. And as a result, I still refused to consider them my friends and preferred not to turn my back on them if I could help it.

And yet to get out of the mess we were in, I had to find something human about them and start seeing them at least as allies, instead of outright enemies.

Lance was an ideal two-handed fighter-duelist, geared for PvP but also capable of dealing heavy damage to mobs. This made him almost indistinguishable from me, except that he was behind in levels. After the carnage in the city, I was already at Level 21, while he was only Level 19. He also preferred European weapons, in contrast to my Asian ones.

T-Rex — tall and broad-shouldered, though still smaller than Simba — was also not averse to fighting. I vividly remembered how the two of them clashed in the MosTech cafeteria on the very first day of the beta. To be fair, he was dumber than my buddy. Simba might seem like a lumbering oaf, but he had a strong entrepreneurial streak and was a decent organizer.

And I would never get over those stupid pink bangs of his. They just didn't make him look very smart and that was that.

T-Rex had to be leveled up as a tank as our party needed at least one of those. For now, however, he could only boast about taking more damage longer than the others. That meant he could make it to a spot the rest of us wouldn't be able to reach — in this case, in the middle of the krogs.

And yet, who even knew how to "level up" anymore? The old skill tree was disabled, replaced by the divine one, and the only way to level up now was to kill members from other Houses. It was obvious where the AI was pushing us, but we needed to make sacrifices to even understand how the new mechanics would work.

Shugga — the little thief — had already surprised me. Quiet and silent, he turned out to be observant, tenacious, and capable of drawing his own conclusions. And I occasionally caught his glances at Anna, which were sometimes interested, sometimes admiring.

I'd never played as a thief, rogue, or assassin, so I had a poor understanding of this class's capabilities. I only guessed he could move stealthily and that attacks from stealth came with hefty multipliers, but I had no idea what these were or how exactly they worked.

Now I made a mental note to talk to him about his abilities later on, although only after we'd accomplished something together and started feeling like a team in reality, not just in name. I doubted I'd get anything useful out of him until then.

Both Shugga and T-Rex were Level 17, the lowest in our party. After a moment's thought, I shifted the party's XP distribution in their favor. When there's too much XP disparity in a party, the lower levels become useless. The speed of a team is determined by its slowest member. My father drilled this into me when we went on family hikes in my childhood. That was so long ago it seemed almost unreal now.

Finally, Anna was our prima donna in combat skills. A real "cat in the bag." Or rather, a tigress. I had no idea who had put a cat in a bag to coin this this proverb, but I figured the cat would come out hissing pissed. And that was Anna's typical state of mind. Even now, she hadn't killed anyone in twenty minutes and you could tell it was making her antsy.

She was Level 22. I had no clue what skills she had and now, divine skills would be added to that... In any case, she was our main strike package. We had only to aim her.

"Shugga, go into stealth and scout what we're dealing with," I ordered. "Once you determine how many there are and where they are, come right back, got it?"

The thief nodded curtly and disappeared into thin air.

"What if they spot him?" Lance asked.

"Then he'll come back from the other side," I shrugged, "just like you did."

But there were no surprises. The little thief reappeared well within the ten minutes I'd allotted him in my head.

"There's a dozen of them," he exhaled. "Three in the trees, the rest on the ground."

"Show us," I squatted down and handed him a broken twig.

Drawing circles and lines in the sand, we sketched our play. We would take down the krogs on the ground by and by. There was no hurry there, especially with our respawn point so close. But the ones in the trees posed a problem. We didn't have anyone who could dps at range. I remembered AngelCake and sighed wistfully. No wonder I'd assigned roles in my previous party. Now we had to improvise.

"Who has any skills in shooting or throwing?"

Silence. As if it was shameful to kill enemies from a distance. "An arrow is a fool, a sword is a hero," so goes the proverb.

"Anna, I saw you throw a wakizashi," I remembered, "what skill was that?"

I decided not to remind her that she had thrown the wakizashi in question at T-Rex's skull.

"*Shuriken*, but it's level 1," she replied. "It's useless, no multipliers, just lets you throw anything and has a random chance to stun."

"That's great!" I was thrilled. "Okay, let's not hold back. Empty your inventories of anything throwable."

I laid out my stilettos and a one-handed Carolingian sword. The others started unloading their inventories too, adding various grades of junk to the pile on the ground. Shugga especially impressed me.

"Look, it's a kaginawa!" I picked up a long thin chain with a hook at the end.

"It's not even a weapon," Shugga started trying to take back "his precious," but didn't make it in time.

"We know what this is," Anna accepted the tool from me and twirled it with a flick of her wrist.

The chain blurred into a semi-transparent circle, emitting a low intermittent hum.

"You'll be fighting with this," I informed Anna.

"Bossy, aren't you," she snorted, "don't forget, I'm still your Goddess! I'll fight as I please."

"Alright, Goddess, then just go and incinerate the lot of them." I didn't argue.

Anna's arrogant expression soured a bit. "Better let's stick to the plan," she backed down. "What's the plan again?"

The first out was Shugga. The sneak vanished again, reappearing two minutes later behind the largest, ugliest, orangest specimen, a Level 22 krog, and hitting him with a Shadow Strike for 3x damage.

I didn't know if krogs had elites, but I decided not to risk it and start on the biggest one first. Shugga's strike didn't kill the creature but it did significantly reduce its health.

The sudden attack sent the other krogs into

a frenzy. Bellowing, they immediately began stabbing both the thief and the nearby krog with their spines, heaping on yet more damage with their friendly fire.

While the krogs dealt with the chaos in their ranks, T-Rex charged out of the gorge with a roar. Taking advantage of the enemies' confusion, he almost made it to the trees, buying us time.

The three of us tucked behind his broad back and ran in a file, then broke into a sprint and plunged into the fray as soon as we got close enough.

I did a *Whirlwind* on the nearest two krogs, turning one into mincemeat and reducing the other's health to the red. A couple more strikes and the mob evaporated, dropping a beautiful red crystal.

Nearby, Anna was using a similar skill to cut a swath through her enemies.

"The trees!" I shouted.

She grimaced but swapped her swords for the hook. The first throw knocked a fat krog to the ground, where we finished it off together.

Lance, who had picked up both his jacket and sword along the way, was fiercely avenging his untimely death. The three of us took down the twelve mobs in about four minutes. T-Rex and Shugga hadn't even made it back from the respawn altar before it was all over.

"Gather up the crystals, T-Rex," I commanded. "You've got the highest Constitution."

There were no complaints, which was an

excellent sign.

"We can use the basket," T-Rex informed me, making me even happier.

He pulled out the "peasant's basket" from his inventory, carefully combed through the grass for the loot crystals and placed them in the basket as if he was gathering berries. The others pitched in and we were soon ready to move on.

The next part of the journey was so uneventful that there's nothing to tell. T-Rex went ahead as bait, and as soon as he came under a hail of spines, Anna would *Dash* to the troublemaker, pull it off the tree, and finish it off on the ground.

T-Rex and Shugga even leveled up, and I would have been happy to keep going like that, but then the forest changed. It became taller, lighter, and the leaves turned greener and more succulent. Colorful butterflies fluttered everywhere, lush bright flowers bloomed right on the trunks, and a couple of times I even saw snakes slithering in colorful ribbons among the trees.

"It looks like the tropics here," Lance observed and I believed him. Unlike me, he'd seen them in person, not just on TV.

Then we spotted some humans.

Slender, colorful figures emerged from the trees and approached us. Boys and girls with wide smiles and no weapons. They stopped when there were about ten steps between us, and a tall, tanned blonde came forward.

Her light hair cascaded in curls over her shoulders; she was barefoot and dressed very lightly, to put it mildly. Anna muttered something like "hussy" under her breath, but maybe I misheard.

The blonde's entire outfit consisted of a bright orange silk ribbon wrapped around her hips and chest and somehow clinging to her body. I wouldn't be surprised if this was none other than the silk that Lance and his bros had collected for the Whisperer. Then again, these people looked nothing like Shiloh's minions.

"Welcome to the Wonder Grove," the blonde said, bowing slightly.

Her breasts bounced, and I felt something bounce inside me and rise to my throat. Judging by the looks on the others' faces, their bodies reacted just as intensely.

"My name is Kaya!" the blonde went on. She took her role so seriously that she reminded me of an NPC. "I am the deputy high priestess of Ji-Bo. I am a priestess of the Eternal Groove!"

Allies! Kaya confirmed my hunch. The followers of the Groove had swapped palm leaves for colorful silk, and their faces were more serene and enlightened, but little had changed since my first visit.

Kaya suddenly approached me decisively and hugged me not at all platonically, pressing her ample chest against me, then took me by the arm and handed me the familiar bottle of silly juice.

This was a signal for the others. Scantily dressed girls latched onto Lance and his bros. Anna didn't lack attention either, with two athletic fellas in skimpy loincloths tending to her. Everyone was giggling and getting to know each other.

At first, I pushed the bottle away, but Kaya looked at me so reproachfully that I gave in. It might have been reckless, but this crazy day had worn us out so much that, finding ourselves among allies — especially such busty, curvy, and accommodating ones — we relaxed completely.

My head buzzed lightly and pleasantly, the rustle of leaves blending into a melody, not aggressively club-like this time, but calm, rhythmic, relaxing. We were seated in a clearing overgrown with bright red flowers. The girls danced, dreamily looking up, sat on the grass next to us, brought more bottles...

The picnic was gaining momentum, and I watched from a distance as the blonde and a redhead began undressing Lance nearby. Somewhere behind me, out of sight, Anna laughed loudly and a bit hoarsely, and I realized it was the first time I'd heard her laugh so freely. Kaya ended up on my lap, her lips on mine. They were soft and tasted of wine and strawberries.

"Where's Ji-Bo?" I tried to stay formal.

"Do you need him?" she laughed, and I realized she was right; I didn't need him at all at that moment.

Then the rustling leaves and sunlight on the grass began to spin faster. Kaya's voice and touch grew distant like it was coming through cotton gauze... or like through water... like I was underwater... like I was drowning... like I was falling and the darkness closed in and over me...

Something clicked in my head and in an instant I became revoltingly sober. It felt like a bucket of ice had been dumped into my brain, freezing everything with a burning cold.

I heard Kaya's voice. The sweet purring notes were gone. Now it was businesslike and a bit nervous.

"Is yours asleep?"

"Knocked out," someone answered from the darkness. "Tough one, though."

"Irma is out again," another voice.

"Stupid unbeliever," Kaya's voice again. "Grab her and take her away quickly. Shit's about to go down here."

CHAPTER 18

"POISONED!" The thought flitted through my hollow head, ringing as if it were bouncing off the walls of my skull. *"Drugged! Roofied by these predators!"*

With a conscious effort, I forced myself to stop panicking. This wasn't reality, where someone could spike your booze with anything. Items didn't just change their properties in here. If you drank "Groove Tree Laughing Juice, +5 to Constitution, -5 to Dexterity," it would inhibit Dexterity and boost Constitution as advertised. It wouldn't poison or stupefy you. If something sneaky had been done to make ordinary juice give debuffs, it would immediately show up in the stats, in our status, and even in the drink's name, for that matter.

That's why I had drunk so calmly to begin with. In fact, I had assumed that my "Favorite of the Gods" trait would block any effects as divine magic anyway. These bitches drank their wine too,

I checked. So, it was only the Eternal Groove itself that could have done all this.

The footsteps receded, and I lay there, eyes shut tight, pretending to be asleep. Maybe it was presumptuous of me, but I was waiting for the promised shitstorm to start. Not out of curiosity, but so I could confront Ji-Bo with all the details later on.

Lying there with my eyes closed was boring and a bit uncomfortable. Who knew what this "shitstorm" entailed? Maybe it was already here, ready to grab me by the ass. So, I carefully squeezed my eyelids and started to peek through the slits.

Something swirled in the air, and it was beautiful. Like thousands of tiny diamonds floating above the ground, sparkling and filling the grove with a diffuse glow. They rose upon the air currents, refracting light and making colors and distances changeable and illusory. The diamond dust filled everything around.

Pollen — that's what it was. Fleshy red flowers had bloomed on the tree trunks, their petals soft and plump like the blonde's lips. Above them, the clouds of glittering sparks were especially dense. They stretched upward like smoke from a fire in calm weather, filling everything around.

The flowers looked predatory and vulgar, like giant sea stars stuck to the trunks. It seemed they might peel off the bark, crawl over to us, and start digesting the sleeping people alive, attaching themselves like leeches.

Our entire party lay on the ground like broken dolls. In ridiculous poses of drunks who'd passed out in mid-celebration. The pollen hung suspended over our bodies and I was sure it was what had drugged us. No wonder those wenches had rushed off. The pollen wasn't pleasant for them either, I guess.

Then the ground beneath me moved. A disgustingly pink tentacle broke through the dense layer of last year's leaves, nodding its pointed, blind head, and began to grope around my leg, evidently searching for it by touch. It looked like an earthworm, but judging by its diameter, it must have been two meters long.

I couldn't pretend to be asleep any longer. Revulsion propelled my body into the air like a spring. Drawing my sword, I slashed the tentacle at its base, and it spun around, thumping on the ground and squirting milky, translucent sap. There were several of these creatures around me; they offered no resistance and burst under my sword like overripe tomatoes.

Lance and his friends were completely entangled in this mess, and Anna was already being pulled underground. I rushed to her and carefully cut the resilient, rapidly hardening loops. They wrapped around her ankles and wrists, pinning her to the grass like shackles, and were growing over with dense scales or... was this bark?!

Only then did I realize what it was. Roots. They were sprouting from the ground to grab their prey and drag it back, slowly draining life from the bodies deep underground. The entire Wonder Grove was a single organism, a killer plant that lured victims in with its gourds of sweet juice, enchanted them with its musical rhythm, lulled them to sleep with its pollen, and then devoured them alive.

Once I managed to cut Anna free from the gushing tendrils, I dragged her aside and began slapping her cheeks. She showed no signs of waking up, however.

Looking up, I saw Kaya in the distance among the ordinary trees. She was watching me with hatred, her fists clenched against her chest. It seemed the priestess was desperately rooting for her carnivorous grove and worried we might escape it.

"Come over here," I yelled, waving my hand. "Help me now or it'll be worse for you later!"

Kaya shook her head vehemently and stayed at a safe distance.

I dashed over to Lance next. His legs were already completely underground, with only the tips of his boots visible on the surface. I hacked away at the offshoots around him until he was free and then ran over to T-Rex...

Sensing I was the only threat, the roots now became bolder. They emerged from the ground all around me, grabbing at my legs, trying to entangle and hold me in place.

Meanwhile, some other spectators had joined Kaya. They were less restrained and squealed with excitement every time I stumbled over another "worm."

It was a test of stamina and sooner or later, I could tell I would lose. In fact, I was already losing. Despite all my efforts, no one in my party was waking up.

Dragging them to safety? No time. I wasn't strong enough to save everyone, and while I was dragging one, the others would be pulled under. I could save Anna as a last resort, but it wasn't a great option.

What had knocked them out? The pollen. It was still rising in spurts above the buds. There weren't many flowers, and they bloomed as if on command, only in the clearing right above us.

I looked around, cut a long pole from the young shoots, and knocked one of the flowers to the ground. Despite its dangerous appearance, it didn't try to crawl away from me. It fell and lay there like a normal uprooted plant. To be sure, I stomped it with my boots and started knocking down the others.

Fighting the flowers, I had to ignore the roots, but I decided to take the risk.

"What the hell?!" I heard T-Rex's voice howl behind me.

He was struggling against the stiffening roots, writhing like he was entangled in the rings of a giant boa constrictor. As I ran past, I freed his right arm with a slash, giving him a chance to free himself.

The others woke up with shouts and curses. Even the normally prim Anna was swearing like a sailor. While I finished off the last buds, they cut each other free from the wooden shackles.

"T-Rex!" I yelled. "Didn't you have an axe?"

The tentacles kept coming out of the ground, and though we were free, I had no intention of fleeing.

"Here it is!" T-Rex pulled a two-handed axe from his inventory. "You mean to...?"

"Yeah! Chop the trunk down!"

T-Rex swung and buried the axe blade deeply into the fleshy trunk of one of the trees. And the grove felt it. We knew because it screamed in pain! All the trunks shook and emitted a low hum, while the roots protruding from the ground thrashed as if electrified.

"Keep chopping!"

We rushed to the trunks, pulling out crappier blades from our inventories, ones we didn't mind damaging on the wood, and began hacking at the grove like a living enemy. And that's what it was after all: The grove was alive, arrogant and over-confident, accustomed to easy victories and defenseless victims. It was an enemy that had never bled before.

Our swords sank into the soft bodies of the trees with a squelch, and light pink sap, like plasma, flowed from the wounds.

And then we saw it. An enormous, ridiculous figure over three meters tall, moving towards us like it was on stilts. Green skin, resembling bark, long arms that hung to its knees like tendrils. Strange, inhuman, yet intelligent, glowing yellow eyes. The Eternal Groove was approaching!

Level 26. Almost on par with our Anna. But who knew what surprises a god in this game had up his sleeve? Though he didn't have sleeves. The Eternal Groove was naked. His absurdly lanky and hunched body was covered in dense green skin, or bark. He looked like a cross between a Tolkien ent and the Jolly Green Giant.

The worst part was that my teammates were still saddled with the "Drowsy" debuff. Though they were awake and moving, they were still torpid and slow, and their stats were reduced. As party leader, I could see it all in my party interface.

So, with my swords drawn, I stepped forward to meet the Eternal Groove, closely watching his jerky, abrupt motions and swaying gait.

One thought kept pounding in my head: Who are you really? A game spirit, another powerful NPC, or is there a player behind this ridiculous exterior? If so, they must be a real freak.

The Groove raised his arm over me, huge and heavy like a club. He didn't bother to fight by the rules, use tactics, or anything else. He swung as if to swat an annoying mosquito.

I was ready to dodge. My mind was weaving together blocks and counters, evasions and parries, retreats and counterattacks. Then the Groove jerked as if his body had a cramp. His attack flailed nowhere near me as if it wasn't a strike at all.

I responded with a quick thrust and a cut to his forearm. Any normal opponent would have lost an arm by now, but the Groove's body only made a dull thud under my blade, as if I'd tried to chop a log with my katana. Damn, how much armor, endurance, and other crap did he have? Could I even kill this thing?

He swung a leg, but twitched again, mid kick. Damn, what's happening?! I glanced away from the fight for a moment and saw my team hacking at the grove.

T-Rex had nearly chopped through one trunk. Anna and Lance, working with simple, cheap hatchets, were hacking another, and Shugga was furiously chopping branches and the few remaining pollen flowers.

Each deep cut made the Groove twitch and freeze. It was hurting him!

"Keep chopping! Faster!" I yelled. "Raze those damn bushes! Hack it all down!"

The Groove stumbled in place. He seemed confused. Instead of fighting, he was flailing, trying to turn to the trees, but I kept pulling his attention back to me.

"Die, bastard!" I felt a giddy thrill.

Whether he was a god or not, it looked like he could be slain just like anyone else. We didn't start this fight, but we'd finish it. Knowing I wasn't doing any damage with regular strikes, I gripped the katana with both hands and used my *Precise Strike*, bringing it down on one of the stilt-like legs of this tree god-monster.

"NOOO!"

It felt like the earth itself was moaning, or a

hurricane howling through the treetops. But it was the Eternal Groove, bellowing deeply and plaintively.

"SPARE MY WONDER GROVE!"

He wasn't fighting anymore, just standing there, shuddering and shaking as if rocked by an invisible wind.

"Finish him!" Lance shouted.

I raised my katana, ready to lop off the Groove's leg and bring him to the ground — but stopped at the last moment.

I couldn't imagine what kind of fantasy had created this character. From whose mind's depths the neural network had pulled this creature, resembling a spindly, undergrown ent.

The more I looked, the more human traits I saw. Even the hands had five fingers, as they should. The face, despite the thick bark-like skin, was contorted in pain. And his features seemed vaguely familiar, though I couldn't guess from where.

"Stop!" I raised my hand, and my team of avenging lumberjacks halted.

Apparently, saving them from the grim prospect of being buried alive had boosted my authority in the team to previously unreachable heights. They listened to me instantly. T-Rex even paused mid-swing with his ax, still brandishing it to make the Groove more cooperative.

Anna approaches, standing next to me with her arms crossed over her chest.

"Well, hello, divine brother," she squeezes

through her teeth. "What the hell are you supposed to be?"

The Groove turns slightly away, as if embarrassed, and tries not to look at Anna.

"Spare my grove..." he mutters, almost to himself, and at that moment, he looks entirely human, almost like a sulking teenager.

"So, this is how they were getting their sacrifices," I say to Anna. "I always wondered how pacifists could survive here. I wonder how many players they've devoured already."

"Aren't we supposed to be allies?" she protests.

"Maybe the chance of having an easy snack turned out to be tastier than the desire to be a good ally," I shrug. "Imagine, both a Goddess and a high priest... Think of all the rewards they'd get for such a sacrifice."

"Exactly," Anna spits angrily at the ground, "One slip here, and you're done for good. Just look at your friend Lance as an example."

"My foressst..." the Groove whines incongruously in the meantime.

Anna squints, peering at him with curiosity, and the Groove turns away again. Meanwhile, I'm racking my brain on what to do. Can we really wipe out an entire divine House like this, and what benefits would it bring me?

Honestly, if I had fire at my disposal, I wouldn't even think twice about it. I'd incinerate this parasitic grove and its strange god with purifying flames. But as it stands, chopping down all these trees by hand... I'd like to believe it was my common sense that prevailed, but laziness and time constraints played a part too.

"Call your people here," I said to the Groove. "I need to talk to them first."

The Groove waved his branch-like arms and made strange noises, something between buzzing and clicking. It did no good however. Some faces flickered among the trees at the edge of the large clearing, I even saw Kaya's blonde head, but they quickly hid again. It didn't seem like they had much respect for their own deity.

"Sorry, buddy," I shrugged. "Looks like they don't value you."

The Groove stomped indignantly, crackled, and buzzed again, addressing the bushes. I thought I heard "excommunicate" and "curse" in his hum, but maybe my imagination was playing tricks on me. After all, what else should he be shouting in this situation?

Whatever it was, it worked. Half-naked figures started appearing from the bushes. They walked slowly and resignedly, knowing nothing good awaited them. Yet still they came forward.

I was a bit out of touch with local realities, but it seemed being excommunicated was worse than any punishment. Kaya came last, stepping carefully over the severed branches with her long, beautiful legs, eyes downcast. There were eighteen people in total: twelve girls and six guys. All, even the guys, were unarmed and wore colorful silk ribbons instead of armor.

They looked at me warily, only to have me fully justify their fears.

"On your knees, every single one of you," I commanded. "I'm about to pass judgment, and I warn you, I have neither the desire nor any reason to show you mercy."

Chapter 19

KAYA WINCES. SHE'S PROUD. I recognize her type immediately. Even when she was fawning over us to lure us into the grove, I noticed her disdainfully pursed lips. It was amusing to watch her try to be hospitable back then.

Now she faces a simple choice: swallow her pride and shove it... wherever she wants. Or tell me to go to hell, die quickly by my sword, and head on back to the respawn point.

Yet she hesitates, most likely, because of her damned pride. Such women can't stand losing; it's not in their programming. It's clear that in Ji-Bo's absence, she's the one in charge here.

And if someone like her made it to the top of the local power structure, she'd fight tooth and nail to keep her position and privilege. I still vividly remember how Marina chased me around my room on her knees. And that was real life, not a game. Here, you can do whatever you want; it's not real, so it doesn't count.

"Think I'm going to kill you?" I nudge her in the right direction. "If you and the others keep acting up, in a couple of hours, your precious grove will be nothing but stumps. You'll be nobody. *Nobody!* A priestess without a god. You'll be of no use to anyone!" I recalled the fear and disgust I felt seeing the root-tentacles and poured all my emotions into my next words: "On your knees, bastards!"

"The grooove..." whimpered the Groove.

He didn't seem to care about his followers at all. Only the fate of his precious parasitic grove concerned him. He probably didn't love nature that much either. More likely, the trees channeled divine experience into him from the killed players. A living altar, so to speak. As for the believers, they'd resurrect and return. If they didn't, new ones would come.

The tree-like god shuddered under Anna's piercing gaze. For some reason, her attention made him uncomfortable. The Groove retreated behind the trees, then turned around and swayed with each step as he walked away, repeating:

"You promiiised..."

For Kaya, this was the last straw. The blonde lowered her eyes, her knees buckled. The others followed suit. T-Rex snickered with satisfaction and began unbuckling his pants. Kaya turned pale.

I glanced at Anna, fearing she might protest, but she watched with curiosity. Judging by her expression, even if all the prisoners were laid out on the grass and passed around, she wouldn't object.

I didn't stop T-Rex; let Kaya comprehend her situation. Only when he reached to grab the blonde priestess by the hair did I intervene.

"Where's Ji-Bo, Kaya?!"

"In the city... at Shiloh's temple..." she answered with gusto like an eager student.

"Does he know what you're doing here?" I took a step, standing next to T-Rex.

Together, we loomed over her. She tried to avoid looking at him, carefully turning towards me.

"He ordered it... We need sacrifices..."

"Even allies?"

"Everyone's an ally now," Kaya sneered. "When it comes to Anima's followers, only the straylings are left in the city. Who would let them travel all the way over here?"

"What did you call them? 'Straylings?!'" The strange word surprised me.

"Those who renounced Anima," Kaya explained. "Shiloh came up with it. They renounced their Goddess and thought they'd be forgiven and accepted into the other Houses. But fat chance! No one wants them. Shiloh suggested boycotting them."

"Why?" Anna joined the conversation.

"We need someone to level up on," Kaya explained calmly. "Everyone needs live flesh for the altars."

"And what about you?" I lifted her chin. "Are you live flesh too?"

"Please, no," Kaya's voice trembled. "I can be useful to you."

I realized she might prove useful indeed. People like her didn't care who they served, as long as they had some power. But they couldn't be trusted. They'd sell you out the moment someone stronger or more promising appeared.

"STAND UP!" I didn't give her time to think, yanking her to her feet. "First, pay for our lives! For five of our lives, five of theirs!" I pointed at those kneeling. "Tell me, who will you give in exchange?"

Kaya thought even less than I expected. I might have underestimated this cunning bitch.

"That one!" she pointed.

I nodded to Lance, and one of the kneeling guys lost his head.

"That one!"

T-Rex delivered a powerful stab, piercing the heart, and kicked the body off his blade.

"And her!"

"You bitch!" A short-haired girl tried to jump up, but Shugga quickly caught her by the throat.

The others waited, patiently staring at the ground, awaiting the end of this mad lottery. For the losers, it was just a flight to the respawn point, which, in the grand scheme of things, was nothing. But something told me that if Kaya took power in the House of the Groove, the victims might not be welcomed back. She was a tenacious one. What was that word she used? Straylings? A good word. I should remember it.

"That one," Kaya didn't even call them by name. They were expendable to her.

Anna looked at me questioningly, then killed her victim with an impressive upward strike, nearly slicing the body in half.

The Groove's followers were all low-level, none except for Kaya were above Level 3, and Kaya was a Level 5. When it came to killing the followers of other Houses, however, XP was awarded differently, on a per-kill basis. I had racked up quite a few in the previous war with Anima's paladins, and I only needed eight more kills to unlock my next divine skill. Now, it was down to seven.

"And this one!"

On a sudden impulse, I crossed my blades in front of me, and like scissors, I beheaded a tall, muscular guy. Blood spurted in a fountain, and his body slumped aside before disintegrating into ashes.

"Do you want to serve us?" I asked, and Kaya nodded frantically. "Then remember the new rules. This grove and everyone who serves it are now trophies of the House of Death. No dependencies, no vassalage. You're our property, bitch. Our *thing.*"

Now that she had tasted power and was closer to us than to her former friends, it was easier for her to make a decision. Kaya nodded, and... nothing happened. No new quest, no system notification. The game didn't react to our agreement at all. It was the same with Theophilia's vassalage.

This new agreement would have to be maintained by force alone.

"Lance," I turned around, "this grove should become our outpost. It's on the way to the Temple of Death. So, you and your guys stay here. Consider yourself the governor or commander of this place, whatever you like. Make these naked asses move," I nodded at Kaya, implying she had no say in the matter. "You have two objectives: Deliver nine sacrifices to the Temple of Death and clear a path through the woods so we don't have to fight krogs every time we go there."

T-Rex's face spread into a blissful smile, while Kaya's grew even paler. I sensed these two would get along just fine once I was safely out of the way. And I was okay with it, as long as it didn't hinder our cause.

"What am I to do with this lot?" Lance nodded at the still-kneeling "Groovers."

"That's not your problem," I replied. "They're quick; let them catch others to take their place. If they don't try hard enough, they'll end up on the altar themselves."

"We'll catch them," Kaya interjected. "We're good at that."

"See? You just need to handle the delivery," I encouraged Lance. "And provide the muscle."

"Just the three of us?" Lance sounded doubtful.

"Recruit people. Who's stopping you?" I replied. "Take a good look at the girls here. They've got more fight in them than the guys. Maybe some newcomers will catch your eye. If these idiots are asserting themselves at the expense of the straylings, then we can use them. We need more than just a clan; we need an army."

"Why?" Accustomed to being a lone warrior, Lance didn't understand what I had in mind.

"To be the strongest, of course," I avoided providing a direct answer.

I knew the real reason. The alliance I had tried to create with Ji-Bo and Shiloh was already falling apart. So, I could only rely on myself.

* * *

It took us about ten minutes to reach the city from the grove. I could have been more precise; the game timer was diligently counting down the time left for the session, but I didn't bother with it. We arrived when we arrived.

On the way, we were attacked by a few fluffy critters of very low levels but outsize aggros. We also passed a grove of silkworms and admired the groups of weavers in straw hats, even exchanging a few words with them before parting peacefully.

From them, we learned that crafting had appeared in the city. So far, only NPCs had mastered it. There was a blacksmith's shop, a leather workshop for light armor, an atelier for fancy clothes, and even an alchemist's shop. I made a mental note to check these vendors out when I got the chance.

Currently, players could only gather

ingredients and buy finished products. There was no training for professions yet, though some odd-balls were already begging at the blacksmith's or alchemist's shop to teach them the basics.

And it was no surprise that Shiloh had taken over all the trading points. The quests for raw materials and selling finished gear went exclusively through him. Initially, a few freethinkers declared the city "free," but they quickly disappeared, and cautious, sensible people replaced them.

The weavers were harvesting silk for good money, with Anima's former followers, hoping to be accepted into the main group, helping them for free.

I shot a quick message to Lance, suggesting he come here to recruit fresh blood, but we didn't linger otherwise: The city was just a few steps away.

*   *   *

I couldn't believe my eyes as Anna and I walked down the street. It felt like we left one game yesterday and entered an entirely new one today. Sure, this world was supposed to change, but not this fast… The only explanation I could think of is the neural network had "listened" to the players' desires and adapted the environment to match.

The shops began offering all kinds of wares, while new options appear in the interfaces. Otherwise, how could a pseudo-medieval game world turn into a vivid futuristic clan-based one in just one day?

The priestesses of Lolf, once eccentric witches with tousled hair and bare breasts, had transformed into arrogant, pretentious bitches. Their black silk robes, ending just above the buttocks, revealed more than they concealed, the exposed skin covered in intricate clan tattoos.

These ladies favored patent leather boots with towering stiletto heels.

The first priestess we saw walked alone, nose hiked in the air, with three businesslike Level 10 spiders scuttling beside her, either as her bodyguards or as her pets.

The next two, young and giggling, were leading a man dressed in black latex shorts with a bare chest.

The man wore a collar with a short chain ending in one of the priestess's hands. He looked like he'd stepped out of a BDSM porn flick. A black latex mask covered his face, leaving only his nostrils and eyes exposed. He trudged after the priestesses obediently.

"What the hell is this?" I turned to Anna, slightly freaked out.

"They're training initiates for their clan," Anna snorted. "The main group is all girls, but they have a male guard. That's the only way you can get in."

"Seems like they enjoy it," I noted.

"Why wouldn't they?" Anna confirmed. "It's a game. Why restrain yourself? They get to feed their inner demons and make money in the form of cold hard cash."

It was like the game was mixing the players in a giant tumbler, bringing out the traits they concealed in meatspace in fear of the consequences, judgment or shame. Here, everyone eventually found their place, even if it was as a killer, a slave, a thief or a whore.

The colorful clusters of Eternal Groove supporters reminded me of the Hare Krishnas I remember seeing in my early childhood during the era of universal freedom and universal poverty. The Hare Krishnas and freedom disappeared, but the poverty and memories remained.

Cheerful and carefree, Groovers of both sexes danced barefoot on the pavement, draped in colorful silk robes to meditative clan music from portable speakers, smiling at everyone and trying to lure them to join their House. I already guessed where these merry companies ended up, but it suited me now, so I winked approvingly at the girls and even clapped in rhythm a few times.

The streets were full of sneaks and thieves, the followers of the Whispering God. Gray cloaks wandered alone and in groups, busily lurking and aimlessly wandering, teasing passersby without much malice, shouting obscene jokes at the spider priestesses from a safe distance, and flirting more boldly with the Groovy girls, sometimes even trailing after them.

Then I saw something interesting. A paladin was walking down the street. He walked calmly, barely glancing around. Next to his name was Anima's mark, and two sneaks walked beside him.

Instead of attacking him, a clear enemy, however, they looked around attentively like seasoned bodyguards.

I wanted to approach and ask what was happening when suddenly a shout echoed down the street:

"The straylings are making a break for it!"

"Head to the square!"

"XP! XP!"

"Crush the straylings!"

The crowd of revelers vanished as if blown away. Even the Groovers disappeared, though I doubted they'd be useful in a fight.

"Shall we go take a look?" Anna asked.

"I doubt there will be much to see," I shook my head. "Whatever it is, half the city is there now."

"Hey, you in black! Stop right there!" I heard suddenly.

I turned with immense surprise. My armor was black indeed, but to yell at us so brazenly, considering our level... These could only be morons or suicides.

"Are you talking to us, boys?" Anna beat me to it.

"Yes, you bitch, and your deaf boy toy too."

A gang of hoods was approaching us leisurely. Calling this group anything else felt wrong. They swaggered, fully confident in their strength.

The guy who did the talking was a Level 15 named Oar, while the rest of his rabble grinned over his shoulder. I squinted slightly, observing their in-game names, and noting a tiny crest next to them — a noose on a blue triangle.

Whether it was a lasso for catching victims or a gallows that awaited every devotee of the Shadow God, I leaned towards the latter. Each House now had its own crest, which could be seen next to their handle.

Anima's followers bore a golden club on a red shield, the Whisper's hoods had the noose on a blue triangle, Lolf's girls had a predictable black spider on a gray spider web, and the Eternal Groove bore a purple bottle on an orange lotus.

As for us humble servants of Death, we sported a white skull on a black rectangle — a sort of Jolly Roger. It might have been a cliché, but it was neat and effective.

"Fellas, are y'all confused?" I asked amicably. "Have you seen our levels?"

"The bigger the tree, the harder it falls," Oar quipped.

"Doesn't it bother you that we're allies?" I tried to reason with this virtual thug, to no avail.

"You don't look like a 'Spider,' and you're not a 'Groover' either. So, you're a strayling," he concluded. "And you're not on the list. Don't think your level will save you. We've taken down fatter pigs than you before. All it takes is some teamwork. So, hand over the cash, loser. Your chick can get all the love she wants for free, but if you want to live — you'll have to pay up."

Anna stepped forward, drawing her sword and planning to end these negotiations, but I stopped her.

"I'll pay, fellas," I replied. "But I want a receipt."

CHAPTER 20

ANNA WAS NOT HAPPY WITH ME. She wrinkled her nose the whole way, like a purebred Siamese cat being fed canned fish in tomato sauce. There was not a diplomatic bone in the girl's body. But I wasn't surprised. I had seen how my deadly friend preferred to solve problems. Moreover, I had been in her path a couple of times and was now very grateful that we were on the same side of the barricade.

Thank heavens, she didn't intend to make a scene or start a public showdown. Surprisingly, oncc she had stepped aside and let me take charge of our clan, she never interfered by voicing her "especially valuable" opinions or "concerned" advice.

Compared to all the other women in my life, from my mom to Marina, who constantly tried to steer me, Anna's behavior was a godsend. It added another feeling to my already extensive range of emotions towards her — respect.

To their credit, the thugs didn't push their luck. Whether our levels did give them pause after all or because Shiloh had instilled serious discipline in his mob, the fact that "the customers" were ready to do business meant that there was no need to press further.

Our brief walk culminated at the doors of the Bedtime Story, which had become the Whisper's temple. For his religious ceremonies, the Whispering God preferred booze, striptease and maybe something stronger, which we hadn't seen yet.

The temple shone with a freshly painted sign, its windows flickered with colorful lights, music thumped behind the door, and two suspicious characters lingered by the entrance. They seemed to be guards, though I wouldn't have trusted them with an ashtray of cigarette butts.

"What's up?" one of them asked Oar.

"Brought these patsies to the boss," Oar nodded importantly.

They completely ignored me but scrutinized Anna with full attention, even smacking their lips in admiration, making her tremble with rage.

"Wait a minute," I stopped them, and they stared at me as if an inanimate object, like a piece of meat, had suddenly spoken. "This is the place where you were taking us?"

"Yeah and..?" Oar didn't get my drift.

"So, what do we need you for anymore?" I smiled, drawing my katana.

Anna beamed as if I had presented her with a

bouquet of a hundred and one roses right in the middle of the street. I barely had time to raise my sword before she set off her *Whirlwind* and instantly turned all four hoods into mincemeat.

"You fucking..." managed to say one of the guards before dying.

The others died silently. We'd have to explain things to Shiloh anyway, so why forego the kills? Then we entered the Whisperer's temple as befits such establishments — by kicking the door open.

Shiloh, or rather his toadies and sycophants, had been busy indeed. The place had a swanky, lurid interior. The bar counter glinted with black marble and chrome, an ample dance floor glowed with colorful squares, while several dancers in varying degrees of undress polished the poles on special pedestals with their bodies. Surprisingly, the audience included many of Anima's flock. Having shed their armor, yesterday's paladins were relaxing, watching the strippers twirl their tits and asses. Dim lighting and purple drapery completed the picture of this half-club, half-brothel.

When we entered, the music stopped, and in the best traditions of yakuza movies, the Whisperer's boys in their dark cloaks jumped to their feet, grabbing their weapons. The boss's table was by the far wall and as we approached it, the sneaks gathered behind us, cutting off our exit.

Shiloh lounged nonchalantly on a couch, before a low table piled with all sorts of food. Next to him, equally relaxed, sat Ji-Bo. Together they made an amusing picture. The round-faced and short plump Shiloh with shifty eyes, and the burly Groover guru with a bushy beard and colorful dreads. Above both their heads were the symbols of their clans, though their levels weren't visible.

Apparently, Ji-Bo had completely forgotten that his current drinking buddy had strangled him with his own hands just yesterday. I had figured at our recent meeting that these two would find common ground. They had too many shared interests out in meatspace. I wouldn't be surprised if the showbiz mogul offered the ambitious DJ some sweet deals, and in return, got him by the balls.

And that meant that the House of the Eternal Groove was no longer independent, to put it mildly. In simpler terms, it was under Shiloh's thumb, working hard to advance his career as a leader. No wonder all the dancers in this place bore the Groove's sigil. Then again, this place would hardly discriminate on religious grounds.

The friendly duo of Shiloh and Ji-Bo was accompanied by four chicks, two apiece. They had cozied up to the bosses like cats, ignoring us completely. Seeing them, I realized I had been hasty about assuming clan affiliations here.

The blonde and brunette pleasing Ji-Bo were "straylings," working off their probation, no doubt. They wore no clothes, but their bodies were covered in bright glitter, thicker in intimate places. In the club's dim light, they glowed like two Christmas ornaments.

On Shiloh's right sat a stunning brunette wrapped in thin silk ribbons like a gift. Only the bow was missing. On his left was a dark-haired "spider" in a latex bra and shorts, covered in intricate tattoos. When we approached, she turned, and I realized I remembered her. One of Theophilia's girls, spirited and talkative, who had sat with us in the basement waiting for Anima's paladins to storm the place.

I smiled widely at her, but found no recognition in her eyes. They were filled with madness; her dilated pupils covered almost the entire iris, but even they weren't entirely black — more like cloudy, as if dark smoke swirled inside them.

"You killed my men!" Shiloh pointed at me.

His eyes were quite different. Fixed on me, they were strict, meaningful, and angry, like gun barrels.

"Oh, come on!" I laughed and plopped down on a low couch across from him. "They'll respawn sooner or later. You should train your mutts better, so they don't bark at the bigger dogs." I leaned back and stretched my legs out. "Now then, top of the morning to you, my dear ally."

Anna sat down next to me, on the edge of the couch, ready to spring into action at any moment. She radiated danger. I, on the other hand, was smiling and casual, as if I was at home, waiting for my slippers to be brought to me.

If I had shown any fear or hesitation, Shiloh might have ordered an attack, and we would have been swarmed. Who knows how it would have ended, but he might have tried. Yet I decided to act unpredictably, giving him a chance to save face...

And the chief sneak relented.

"Hello, TargetAi, though it's hardly morning." Shiloh stretched his lips into a smile. "And greetings to you, Goddess of Death." He nodded to my companion and pushed two wide cocktail glasses filled with the familiar laughing juice towards us. "Please have a drink, my dear guests."

"I don't drink on the job," I declined.

Anna didn't even deign to respond to Shiloh. Since our arrival, she hadn't said a word, only glancing around with a mixture of curiosity and disdain, as if calculating how convenient it would be to burn everything down and what it would take to do it. Conversations weren't her forte, and she had delegated all diplomacy to me.

"You're missing out," Shiloh noted.

He pulled out a green capsule, like those used by the spider priestesses, and dropped it into the glass. It dissolved instantly, releasing a swarm of tiny fizzing bubbles and turning the contents a deep emerald color.

"How about this?" he asked.

"Even more so," I grimaced.

"Then watch."

Shiloh raised the glass and brought it to the nose of the "spider." She didn't see it so much as smelled it — and lunged at it like a dog at a hunk of smoked sausage. The chief sneak teased her, pulling the glass away, then grabbing her hair with his other hand and holding her at bay.

"This is Caprice," Shiloh announced in a sophisticated tone, "the official ambassador of the

Lolf clan to our humble temple."

Hearing this, Ji-Bo laughed approvingly. The other girls also smelled the drink and turned excitedly towards Shiloh — like animals, I noted, not people.

The priestess whined pitifully, almost like a dog, and kept straining for the drink despite the pain she felt. Tears welled up in her eyes.

"We call it 'Lotus Nectar,'" Shiloh said, pleased with the display. "We have a smart guy who knows how to make things sound nice. This stuff has a fantastic effect on the girls. They become obedient, horny, and best of all, they don't remember a thing afterward."

"Don't remember a thing?" I asked, surprised.

"Who the hell knows," Shiloh replied indifferently. "Maybe they lie and remember everything. But they claim not to, and it's nicer that way, less creepy. Like 'it's not my fault.' What they do remember is how the drink tastes all right. They come running here as if it's smeared with honey."

He finally gave the glass to Caprice and she gulped it down in one go, then began to rub against the sneak, ignoring everyone around. Her fingers slipped under Shiloh's cloak, and her sharp, agile tongue left a wet trail on his neck.

"And you think the AI will approve of this?!"

"It already has!" Shiloh leaned forward, pushing the annoying "Spider" away. "It approves EVERYTHING that happens here! Otherwise, it wouldn't allow it. As soon as those crazies," he nodded at Caprice, "started putting men on leashes, the shop immediately stocked all the necessary gear: collars, muzzles... All that kinky shit. When we decided to build a club, we threw it together in a day, out of shit and sticks... The next morning, we come back, and everything's right out of a dream... couches... stripper poles... You haven't even seen the private rooms. Fuckin' Brazzers would be jealous. This AI grants us ANY wish we dream up. Who are we to object?!"

Shiloh, very pleased with himself, fell silent, while Ji-Bo mumbled something and raised his glass as if to second him. I looked at these people and marveled at their ability to arrange their lives. While we were running around the woods, killing porcupines and leveling up, they got on with the simple business of living their lives, building a system that would work for them. While I bounced from one fight to another, Shiloh had taken over the entire town. And now, I couldn't even say who had more power here, him or the mayor himself.

"Look here, TargetAi," Shiloh mistook my silence for doubt and switched to a heartfelt tone, "the only thing that keeps people in check is fear. Fear of being imprisoned, fired, judged, called a whore... But here you can do anything! ANYTHING AT ALL! Want to kill? Go ahead! No one will hold you accountable, your victim will respawn, and that's it. Get killed instead? So what? It's temporary. Want to have sex? Go ahead! No pregnancies, no diseases, no old ladies at the entrance judging you, no one leaking anything to Instagram. Want to get high? Forget everything and relax? Here's your Lotus Nectar! And that's just the beginning. My guys here are smart... They're trying out all kinds of chemical combinations... you'd be amazed. And yet when you pop out to meatspace — nothing! No withdrawal, no addiction! This is heaven, Targe, the land where dreams come true. Nothing to do, nothing to worry about. Just enjoy life while the money flows in. Big money, good and stable. Do you know what everyone here fears the most? Being kicked out. They'll do anything to keep their place at the trough, to enjoy another day at someone else's expense."

As he spoke, I began to understand who my allies really were: Lolf was a drug pusher, the Whisperer was a crime lord, and the Groove was a pimp. What a wonderful company I had chosen for myself. Just the right group to break the system. I remembered Simba and his paladins, the warriors of light. Had I chosen the right side? After Anima revealed herself, I was sure she would be a force under the AI's control.

Yet now I also began to understand why the neural network wanted to destroy the players. I would have gladly squashed someone like Shiloh myself.

Most importantly, all his arguments ignored the fact that the AI wasn't going to submit to anyone. Shiloh saw it as another whore to bend to his will. But in the end, the AI would do the screwing and screw him, not the other way around.

Playing with people's minds was what had plunged the alpha into the abyss, that much I remembered, and I tensed up as soon as Shiloh said that the women didn't "remember a thing afterward." Who could guarantee that their memories would return and their minds wouldn't get stuck in the game, leaving them drooling, incontinent dolls out in meatspace? Such a risk wouldn't stop someone like Shiloh, however, even if he could be persuaded that it was real. He didn't consume the potion himself, and he didn't care what happened to others.

"The Groove and the Spiders give you the wine and the gas," I feigned interest. "What do you give them in return?"

Shiloh glanced around and gestured for his supporters to move away. They had already relaxed, seeing our calm conversation, and now they settled back down. The Whisperer's priest cautiously glanced around again, then whispered loudly:

"Sacrifices."

"What?!"

"Sacrifices," he repeated louder. "We're the hunters, the catchers. For the clans to grow, for their gods to prosper, their altars need sacrifices. We deliver whole caravans of players. Our business is persuasion and we know how to persuade. Players are the best currency."

"You catch them at the respawn point?" I guessed.

Shiloh looked at me as if I were insane.

"Sacrifices don't respawn. They're kicked out of the game until the next round. It's harsh but fair; otherwise what would be their value?" Shiloh laughed. "A hot commodity."

"I'm afraid you'll have to reconsider your agreement with the Eternal Groove then," I remarked.

"Why's that?!" Ji-Bo butted in.

Honestly, I expected him, not Shiloh, to confront me from the get go. I thought he'd want answers about what happened in the grove. But his followers' loyalty was so low that they hadn't even messaged him. Well, let's play the surprise card.

"I spoke to your jolly green boss," I shrugged. "He asked me to tell you that you're fired."

"Wha...?!" roared the High Priest of the Groove. "What's this bullshit you're spouting?!"

Ji-Bo jumped up, nearly knocking his girls to the floor. At almost six and a half feet tall, he loomed over me, waving his arms and sputtering saliva.

"Shiloh, don't you think this has gone too far?!"

Shiloh didn't have time to answer; Anna was faster.

"If any of yours interfere, you'll all die," she warned, placing her katana against the head thief's throat.

No one moved but Ji-Bo: He pulled a strange weapon from his inventory, a blade on a long stick, resembling a Chinese guandao or a Japanese naginata. A terrifying weapon if you know how to use it.

I doubted Ji-Bo's skills with it, but games had

different rules. Maybe he had picked up enough skills to fight like a hidden dragon?

Ji-Bo struck immediately, without preparation, point-blank. He was standing right next to me, and I had to *Dash* away to create distance, landing in the middle of the hall. The Groove's priest casually leaped over a couch and advanced on me, spinning his blade like the rotors of a cargo helicopter. And then, completely out of nowhere, the game began sending me notifications:

YOU ARE ENTERING A DUEL WITH THE HIGH PRIEST OF ANOTHER GOD.

SHOULD THIS FIGHT BE CONSIDERED A DUEL OF FAITH?

IF VICTORIOUS, YOU WILL DEPOSE YOUR OPPONENT AND WILL EARN THE RIGHT TO APPOINT A NEW HIGH PRIEST.

IF DEFEATED, YOU WILL BE DEPOSED.

BEGIN THE DUEL? (YES / NO)

Yes, damn it! I desperately swiped the notifications away. Ji-Bo was already closing in, and only then did I see the level counter above his head: The Groove's guru was Level 28.

CHAPTER 21

JI-BO HAD LANKY ARMS and was almost two meters tall. He loomed over me like a gorilla. And he wielded a weapon on a long shaft. The range on his damned naginata, which he swung like a twig, didn't give me even the slightest chance to get close to him. I retreated, and a self-satisfied smile spread across his face. Ji-Bo thought I was afraid of him. Naive fool.

I was indeed biding my time. For someone who knows how to "watch" their opponent, every extra second before the fight is invaluable. Every Gladiator, even in the junior leagues, studied their future adversary. We watched videos, read coaches' reports, and yet nothing ever came close to seeing our opponents fight firsthand.

To spot the weakness in another and not reveal your own: This was why duels in esports started abruptly and often ended quickly. The first player to spot their opponent's weakness, the key to their defense, their weak spot or even just a hint of something to exploit, would launch the attack before their enemy could do the same.

I had wanted this fight and deliberately provoked Ji-Bo into it. I had to teach him a lesson after what happened in the grove and not just any lesson, but a demonstrative one. No one was allowed to raise a hand against the House of Death, and I would never believe that the High Priest was unaware of what was happening in his sacred place.

But still... Level 28? How in the hell?! This was supposed to be the hippy clan... I'd never even seen Ji-Bo fight. So how? Had the Groover girls seduced him? Or, was this just XP that the sacred grove had absorbed from other players. It was no coincidence that everyone else in his clan had such low levels. Ji-Bo must have taken the XP from those sacrifices flowing into his living, cannibalistic altar all for himself.

And this drastically changed my plans. There would be no "demonstrative thrashing," no easy victory. There was an eight-level gap between us and it wasn't in my favor. Of course, the higher the levels in general, the less this gap played a role. If Level 2 was at least twice as strong as Level 1, Ji-Bo's current advantage was no more than 25% or so now.

On the other hand, he didn't know a thing about fighting and had no clue what to expect from me. Meanwhile, I read this fool like an open book.

He swung his naginata broadly, like a peasant with an axe. To him, it was an axe, just a pretty one, and on a long handle, and his strikes were the most basic, from the top right down.

The rest of his moves were automatic, as if they were a scripted skill. And he did these with conviction, believing that this was how he should finish me. Ji-Bo had probably dumped all his points into his Strength stat — that was natural for a newbie and it fit his character. His movements lacked elegance, clearly favoring power over agility.

But how much he invested in Constitution and how much HP he had remained a mystery. My interface displayed only a green bar above his head.

There were probably special skills that would allow me to see more info, but I hadn't unlocked them. I hadn't unlocked anything lately in fact. And I had only attended the training camp once. As for divine skills, I only had *Ritual Suicide* available. A real handy skill that one. Should I just kill myself out of spite?

I retreated further and felt the crowd behind me give way. We were surrounded; the patrons had jumped up from their seats, even the whores had slid off the poles and squealed with excitement. It wasn't every day they got to see such a spectacle. I wondered if they were placing bets? Shiloh was probably making money off that too. Damn, what was I thinking?! "Every second is invaluable for a professional fighter..." I wondered who they bet on more?

Time froze. I saw the entire hall at once. Shiloh grinned; so far, everything that was happening played into his hands. The spider whore next to him laughed. The eyes of the red-haired Groover girl burned with undisguised hatred. However, her gaze was directed not at me, but at Ji-Bo's back. That was somehow important, but I couldn't figure out why.

Anna held her sword at Shiloh's throat but watched me closely. I shook my head slightly. No, I didn't need help. Who knows how the AI would react to interference, and I wasn't about to find out. The stakes were too high. If I lost now, the House of Death would fall. I didn't know what that would look like technically, but nothing good would come of it.

"What, you scared, little bitch?" Ji-Bo taunted.

He had cornered me on the dance floor. If this were a Hollywood movie, the DJ would cue a killer track right now. I had learned everything I could about him and in a regular gladiator fight, I would have butchered him like a lamb. Even his levels were inflated. He hadn't earned them in real combat, so he didn't know how to properly use his weapon. But here, besides his superior stats, he also had his character's skills. And that meant 28 aces up his sleeve, which I couldn't see and had to infer.

He wore no armor and didn't had base Agility, so there would likely be some form of "mental" or "spiritual" protection. What else? He had boosted Strength, so there would be extra power to his attack. No way could I let him get close — he could one-shot me. What about AoE? Unlikely. He didn't have to grind for his levels. As for mind control and stuns — considering the kind of god he served — definitely. And finally, illusions — possibly…

Just then, Ji-Bo grew tired of playing cat and mouse. He switched his naginata to his right hand and lashed out with his left. Dust! A cloud of silvery pollen bloomed towards me. It sparkled beautifully in the club lights and enveloped my head. A burning sensation flared on my chest.

MIND CONTROL ATTACK BLOCKED: "KALI'S SIGH."

Damn, how is this spell supposed to work?! How do I feign its effects? Should I collapse or stay put? Just in case, I froze with the most idiotic look on my face, and it worked. Ji-Bo swung his naginata like a butcher, aiming to cleave me in half with one blow from the top right.

I waited until the last moment and just as the blade almost touched my neck, I dodged to the right. I saw the naginata's blade glow red. Definitely some kind of boost to it, like a *Precise Strike* with extra damage. Someone should have told this idiot that his weapon could be used for thrusting as well, though I'm glad no one had because it would've been way more dangerous.

Ji-Bo "followed through" after the strike, and I helped his inertia by striking the shaft of his weapon with my blade. The naginata's blade clanged against the floor, and I, working the crowd a bit, spun behind him as if dancing a romantic waltz and drove my second short sword right into his side. Once… twice… three times… On the third strike, I slipped behind him, my blade slicing through his body, releasing a spray of blood.

"R-r-raa!" Ji-Bo roared, not from pain, but from rage.

I didn't care about his emotions. I glanced up at his life bar and a chill ran down my spine. It was still green. My flurry of strikes — which once cut Level 20 Anna's HP by half — had barely scratched this monster. What the hell would I need to kill him?!

Ji-Bo turned and attacked again. He pressed me, chasing me across the dance floor like an enraged bull chasing a nimble terrier. I dodged easily, but I couldn't reach him either. His lanky arms and polearm kept me at bay.

"I'mma get you, little shit," Ji-Bo growled through his teeth. "You thought you could set your own rules? Take over my grove?!"

"We even fucked all the girls there," I gleefully told him. "We fucked your precious Kaya… and the others too… And you know what?! They begged for more… Said you're useless, an impotent old husk!"

The dead silence in the club was shattered suddenly by Shiloh, laughing and clapping his hands. The others joined in, giggling obsequiously. Ji-Bo's face turned a furious red and he set upon me with a flurry of strikes.

Dash and I'm behind him. I grip my katana

with both hands... *Precise Strike!*

Now can I see his damn "armor." The sword pierces it like transparent film, as if the air itself had become so dense it wouldn't let the blade through. A crit! Ji-Bo's health drops into the yellow. I break the distance to avoid a wild counterattack from one of his skills. The score's 2-0 now.

It's hard to believe this guy once seemed like a pacifist to me. Ji-Bo's eyes are narrowed like slits and his nostrils flare like those of an enraged rhinoceros. He advances and I retreat again. I've already figured out that it's better to catch him on counterattacks, so let him rage. It seems he's also realized that victory won't be easy.

Clap! There are suddenly two Ji-Bos in front of me. Both sneering evilly, both holding the naginata forward. Cautious steps, one to the right, the other to the left, both start circling me from opposite sides. They are completely *identical*, damn it!

I know it's an illusion, but I can't tell one from the other at all. I think one hit would be enough to dispel the illusion, just a touch to the right or wrong opponent and he'll reveal himself.

But I can't take the chance. If I guess wrong, I'll take a hit. Left or right? Well, decide already! They're circling, leaving me less and less room to maneuver. They're coming around from both sides and soon one of them will be behind me. And under Murphy's Law, that'll be the real enemy.

"Die already, you bastard!" A red-haired blur crashes into one of the figures.

The girl, who was lounging by Shiloh, the one

in bright golden ribbons, throws herself at Ji-Bo and clings to him. Whether she identified the real high priest by some sign or just got lucky, the illusion instantly vanishes, and Ji-Bo desperately tries to shake off the crazed girl.

He knocks her to the ground with the shaft of his naginata, but she clings to his leg, weighing him down. He raises his blade to finish her...

Ignoring all aesthetics and duel etiquette, I make a desperate leap, landing on Ji-Bo's back and clinging to it like a rider to a camel.

Instead of finishing the girl off, Ji-Bo kicks her aside and starts spinning wildly, trying to shake me off.

"Take that, you bastard... Die... Die!" I deliver several quick blows to his collarbone, watching Ji-Bo's health plummet into the red.

His damn invisible armor doesn't work at such close range. The girl, Mira, or Mirta... I didn't have time to properly read her name, is dragged away by Shiloh's henchmen. The game's AI stays silent, however, deeming her intervention acceptable to the rules of our duel. If only I had known all these rules in advance...

Ji-Bo finally throws me off. I roll and stand back up in a fighting stance. The score's 3-0 now and my opponent is seriously hurt. His back and neck are streaked with congealing brown blood. His health bar has dropped more than three-quarters and is flashing red. Just a bit more... I just need to finish him off...

Ji-Bo must have read my mind. He grabs one

of the vials from his belt. An ordinary bottle, like those growing on the vines in the predatory grove. The Groove's priest tilts his head back, and his life bar start growing visibly. It's already yellow… now it's passed halfway… And now it's glowing green and nearly full.

Health potions! The damn sneaks have learned how to create health potions! No wonder Shiloh bragged about his pharmacological lab. They're not just making drugs there.

Ji-Bo laughs. Of course he has reason to be happy. He'll wear me down until my stamina drops to zero and then finish me off. And it serves me right — I shouldn't have jumped into a duel without properly learning about my opponent. For the second time in this fight, a sense of hopelessness washes over me, now even stronger than when I first saw his level.

My opponent gestures with his hand, and I stumble. What the hell?! I glance down: Roots from the sacred grove are sprouting from the dance floor tiles. One of them has coiled around my ankle. I cut it off with disgust while barely managing to deflect Ji-Bo's blow with my wakizashi, which shatters with a soft chime.

I don't even have time to mourn the loss of one of my swords. Another rush, and I'm knocked to the floor. The damn tendrils, like giant worms, are writhing all around me. Finding me, one of them yanks me down. Ji-Bo raises his weapon over his head like a club, intending to pin me to the floor.

Ding! My katana whines sadly before shattering to fragments in my hands.

You bastard! If I go now, I'll find and gank you later! And I'll keep ganking you over and over again for breaking my unique swords. That is, if there even will be a "later."

Ji-Bo raises his blade... and I realize I'm out of options.

"Catch!" Anna yells, and a thin strip of blued steel slides towards me across the floor.

I grab it without looking and drive it into the stomach of the High Priest of the Eternal Groove. The House of Death doesn't have many skills or sacred items. We don't have monster-like gods like Lolf, or noxious gases, or health potions... But what we do have is Death, swift and merciful. The sacred tantō knife of the very Goddess of Death. One shot, one kill.

Ji-Bo disintegrates into dust to the grave silence of everyone present. And I'm hit by an incredible high. Even a blowjob from Marina didn't come close to this feeling, and I used to think nothing could be more pleasurable.

NEW LEVEL GAINED! LEVEL 21...

NEW LEVEL GAINED! LEVEL 22...

NEW LEVEL GAINED! LEVEL 23!

Three levels at once for that overgrown pig. Coming to my senses ever so slightly, I grab the naginata from the floor and walk towards Shiloh, leaning on the shaft like a staff. Every hair on my body is standing on end from the thrill of the fight.

"Is there anyone here who challenges my

victory?!" I proclaim, sweeping my gaze across the hall.

Silence. The sneaks avert their eyes, their fighting enthusiasm evaporated. Even Shiloh tenses slightly. He is sure to have known about the health potions, so he was confident in my defeat and prepared to benefit from it.

"Is there anyone here willing to challenge me?!"

More silence. Then a flood of system notifications overwhelms me.

YOU HAVE WON THE DUEL OF FAITH!

THE HOUSE OF THE ETERNAL GROOVE IS DISGRACED!

HIGH PRIEST JI-BO IS DEPOSED!

DO YOU WISH TO SELECT A NEW HIGH PRIEST?

A list of several dozen names appears before me. Most of them I've never seen in my life. The House of the Eternal Groove turns out to be quite large. Kaya's name is near the top. She was who I planned to put in Ji-Bo's place simply because I didn't know any other candidates. But now I have options.

"Hey, you, Mirta, come here!"

The girl is huddled in a corner by the couch, sitting on her haunches like a frightened animal. Ji-Bo almost managed to finish her off. Hearing my voice, Mirta jumps up and, after a few steps, falls to her knees before me.

"Yes, Lord."

Her address grates on me, but I continue.

"Who are you, Mirta?"

"I am the ambassador of the House of the Eternal Groove in the House of the Whisperer," she recites mechanically.

"Why did you help me?"

Mirta raises her head and looks me straight in the eyes.

"I wanted him to die. He tricked us into coming here. Said it was a party," the brunette speaks haltingly, nervously. "Then they plied the girls full of that juice and they shut down, like they weren't even themselves, just dumb NPCs."

Another alarm rings in my head. "Like dumb NPCs" — it might just be a figure of speech, or it might be another attempt to mess with the players' consciousness. In any case, I need to find my way into Shiloh's lab. They're clearly brewing some nefarious substances there.

Anna stands beside me, scrutinizing the girl.

"What about you?" she asks distrustfully.

"It doesn't affect me," Mirta explains. "I have immunity."

"Will you come with us, Mirta?" I ask.

"No," she shakes her head. "I won't leave the other girls here."

"ENOUGH!" bellows Shiloh. "I've had it with this circus! Grab them, all three of them!"

CHAPTER 22

A RADIANT SMILE SPREAD ACROSS Anna's face. Damn, she seemed really happy about this turn of events. Without any killing to do, the poor thing had been bored stiff.

Seeing the expression on her face, the sneaks surrounding us seemed to falter and slow down. But what the hell is Shiloh doing? Doesn't he realize that we could tear this place apart right now? And we definitely have the levels for it, no doubt about that.

But then along with this club — or the Bedtime Story temple — we'd bury the entire idea of our alliance. Shaky and flawed as it was, it still ensured some semblance of peace in the game.

So, what was this then? A desperate move? Is he that afraid of us? Or maybe he just doesn't understand what's happening?

Shiloh likely isn't aware that we were

attacked by the Groove. It's not the kind of thing Ji-Bo would tell him. The old Groover no doubt aimed to get our XP all for himself, which would have guaranteed him becoming the strongest player. So damaging relations with the Whisperers isn't in our best interest right now.

"Calm down, friend!" I put the naginata into my inventory and raise my palms in a peaceful gesture. "Ji-Bo was a rat and deserved what he got. I'll prove it! You shouldn't repeat his mistake."

Everyone stared at me. Mirta with fear, worried she'd be sent back to the sneaks, Anna with disappointment, like a child whose candy was being taken away, and Shiloh... Shiloh with curiosity and... hope? This weasel was eager to let things slide, so I needed to meet him halfway.

"Words need backing," Shiloh said cautiously.

He liked the role of the fixer far more than that of a potential victim.

"I'll back them up, don't you worry."

I actually didn't care what he decided. If my explanations didn't satisfy him, we'd just cut them all down. But the sneaks would respawn and become our worst enemies. The alliance was already on the brink, so I needed to be persuasive.

Proof... proof... How to prove that the Groove had lured us to that predatory grove? No evidence remained, except...

"Mirta, tell me... is your temple a grove?" I asked. "Stand up and answer. And don't even think about lying."

"Yes, it's a grove," the green-eyed girl rose from her knees, speaking reluctantly. It was undoubtedly a clan secret.

"Is there something... unusual about this grove?" I carefully chose my words, hoping the girl would start revealing the truth gradually.

"Yes," Mirta blushed.

"What difference does it make?!" Shiloh exploded again. "What's so unusual about that grove? Do they screw in there or something?!"

"Wait a minute, you'll understand everything in a second," I nodded at the sneak and continued questioning the girl. "What does this grove do to... anyone who wanders through it?"

"It puts them to sleep," Mirta said, not taking her eyes off me, "and then roots come out of the ground and..."

"...AND DEVOUR THEM!" I finished, turning to Shiloh. "What do you think, my dear aly, how do I know this?! We were nearly eaten by those very roots — by order of your buddy Ji-Bo! Would you say he was acting within our alliance when he ordered that?!"

"No," Mirta's voice replied quietly but audibly to every corner of the club. "Ji-Bo ordered us to capture everyone. They don't remember anything afterward anyway. Some return several times. But not in the same beta round because victims don't go to the respawn loop. They're kicked out of the game."

"You bitch!" A shout erupted from the hall's other side, followed by a loud scream. One of the sneaks pinned a dancer to the floor, trying to strangle her, in his rage forgetting all about his weapon. "You said I'd gain strength in your grove, then told me some tale of a 'system glitch!' And then you fed me to your trees!"

He was pulled away. The girl remained sitting on the floor, whimpering and smearing tears over her cheeks. The blackness and bravado in her eyes gave way to the cowed fear of a beaten dog.

"Kill them..." voices yelled now. "Execute all the whores...!"

And something even more curious:

"Hang them... Hang them!"

Was this a hint about how the Whisperer accepted his sacrifices?

"How do you think I know this?" I addressed Shiloh again, raising my voice to drown out the shouts. "We were in that very grove, under those very trees. But we fought our way out! And now I can appoint a new High Priest for the Eternal Groove. That House is under our control!"

I lied a bit here. My ability to appoint a new leader had come later, and not for the victory in the grove, but Shiloh didn't need to know that. Nor about the duels between high priests or how that mechanic worked.

"We'll see what Ji-Bo says about that when he comes back," Shiloh replied evasively.

"Ji-Bo?!" I laughed. "Who needs *that* clown? The new High Priest of the Eternal Groove is Mirta! You'll deal with her now."

I saw Shiloh's face contort. His recent pet,

who had eaten from his hand, was now his equal. There's a good chance these two won't conspire behind my back.

"Thank you, TargetAi!" Mirta fell at my feet again, trying to kiss my hand.

Anna looked surprised. She likely thought I'd choose Kaya, given the opportunity. Kaya had proven herself a decent organizer and, alongside Lance, was our main contact person in the Groove's sacred grove.

But I preferred personal loyalty. Mirta helped me in my duel with Ji-Bo and clearly expressed her allegiance. Such impulses should be rewarded, so everyone would see that the House of Death was generous and fair.

"Well now, Shiloh, my dear ally," I said, reclining in the couch and propping my boots on the coffee table, "at last we can talk in peace."

* * *

As I suspected, Ji-Bo had sold out his clan to the sneaks in return for perks in meatspace. Shiloh paid for the alcohol with captives for sacrifice, but the Groover girls danced for free in Shiloh's club and even ended up owing money from getting hooked on the narcotic brew.

Even now, three of them refused to leave. Mirta tried to persuade each one, but they just stubbornly shook their heads, and one even told her would-be savior to go to hell.

Shiloh tried to argue, but I supported the new

High Priestess. I needed them on the streets, bringing sacrifices to our temples, not warming the beds of the Whisperer's thugs. Still Shiloh argued for appearances' sake and then gave in, although the looks he threw my way grew less and less friendly.

Mirta quickly adapted to her leadership role. It wasn't a coincidence she'd been named an "ambassador," as Shiloh put it, meaning either an envoy or a go-between for the two clans. She comforted some of her subordinates, slapped around some others, then lined everybody up all ready to set out for the Wonder Grove.

I looked over this group of scantily-dressed girls, whose highest level was Level 3, and realized they'd be lucky to make it past the first corner. They'd end up back in the Whisperer's temple one way or another.

"Anna, would you escort the girls please?" I asked simply.

"What?" The Goddess of Death seemed shocked at my words. "And where are you going?"

"I want to check out a hunch I have," I replied.

With less than ten minutes left in the beta round, I sprinted out of the Whisperer's temple. After Level 21, a player could conceal the level counter above their head. That's why I hadn't been able to see the levels of Shiloh and Ji-Bo back there. And honestly, Shiloh must be among the top players by now. He wasn't one to shortchange himself. Now, however, I intentionally displayed my level. Let anyone who crossed my path fear me and stay out of my way.

The thing was that I couldn't shake something Mirta had said back there: "victims don't go to the respawn loop." In that case, what happened to Sibyl then? She had died on Death's altar and didn't respawn. That meant that whoever was playing her character couldn't log into the game again during this beta round. Yet in order to verify this, I had to go to the mayor's palace.

The guards let me in without objection, my reputation still working in my favor. But I had to wait for the mayor himself. The reception hall was empty, its all doors closed. Finally, the main NPC of the game deigned to appear.

"Your Grace!" I began briskly. "I have urgent business with Lady Sibyl."

"What, you don't know, my friend?" The mayor dabbed his eyes with a handkerchief, and I noticed they were red and swollen. "Lady Sibyl is dead. Someone dispatched her in the most cruel of ways. We will surely find the assassin and punish him to the fullest extent of the law!"

NEW QUEST: "A COURT LADY'S DEMISE."

FIND LADY SIBYL'S ASSASSIN AND REPORT HIS NAME TO THE MAYOR.

REWARD: +10 REPUTATION WITH THE MAYOR AND A UNIQUE ITEM FROM THE TREASURY.

FAILURE PENALTY: -10 REPUTATION WITH THE MAYOR.

"I believe in you, my friend!" The mayor shook my hand firmly, and I was ready to howl at the game's treachery. Why the hell did I come to this palace?! To confirm my hunch? Well, there you have it. It's confirmed. And now what do I do? Either fail the quest or confess and get hanged?!

With clenched teeth, I exited to the real world.

Shuffling across the slippery floor in wet slippers, I tried to run to the locker room, but I felt like I was moving at a snail's pace. I could have spent an extra two minutes to dry off properly, but no… I bolted as soon as I got out of the VR pod, dripping saline solution and ignoring the technicians' shouts, ran into the corridor, wrapping myself in a robe on the way.

I slipped and fell, hitting my knee painfully, but barely noticed. I couldn't manage to unlock my phone with my wet fingers, so finally I cursed, wiped my hands thoroughly, and dialed the number I needed.

"I gotta see you right away."

"I missed you too…" Marina purred over the phone.

"Marina, this is business. Important business." I tried to cool her down, lest she decide to touch up her makeup or curl her hair before heading out.

"I get it," the blonde sighed. "You're saving the world again."

"Let's meet downstairs in the lobby by the doors in five minutes," I stayed serious, resisting her provocation.

"Okay," Marina replied and hung up.

Shower, clothes, elevator… Screw the

elevator... Down the stairs... I was almost at the lobby, just one turn left, when an office chick I didn't recognize blocked my way with a bouncer built like a wardrobe over her shoulder.

"Andrew Severyanov?" she asked.

"What?" I tried to rush past her in my haste, then nodded. "Yes, that's me."

"You need to fill out some forms..."

"Later," I tried to slip past her again. "I'm in a hurry."

"We insist," the security guy spoke up. "With all due respect... These forms need to be signed now."

I sighed and relented. No point in starting a fight in the corridor, especially with the odds against me. And I had a pretty good idea what these forms would be. After all, I was the one who'd cooked them up early this morning and now I would have to deal with them.

"Fine, let's go," I agreed.

We went into a tiny room with a single table and a few chairs. I wondered if it was a negotiation room or an interrogation room? What did they use such rooms for at MosTech?

The girl spread several colorful forms in front of me like a game of solitaire. They looked professionally done, you'd never guess I had typed all this up last night and shown it to the Master this morning.

"By signing this, you confirm that any physical, verbal, symbolic, or indirect action towards you in the game is done with your consent and you waive any claims…"

"You acknowledge that being in the game may have negative health effects, including tachycardia, hypertension, neurosis, mental disorders…"

"Disclosing any information about what happens during the beta test, both in the virtual and real world, is considered a trade secret, and any intentional or accidental disclosure is punishable…"

I had convinced the Master that players needed to be aware of the game's dangers and go on with the beta test with full knowledge of the risks they faced. Besides these points, which undoubtedly benefited the Corporation by covering its legal bases first and foremost, there were also terms of proportional payment. The higher the level, the greater the payout.

The Master had smirked that morning when he first heard my idea. He thought I wanted more money for myself. Naturally, I did, but I also wanted the others to keep leveling up and growing. Money was a great incentive to push the limits and the stronger the players, the easier it would be to resist the AI.

Another point I insisted on was extending the beta rounds to eight hours. Why not? Ordinary workers spend as much at a counter or on a conveyor line, so why couldn't we handle a regular shift in cyberspace?

I aimed this change against the NPCs and "illegals" who, I was sure, were entering the game and leveling up all day while we waited for our turn in the VR pods.

"Are you reading everything over carefully?" the security guy asked, surprised as I signed sheet after sheet.

"Yes, of course," I replied without looking up.

"I wrote it myself," was what I wanted to say, but kept silent. No need to throw pearls before swine. MosTech's lawyers had added some details and jaw-breaking phrases, but the core of it was mine.

My phone vibrated. Marina was looking for me.

"Where are you?" I heard her voice on the phone and, simultaneously, in the corridor outside the door.

"Almost there, just finishing up!"

"I'd like you to finish everything first, and then you can leave," the security guy interrupted.

But it was too late. Hearing my voice, Marina burst through the door.

"Andrew? What are you doing here?" She stormed in, ready for action.

Whether it was to chew me out or pull the hair of a rival... Marina always faced danger head-on, and at that moment, I admired her for it. Her cheeks were flushed... her coat was open... her chest heaved under her blouse...

"You aren't allowed in here, Ms. Skvortsova!" the chick behind the table jumped up, pushing out her chest, which was at most a third, if not a quarter, the size of Marina's.

"Have you lost your mind, Svetlana?!" Marina

gave her a once-over. "It's been a while since you've done inventory out in the company warehouses, is that it? I can arrange to have you sent back."

The mysterious Svetlana shrank back, shedding about two sizes and ten centimeters in height, while I glanced at the security guy, who seemed reasonable, and said curtly:

"Give me two minutes and I'll be back."

He thought for a moment and nodded. I pushed Marina into the corridor. As soon as the door closed, she wrapped her arms around me and buried her nose in my shoulder.

"What's wrong?" I asked, surprised.

"I'm scared, Andryusha." It was the first time she'd used that name for me, and it didn't bother me.

"What are you scared of, silly?"

"Yes, I'm silly!" She pulled back, staring into my eyes. "I know what's happening in this damn game... I saw them take Xavier away in an ambulance... Andrew, I don't want... Every day, I'm worried sick... What if you stay in there?! What if everyone comes out, but you'll stay, lying in there... drooling... not recognizing me... and... and THAT'LL BE IT!"

Marina buried her face in my shoulder again, sobbing. I stroked her hair awkwardly, unaccustomed to such gestures.

"Come on, stop it... They'll see us here... That Svetlana of yours is probably eavesdropping... Nothing will happen to me. I know this monster better than anyone... I know what to expect... Very soon, I'll beat it... WE will beat it... Together..."

"What did you call me here for?" Marina asked, once she'd calmed down a bit. "It's not 'cause you missed me."

I felt a bit guilty using her like this — now for my plans and later in bed, at her place... But the guilt, more like a slight awkwardness, vanished immediately. I was helping Marina do her job, not the other way around. That's how I saw it.

"Today, at approximately 12:35," I matched the game time to real time, "a player was kicked out of the game. He or she couldn't get back in. That means that he or she got out of the VR pod. There are no cameras in the VIP pod room on the fifth floor..."

"But there are in the corridor!" Marina finished for me. "I'll get the recordings... I know where..."

"Hurry before they're destroyed, in case someone else is as smart as us," I kissed her cheek. "See you tonight!"

"See you tonight!" she shouted, already running off, her suede boots clicking on the floor.

I felt a sense of hope as I watched her depart. Finally, we would have a chance to see our unknown enemy's face. When Marina disappeared around the corner of the office corridor, I returned and quickly finished signing the release forms.

For the first time in a while, I was at a loss when I stepped out of MosTech's building. Marina's Mazda stood in its usual spot, lightly dusted with snow, but waiting for her was pointless. Who

knew how long it would take her to get the information we needed from the security department.

Anna's motorcycle was parked a bit further
on. Despite the icy roads, she remained loyal to
her two-wheeled steed. Lance's Tesla was two rows
over. They were probably still going over the new
release forms as well. I knew them almost by heart,
but for them, it would all be new and would take
them some time.

I considered calling a taxi but decided that a
walk would be better than standing around, so I
stuffed my hands in my pockets and headed to the
electric bus stop.

"Hold it! Don't move!" I was grabbed roughly
by the arms, preventing me from struggling.
"Someone wants to talk to you!"

A black van's door suddenly appeared in front
of me. It slid open silently and two burly men
tossed me inside.

CHAPTER 23

TO MY SURPRISE, THE VAN turned out to be quite cozy. I expected... well, hell, I didn't expect anything. I hadn't had a single thought in my head from the moment those thugs grabbed me from both sides and shoved me into the van.

Yet the interior here was clearly recently refinished. It looked like the inside of a limousine from movies about rich people. The mood lighting made it impossible to tell where the lights were, as if the light was coming from everywhere at once. A low table stood in the middle, like in a train compartment, and there were soft sofas upholstered in dark cherry leather for sitting.

The thugs sat me on the back sofa, squishing me from both sides with their shoulders. Sitting across from me, Shiloh looked at me sternly. I was surprised to see him in a dark suit and black shirt with an open collar instead of his usual coat. The thief's hood he wore in-game suited him much more. Or perhaps I was just used to it.

I looked around the cabin again, noting the expensive upholstery and the impressive video panel on the wall, and then stared back at Shiloh. Modest Slonimsky didn't say anything. The only sound was that of his guards breathing heavily.

I realized that my situation was unpleasant and that here in the real world, a person like him could seriously mess up my life, possibly starting right now. You don't become a nightclub owner just like that, and you don't ride around vehicles like this one for nothing.

They'd give me a good beating and dump me somewhere outside the city, and then I'd have to survive in the cold however I could. If I didn't survive, well, that was my problem. All of this was clearly imprinted in my mind, but for some reason, I wasn't scared.

"12 Red Commune St.," I said. "Building 2."

"Huh?!" Slonimsky was dumbfounded.

"Well, you're giving me a lift, aren't you?" I asked naively. "Thanks, by the way. I'd freeze completely waiting for the electric bus in this weather."

Modest forced a smile.

"Sure, why not? Want a drink?" he asked in a friendly manner. "No status effects here, don't worry."

I shrugged. I didn't plan on any further heroic deeds today, and the alcohol would do me good.

"I won't refuse."

Modest pulled back a wide armrest, revealing

a minibar underneath with bottle necks wrapped in colorful foil sticking out. Something pink and lacy was hanging from one of them, suspiciously resembling women's panties.

"No champagne though," I protested. "It's useless, just gives me a headache later."

Slonimsky's face twisted slightly. Turning around, he knocked irritably on the glass separating us from the driver and waited for the partition to slide down.

"Was Ronnie picking up whores in the van again?" he asked the driver angrily.

The driver mumbled something in response, which I couldn't hear from my seat. Modest turned back to me, now extremely irritated. The image of a mafioso intimidating a competitor was falling apart before my eyes.

"Do you really commute to the beta test in this thing every morning?" I tried to lighten the mood.

"And if I do? What's wrong with that?" Modest sounded offended. "It's a great car. We use it to transport our VIPs to shows. They like it. Why let a good thing go to waste?"

I wasn't too convinced by his explanation. It felt like he brought his limo van specifically to impress me. He definitely didn't always have the thugs with him. So this conversation was going to be serious.

"Yeah, your girls must be thrilled," I agreed, causing another grimace from Slonimsky.

"Andrew," Modest got to the point, "I can see

you're a smart guy. I appreciated your idea of an alliance, and as you can see, I was actively pursuing it while you went missing in action."

So, the accusations began.

"Does it look like I went missing in action? Really?" I raised my eyebrows in surprise. "I found a rat in our ranks and punished it — the one you, by the way, had taken under your wing."

The thugs squeezed my shoulders ominously. They weren't used to people talking to their boss in such a tone. The effect was unpleasant — as if the air was knocked out of me.

"Let him go," Modest said majestically. He leaned closer to me, resting his elbows on the table, and his eyes became very kind. "You're smart, Andrew... but you're still oh so young. Let me explain to you how things work in real life."

"And how is that?"

My question sounded brave, but a bit hoarse. I was struggling to catch my breath.

"Some cloud-dwelling people descended into our mortal world. I don't care about them. They have their level, I have mine, and I'm completely satisfied with mine. They play their silly games and throw around money they have in abundance. Including giving it to people who have never seen such money before and are fundamentally unworthy of it. Don't make faces... I know you didn't come from the street either. Your girlfriend got you into this revenue stream, and she did the right thing. Don't be shy, I'll keep quiet... I won't tell anyone. It's not my business."

So, Shiloh knows about my relationship with Marina. It's not surprising, we didn't really hide it. But he's clearly interpreted it in his own way. Is this good or bad? He definitely doesn't know that I have access to the MosTech executives. Otherwise, he wouldn't try to scare me with such basic blackmail. The question was, should I drop the hint or not? I really wanted to show off my acquaintance with the Master or Doc. At least so these two meatheads would stop messing with me.

By sheer willpower, I suppressed the childish desire to show off in front of the mobster only to see some fear or doubt flicker across his smug face. I couldn't predict what Slonimsky was capable of if he got scared. What if he decided that — given my connections — I was too dangerous and dumped me in the forest without any vital signs? I didn't know anything about him, but I was damn sure that kind people didn't survive in his line of work. So, I had better keep playing the role of Joe Shmoe, average Andy, who'd gotten a spot at the trough and who was eager to hear his words of wisdom.

Meanwhile, Slonimsky interpreted my silence in his own way:

"Don't worry, Andrew, we're on the same crew!" he laughed, "I don't rat out my own... until they become strangers. So now, about these revenue streams, one of which you've latched onto: Our job is to reroute any revenue streams we encounter in the right direction — into our pockets! There's a bunch of losers that log into that game every day and hide in its nooks and crannies, hoping not to get robbed, killed, screwed, or all three at once. And they get paid huge bucks for it! Not a single whore of mine can blow that much in one night!"

Slonimsky smiled, signaling that he had made a joke, and the thugs laughed obsequiously.

"And what are you suggesting?" I asked with genuine curiosity.

I figured his explanation might shed some light on what the "Animaniacs" were doing in the Bedtime Story.

"Suggesting?!" Slonimsky adopted a preachy tone. "I've been doing everything for a long time! Peace! Security! Safety! Entertainment! Bread and Circuses!" He gesticulated like a seasoned tribune addressing his constituency. "For a measly half a day's salary, you can play in peace and forget all your problems. That way, everyone is happy! The losers of yesterday get an all-inclusive package, complete with girls, thrills and in-game respect. Meanwhile, back in meatspace the mullah flows in, more and more of it by the day. We ensure order in the game. There's no violence, slaughter or bloodshed on our watch. Everything is neat and nice."

"And the admins?"

"What the admins don't know, doesn't hurt them," Shiloh cut me off. "We operate within the rules and what happens in the real world is not their concern. I hope you're not stupid enough to chop down the branch you're sitting on? And neither is that in-game girlfriend of yours. She isn't stupid either. By the way, we offer a 'Safety' package for beauties like her, provided she works in our temple of course." Modest smacked his lips in pleasure. "And they're all beautiful in this game! Do you know why?"

I actually did know. It caught me off guard when I first noticed it, but all the girls in the beta were good-looking. In a regular MMORPG this makes sense because there's a character editor, and anyone can make themselves a beauty. But here everyone appeared as they looked in real life, and all the girls were at least pretty, while plenty more were outright beautiful. I asked Marina about it, and after she interrogated me for fifteen minutes about "which bitch caught my eye," she finally revealed the truth to me.

"The chicks were filtered through a face check," I explained, "Only the cute ones were selected. They did it so that the photos would turn out nice — for the review shows and magazines."

"So that's how it is?" Modest rubbed his hands gleefully. "All the better for us. More competition for them means they show off less."

"And do they consent?"

"Consent to what?" Slonimsky didn't understand.

"To work in exchange for your 'Safety' package?"

"Oh most willingly and eagerly!" Modest leaned back on the couch, as if explaining elementary truths to me. "You're still a greenhorn,

Andrew, even though you do show promise. But you don't know nothing about women! The most important thing for a woman is stability and that no one is gossiping behind her back. And here we have complete anonymity. 'What happens in Vegas, stays in Vegas.' Money flows... There's no neighbors to call her a whore... And when it comes to their fantasies, every other woman roleplays a slut... if not all of them. So, again, everyone's happy."

"I remember you talking about this," I grimaced.

Even though I had lost many illusions about girls over the past few weeks, Modest's words sounded... not exactly cynical, but rather too simplistic.

I didn't believe for a second that Anna, for instance, would offer VR sex services in exchange for VR stability and earnings. Why, she'd bury anyone even suggesting such a thing — and not just in the game. As for Stacy-Anima, she'd knee him in the balls or smash him on the head with her divine club. And Sofia-Theophilia, despite her slutty nature, wouldn't have agreed either — she valued herself too highly. So, Modest's math just didn't add up...

Although maybe he had enough chicks who did agree to his simple terms and didn't care about the rest.

"Do you get where I'm going with this, Andrew?"

"Not really..." I said honestly.

"Look, Eugene aka 'Ji-Bo,' is certainly an asshole," Modest said, "but he is also a useful guy. You shouldn't have treated him like you did. I know, I know..." He raised his hand, anticipating my objection. "He started it, you had to maintain your reputation... But next time don't act so rashly... come alone... consult with us... we could've talked it over... resolved it... So a couple of losers got eaten by some trees, what's the big loss? Especially since they don't remember anything afterward... Eugene... Eugene's a reliable guy... he delivers whatever you need... booze... girls... ingredients..."

"For whom? For you?" I couldn't hold back.

"You didn't ask anything, just jumped into a fight, hotheaded," Modest laughed. "I appreciate that... Well, you taught that dummy a lesson, put him in his place, fine. But now you've promoted that ninny Mirta to high priest... who knows how we're going to deal with her... But it's okay... we've dealt with worse."

Modest seemed to be talking to himself, and I interrupted his musings again.

"Look, what do you want from me? To take Ji-Bo back? That won't happen."

"To hell with him," Slonimsky waved his hand, "I'm offering you an alliance, not like the one we discussed yesterday. That was just talk and show. A real alliance — just you and me."

"Interesting, and how will it be different from yesterday's?"

"You know how to fight, Andrew." Modest

stared directly into my eyes, and once again I no longer saw the relaxed, successful businessman named Slonimsky, but Shiloh, the head of the thieves' guild. "I know what I'm talking about. I've seen many people in my day. Like your buddy, Lance, for example. He's good, but weaker…"

"He's a champion…"

"He lacks anger. He's playing a game in there, but you're living it. Andrew, I can see right through people. My job is to see through people and put them to work. To make sure the most capable person is in the right place. Because it's only then that everyone…"

"That everyone's happy."

"That's right!" Modest raised his finger happily. "You're starting to understand me. That means we'll work well together. You have game experience… I have life experience… You'll grow stronger yet… much stronger than now… And I'll turn that strength into money. Your 'goddess' isn't a problem, she follows you around and looks up to you. Together we'll take over the whole game… No one in there will dare take a breath without our permission. And you'll become a rich man, Andrew. That amount in the envelope that you get from MosTech, multiply it by five, maybe more. We'll discuss that. We need to shear the sheep, my young friend. If we don't do it, someone else will. That's the fate of sheep — to be shorn. Without it, they just bleat miserably: '*Baa ram ewe… Baa ram ewe…*'"

The thugs laughed again and even I smiled.

The pompous Slonimsky was very amusing. Not that I didn't understand his arguments. I had after all entered the beta with only one goal — to make money. I didn't care about the goals and aspirations of the other players. If they're willing to pay for security, great! I wasn't planning on saving the world or educating the people living in it. And I couldn't deny that Slonimsky's praise was flattering.

For a guy who was until recently unloading trucks of vodka for a living, this offer was extremely enticing. Even now, all those lofty people... the Master... Dr. Kotov... Anna... The only reason any of them talk to me is because I'm needed. As soon as the test is over, within an hour, they'll forget I exist. Even Marina's sudden passion for me... I mean, she fell for the player TargetAi, not Andrew the college freshman. Once midnight strikes, this whole world will turn into a damn pumpkin.

Meanwhile, cash money was reliable... Cash money was something real. If I had it, I could get established. Who knows? Maybe I could get a job with Slonimsky? Maybe I could live a wild, carefree and wealthy life, like the one I'd always dreamed of?

The only problem was that Modest's entire business plan was "built on sand." The game would never allow the players to live peacefully, and any "order" would turn to its advantage. The shadow empire Shiloh had imagined wouldn't last more than a few days.

I could see how rapidly the game world was

growing. If we spent the tine we had extorting money from dummies, instead of coming up with a plan to beat the AI, we'd all end up stuck in there forever. What does a vegetable care about how much money it has in its bank account.

"Have you read the new forms they gave you today?" I asked, abruptly changing the subject.

"I took them with me in order to study them closer," Modest said, surprised. "I don't sign anything without a lawyer."

This response shocked me slightly. So, I wasn't allowed to leave even for a minute to meet Marina, but this guy calmly takes practically secret documents with him. Apparently, I wasn't the only one with connections at MosTech, and it was good I had kept quiet about my own contacts. But at least it became clear why Slonimsky got to the street before I did.

"Well when you do read them, pay attention to the clause that says: 'You acknowledge that being in the game may have negative effects on your health...'"

"That? So what? They always write that," Modest waved me off. "It's a standard liability waiver. In case someone's heart acts up, *bam* — and their time is up. They're practically forced to include that stuff to avoid any possible liability."

"Don't you get it?!" I yelled, losing my patience. Modest's impenetrability was astonishing. He had already built his business scheme in his head and saw any other possibility as a mere obstacle. "This game KILLS! It's INTELLIGENT! It's evolving and looking for ways to DESTROY the players. And it's already close to figuring out how to do so! We need to resist it, not help it!"

"I don't know who messed up your head…"

"Modest, believe me! I've seen it. A girl from my party ended up in a coma, and her in-game character became an NPC. We barely saved Lance's guys, and one of them is still in the hospital. The AI won't stop. It will keep finding new weak spots in the players' minds. I'm already telling you more than I should. I just… I need an ally."

"I'm disappointed in you, Andrew," Slonimsky looked at me with pity, "You're either a fool or a very naive person. Neither suits me. You still have time to reconsider. I'll give you until tomorrow morning. But keep in mind… if you get the dumb idea to interfere with my plans, I'll destroy you! This conversation is over!"

The van skidded to a halt and I was pushed out. The door slid shut behind me, and I was left alone, not knowing where I was. Some industrial lot… with rows of identical snow-covered warehouses… dogs barking in the distance.

Thankfully my phone was still working. As I fiddled with my maps app, an incoming call came through.

"Where are you?" Anna asked.

"Hell if I know," I answered honestly, "want me to give you the address?"

"Yes, I want to introduce you to someone."

This option was even better than a taxi, because it was faster and free. Less than fifteen minutes later, Anna braked sharply next to me, dousing me with snow.

"Here," she handed me a passenger's helmet and I slipped it on almost instinctively.

We sped through intersections, traffic jams, and bridges. During this ride, I began to enjoy the cars flashing inches away from us, the sharp sting of snow on my cheeks (my helmet had no visor), and the exhilarating feeling of flying, as if the bike was held on the road solely by the driver's will and not by the laws of physics. All it took was to mentally step onto the path of the samurai. Live as if you're already dead.

Anna stopped in front of a burger joint I didn't recognize and parked between a Range Rover and a Porsche Cayenne. I figured the burgers here were sure to be more expensive than at McDonald's.

The place was decorated like an American roadside diner. A whole row of separate "booths" made up of two sofas and a table in the middle. Bright pin-up posters with voluptuous cuties adorned the walls. The waitresses wore checkered aprons and carried coffee pots. It felt like being in a movie, and any second now, someone might pull out a gun and yell, "All right, everybody be cool, this is a robbery!"

By the way, judging by our appearance, that could've easily been Anna and me. She walked past the coat check, her leather jacket crunching as she removed her helmet, and headed straight for the farthest table.

"Meet Andrew..."

"Yes, we're already acquainted..." I said with some surprise, gazing at the man who had just bitten into a giant triple burger — as evidenced by the dollop of mustard on his mustache.

"No, you don't get it," Anna interrupted me. "Meet *the* Eternal Groove!"

CHAPTER 24

THE GOD OF PREDATORY TREES and the patron of frivolous dancers was as stunned as I was. First, he nearly dropped the burger he was about to bite into. Then he extended his hand to me, noticed it was covered in mustard, pulled it back, and started wiping it with a napkin.

Meanwhile, Anna folded her arms across her chest and silently admired the slapstick she'd caused.

"How did you figure it out?" Groove asked once all the greetings had been made and we had all sat down.

"We lived in the same building for seven years," Anna snorted, "did you think I wouldn't recognize you? This guy wanted to be a DJ in high school," she went on, turning to me, "with no rhythm whatsoever... His remixes would make the cats flee the house, and my mom's ficuses would wilt…"

I was sure I saw Benjamin Zvyagin blush at these words. Even I felt a bit embarrassed by these revelations of family secrets. We were saved by a waitress who suddenly appeared at our table.

"Ready to order?" she interrupted Anna.

"No," Anna waved her off irritably.

"That's not allowed," the waitress replied, not budging.

"What do you mean?" Now all three of us stared at her.

The young, round-faced, tall girl looked at us with bold light-blue eyes. I would've even called her pretty if not for the overly chubby cheeks and a roll of fat that was beginning to swell at her neck. It was clear she ate well but didn't work out.

"But I've already ordered…" Benjamin tried to smooth things over politely.

"They haven't," the waitress retorted. "This is a respectable establishment, not a park bench. Order something or leave!"

Anna was on the verge of exploding with righteous fury. She was ready to stand up and explain to this turkey what "a respectable establishment" even meant, but I didn't want to waste time on this.

"I'll have the same burger as him," I pointed to Benjamin's plate, "and a cola. The lady will have a blackberry cascara."

"We only have drip coffee!" the waitress snapped.

I glanced at her name tag. "Jean," it said. I

pulled out an envelope from my pocket, which I hadn't even opened today, and took out a fifty-euro bill without looking inside.

"Jean, be a dear," I placed the bill on the table and slid it towards her, "go fetch us one from the nearest cafe!"

The struggle between rudeness and greed lasted about ten seconds. Then the bill vanished as if by magic and Jean darted away from our table, demonstrating efficiency with every movement of her plump hips.

"What the hell," Benjamin muttered, "I thought this was a respectable establishment."

"Everyone has different notions of 'respectable,'" I shrugged. "If you ask me for instance, meddling in the game process is hardly respectable. But at MosTech, that kind of thing is done regularly."

"I'm not discussing this," Zvyagin pouted. "That's classified information."

"Classified for whom?! For your new buddies on the Board of Directors?" Anna joined in. "Do you sneak into the game, or do they know?"

"They're not my 'new buddies,' I've been on the Board for two years! And you'd be there too if it weren't for your ridiculous rebelliousness."

"I don't trust them!"

"You need to grow up!"

I listened as the siblings squabbled, waiting for a pause to interject. Finally, I lost my patience.

"Quiet!" I clapped my hands, and they both looked at me in astonishment.

It hadn't occurred to them that someone could interrupt their extremely important bickering.

"What do you think you're..."

"Benjamin, listen," I interrupted him. "She's ALREADY playing. Your sister is ALREADY in the game. And she won't back down. You won't convince her with shouts or reproaches. THAT won't save her, understand?!" I could tell by his expression that I had hit the mark and now began hammering my point home. "You didn't want Anna to be in there playing, right? Especially since she's trying to win? But you can't keep her out either. So did you decide to intentionally sabotage her? Is Sibyl working for you somehow? Did she deliberately turn the town against us? Tell me, who is she?!"

"I don't know," Zvyagin confessed.

"Benjamin," I pressed on, "the only way to protect your sister is to help us. Tell us everything you know."

"But the game process..."

"To hell with the game process! You yourselves interfered with it and stomped all over it with your dirty boots. Now it's not players competing, but people against the neural network. So whose side are you on?!"

"Why the hell did you go in there, you fool?!" Benjamin shouted so loudly that people turned to look at us. "That thing killed our dad! I won't let it destroy you too!"

"Our dad is alive!" Anna pounded the table

with her fist.

There was such desperate belief in her gesture that it even choked me up.

"I really don't know who Sibyl is," Benjamin insisted. "That's what I was trying to find out in the game."

"How is that possible?" I didn't believe him. "You run the entire technical side. You should have access to logs about anyone who enters the virtual world."

"I do," Benny confirmed. "Anyone except the VIPs logging in from the VIP room. All the pods in there are rooted. They don't track anything, whether recording the game session or logging the users' fingerprints or face IDs. At first, I couldn't even detect an outsider. Sibyl is an NPC, embedded in the 'core' of the game, like the 'dollhouse' our father created for Anna. Only later did I realize that an adult Sibyl couldn't exist in the game. The town is being rebuilt. The governor's daughter should be a child. The only child in the entire virtual town."

"But how did they know what she'd look like as an adult?!" Anna turned pale as chalk.

"Before launching the beta, while you were in Austria, we logged into your game," Benjamin said guiltily. "We all went to our house and took turns immersing ourselves. We studied how the AI worked. Well, I mean, it's my house too after all." Benny raised his chin stubbornly. "No one thought you'd ever come back."

"So Sibyl was created by one of the

executives?" I clarified.

"Yes, or at their behest," Benjamin confirmed. "Someone entered the beta early on, killed the little girl in the mayor's house, and took her place. The NPCs accepted her as one of their own. The AI doesn't actually differentiate between NPCs and players. It simply tries to eliminate them."

When Benjamin realized that Sibyl couldn't be an NPC, his first instinct was to go tell Dr. Kotov. But in the corridor, on the way to the CEO's office, Benny had stopped mid-stride.

This theory of his simply sounded so outlandish. It effectively implied that one of the three remaining Board members was secretly interfering with the experiment. But who was it?! And what if Benjamin was about to share his suspicions with the actual impostor?

What was "Sibyl's" goal? What did he or she want to accomplish? Benjamin couldn't help be intrigued about that too.

Finally, what if he was right and even managed to expose the impostor? Even then, it would only be his word against another executive's. And he hadn't any evidence!

So Benjamin decided to spy on Sibyl in the game. That's why he created the Eternal Groove.

"So you created the gods and not the players?!" I asked, surprised. "Then did the Master lie to me?!"

"No, what he said was true," Zvyagin raised his eyebrows, revealing his surprise at my close acquaintance with the Master. "The gods were created by you, the players. In the alpha, the bigger world before this one, there were gods too. But we disabled that feature, along with magic, for the beta. You can think whatever you want, but we're not idiots or scoundrels. We didn't want problems or players in comas. We wanted winners, not victims."

"Well maybe you don't want victims, but someone else clearly thinks otherwise," I thought. Someone was intentionally provoking the AI — no doubt the same person that had inserted Sibyl into the game.

"Why the Eternal Groove though?"

"Why not?" Benjamin retorted. "Do you think it's possible to introduce a new character into the game, while going unobserved by my top-notch mod team? Sibyl slipped through because she killed her in-game alter ego. But there were no other 'vacancies.' And then the gods appeared! It was like a miracle!" Zvyagin's voice filled with the enthusiasm of a scientist discussing the beauty and perfection of the cholera virus. "The players' consciousnesses create images, imbue them with power, and literally bring them to life! Lolf, the Spider Queen, was just a dumb raid boss until those fangirls pumped her full of divine power. Now she's developing a pseudo-consciousness! She's becoming sentient! It's the same story with that carnivorous grove. Ji-Bo was tripping in the thicket one day and thought he saw something, so he started telling other players, and they BELIEVED him! All I had to do was take control of a wild ent and appear a few times to the Groovers. After that they started feeding me divine XP. Their god was born and no one ever suspected that it might be a player instead of an NPC."

At this point, Jean, polite to a tee, returned from the café across the street. She handed Anna the cascara, and, "forgetting" to give back the change, disappeared into the kitchen. Her appearance interrupted Benjamin's tale. Zvyagin seemed to come to his senses and fell silent.

"Tell me," I sensed that he was in a talkative mood and decided to extract the information I needed most. "What's needed to level up a god? Why is Lolf so powerful? Why are you and your grove getting fat so quickly? And what's wrong with Anna?"

"It's simple," Zvyagin smirked, "for a deity to grow stronger, players have to believe in her."

I could tell he was ready to share a lot more interesting information, but just then my phone vibrated in my pocket. It was Mom calling.

"I'll call you later," I sent her an auto-text message, but a minute later, the phone buzzed again.

"Mom, I'm in the middle of an important conversation. I'll call you back."

"Andryusha, what have you gotten yourself into?!" Mom insisted. "How could you?! I knew we shouldn't have taken that money!"

"What money, what are you talking about?!" I could hear tears in my mom's voice but couldn't understand what was happening.

"They told me you borrowed money from very dangerous people! I told you your games wouldn't lead to anything good! Now they're going to take our apartment..."

I heard a stream of incoherent words in the background. What new nonsense was this? One thing was clear: I needed to go home urgently.

"Sorry, Benny!" I jumped up from the table. "Urgent family matters."

Zvyagin snorted incredulously but shook my hand.

"Where are you going?!" Anna caught up with me at the door.

"Sorry, now's not the time." I waved her off, "I need to go home ASAP. Something bad happened to my family."

"I'll drive you," she offered immediately.

"Are you sure?" I asked. "Why? I can take a taxi. Shouldn't you talk to Benjamin some more. Maybe you'll learn something else?"

"Family is important," Anna said solemnly, "you have to cherish it while you still have it."

I didn't know how to respond, so I just nodded. We raced through the snowy streets, but this time I didn't feel the thrill or the excitement of the ride. All my thoughts were at home, with my parents, whom I had so quickly forgotten about as soon as the light of a beautiful life had begun to glow around me.

We left the bike on the street near the shopping center. At least there were cameras watching over the parking lot there. Flashing a bike in front of the local thugs didn't seem like a good idea.

We reached the building's entrance without running into anyone unsavory. Anna looked around curiously at the bent mailboxes, the walls covered in marker graffiti, and the broken railings. I realized that this girl who had been born with a silver spoon in her mouth had probably never been to places like my native apartment block.

But whereas in front of Marina I felt embarrassed about my unpretentious lifestyle, Anna's reaction would probably only amuse me. It dawned on me that a person's worth isn't determined by where they live or how much they can spend on a cup of coffee.

A person's value lies in their will and actions. And everything else around them — the houses, the cars, even the women — are just attributes of their status and the consequences of their will and actions.

"Who is this?" Despite her tear-stained eyes, my mom remained true to herself and met Anna with a disapproving look.

To my mom, the motorcycle black leather that Anna was wrapped in had nothing on Marina's feminine outfits.

"This is Anna. She works with me," I said quickly, not giving Anna a chance to speak a word, lest she mess things up further. "She just gave me a ride. It was on the way."

Understanding that no one was threatening Marina's place in my life, Mom calmed down a bit. She had already designated Marina as the mother of her grandchildren and perceived any threat to this fantasy as a great danger.

"Now what are these debts you were telling me about?"

"Here!" she shoved a phone in my face.

MY PHONE! The very one that disappeared from my pocket when I got clocked on the head the other night. I was stunned by the audacity of the thieves, but that turned out to be just the beginning. On the screen was a screenshot of a conversation, allegedly from my number, where I was begging an unknown contact to lend me ten thousand euros.

"They said 'the meter is running,'" mom's hands trembled, and another tear rolled down her cheek. "If we don't pay, they'll take the apartment. They said going to the police is useless. They have everything covered! What have you done, Andrew? Why did you lie to me?! I already gave them your cursed euros, but they say we need the same amount again. Why?! Why did you take it?! We were poor but we were honest... It's all because of your games!"

"I didn't take anything, mom! It's nonsense! I earned that money!"

"Here's the proof!" She waved the screenshot in front of me. "This is your phone and your inbox! Now stop lying to your mother!"

Breaking down, she slumped into a chair and covered her face with her hands. She cried quietly, silently, her thin, frail shoulders shaking under the shawl she had thrown on.

Out of nowhere a wild, furious rage filled me to the brim, spilling over — not at mom, who believed anyone but her own son and always knew "what was best," even though her advice only led to poverty and despair — no, my rage was directed at the scum who had ruined my family's life. Those who had slandered and imprisoned my father. Those who were terrorizing my mom now. Those who bulldoze through people's lives without a second thought if they felt like they could turn the slightest profit.

"It's fake," Anna said after barely glancing at the screen.

"What?" Mom's voice was sharp and scratchy, like a stone scraping against glass. "Are you trying to defend him? You're probably all in the same gang... You deadbeats!"

"Mom, Anna is a security specialist," I seized the opportunity. "If she says it's fake, it's fake. She knows what she's talking about."

If Anna was surprised by her new job title, she didn't show it.

"A screenshot is not evidence of anything. For example, no court would accept it," she said confidently. "And Andrew doesn't need to borrow money. He's a highly paid specialist. Whoever gave this to you is a scammer. I advise you to go to the police. Then you'll see that your son isn't lying to you."

"I'm not going anywhere!" Mom stopped crying and crossed her arms stubbornly. "You go talk to them yourself."

"Mom, who was it? Who did you talk to?!"

"Your friend! Don't you remember who you borrowed money from?" She pursed her lips in sarcasm.

"I didn't borrow..." I started again and cut myself off. It was useless. "Wait, which friend?"

"Victor Sulenovsky. You went to school together," Mom sighed. "He was kind enough to tell me everything. He said, 'Let's help your Andrew together. Let him come to me, and I'll put in a good word with the right people. Maybe they'll adjust what he owes.'"

SULLEN! That bastard just wouldn't quit! If I was burning with rage before, now it had a target. Crush the bastard, destroy him, grind him into the ground!

I jumped up and rushed out the door, running into the hallway. And it was my own fault. I should have dealt with that scumbag when he hit me on the head. You can't forgive things like that. These scumbags see it as weakness and push further. Instead of dealing with him, I was preoccupied fighting virtual wars in fairyland. The Soul Reaper couldn't even protect his own family.

"Stop! What are you going to do?!" I felt someone pulling on my sleeve. Anna. In my rage, I had forgotten she was even there.

"I'm going to crush that scumbag! Maim him!"

"Did you ever think," Anna spoke softly and steadily, her calmness breaking through my waves of rage, "that this is exactly what they want from you? If you injure him, he'll take you to court...

Then you'll get kicked out of the beta..."

"I don't care!" I shrugged my shoulder to break free and leave.

"Wait," Anna paused for a second and then suddenly smiled. "I have another idea. Trust me, you won't be disappointed."

Chapter 25

ALL HIS LIFE, VICTOR SULENOVSKY dreamed of being like his father. As a small child, unable to walk on his own, he would reach out his frail hands to grab his father's hand and take a few awkward steps with him.

Victor valued female company much less and would scream desperately when held by his mother and grandmother. His father, however, filled him with awe. He was immense, boisterous and he reeked of confidence and strong tobacco.

He always walked with a swagger, afraid of nothing. His body was adorned with beautiful tattoos: a creepy skull, a dangerous-looking dagger, a playful mermaid, a deck of cards.

He spoke loudly and laughed loudly, and everyone around him seemed to shrink in his presence. They would respectfully shake his hand, call him Mr. Sulenovsky, seek his advice or opinion, invite him to share a bottle of wine or offer him cigarettes courteously.

"Fear means respect," his father used to say, and little Vic took this lesson to heart.

Vic mimicked his father's walk, his way of looking at people with grim audacity, his ability to sneer his words through his lips. He adored his father, and yet his father showed no interest in his progeny.

Victor grew up weak and sickly, he started speaking late, and had a severe slouch even in kindergarten. Watching young Sullen, his father would shake his head, spit a long stream of saliva, slam the apartment door, and immediately forget about his son's existence.

Victor didn't know what he had done wrong. He persistently tried to get his father's attention during the rare moments he was home, but his father would only brush off the annoying child, yell at his mother and grandmother for not raising him properly, and then disappear for days at a time.

One day, his father disappeared for good. His mother said he had gone on a business trip to the north, but the neighbors told Victor that his father was "doing time," and later those same kindhearted people informed him that his parents had divorced.

Victor's mother began coming home later and later, her skirts grew shorter and her makeup grew brighter. Eventually, she too disappeared in search of a better life. Victor was a ball and chain as far as she was concerned, and she didn't need him in her new life.

Thus Vic was left in the care of his grandmother. Not yet an old woman, barely fifty, she completely gave up on her own future in order to "raise" her grandson. By day she worked in a research library and in the evenings she cleaned floors as a custodian. She did all this to clothe and feed Victor, so that the boy "wouldn't wear hand-me-downs."

But instead of gratitude, she received only burning hatred, which grew hotter and hotter as Victor grew older. He took out all his resentment for being abandoned on his grandmother, initially expressing it through tantrums and fits, then through swearing, until eventually, he even began to physically abuse the old woman and stole her retirement savings.

No one of his peers actually liked Victor. His nickname "Sullen" had stuck to him since kindergarten, not only due to his last name but also due to his sullen demeanor.

His classmates avoided him and didn't include him in their games, sensing with their infallible kids' instincts some internal rot.

His attempts to boss them around and impose his own rules, as he did with his submissive grandmother, were quickly and harshly stopped by the boys in the class, who beat up little Sullen multiple times.

His hatred for his grandmother gradually spread to the entire world around him. He hated the neighbors who pitied the "orphan" and his kindergarten teachers for trying to help him: They fed him because he was so frail, prompting a storm of mean-spirited teasing from his peers. Eventually, however, Sullen learned to hide his hatred deep inside.

The only real joy he felt was when being a jerk. Tripping a jogger, throwing another's possession in the mud, shoving, spitting, breaking something.

Sullen understood that he was physically weaker than the others and started finding fellow outcasts who were also rejected by the rest. The first of these was Nikolai Stroev, nicknamed "Hammer." He owed his nickname to a kind elementary school teacher who once joked, "Seems all your head is good for is hammering nails, not solving problems."

Nikolai was indeed a bit slow-witted but he was strong. In second grade he was already the size of a fifth-grader. "Brock," "Dumbo," and "Big Pun" were just some of the names his classmates called him. Yet despite his size, Nikolai was a wimp and slow on the uptake: Whenever he was insulted, he seemed either too scared to respond or simply didn't know how.

Nikolai became Sullen's muscle. They began ambushing the most arrogant kids after school, and soon, few dared to open their mouths not only against Hammer but also against Sullen himself.

Once his pride no longer stung, Victor decided to improve his financial situation. By fifth grade, Sullen had formed a gang of like-minded individuals around him and they started shaking down the younger kids.

That's when Sullen overdid it for the first time: He took the phone of a second-grader, a cry-baby and a whiner. Sullen thought it was unfair that this kid had an iPhone while he only had a Nokia.

The kid's father turned out to be a prosecutor, while his mother worked in the local city hall. Victor's grandmother had to beg them on her knees not to ruin the boy's life. Eventually, they relented and forgave the boy, assuming that he had "learned his lesson."

And Victor did learn his lesson. From then on, he carefully studied his targets. Like a real predator stalking the weaker, sicker prey, Sullen chose those who couldn't fight back. And not all of them came from poor families, although Sullen and his gang weren't picky.

Typically Sullen's victims were too afraid to tell their parents about the beatings and extortion they suffered and were willing to pay a bit of protection money for some peace of mind. Those who naively thought they could stop such payments were severely beaten as a lesson to the others.

Sullen's gang gained strength. New "soldiers" began asking to join. With Sullen, they could make money while drinking and smoking to their hearts' content. Sullen knew who to sell the stolen goods to. His guys shook down the suckers and molested the frightened, compliant girls. People began to fear Sullen, which he interpreted as respect.

Sullen hated that scumbag Andrew Severyanov since they were in school together. One day, back in seventh grade, he miscalculated and led his gang to extort Severyanov. But Andrew simply socked Sullen in the jaw, knocking him out for a few minutes, while the others scattered.

Sullen played it off as if nothing had happened, although he held a grudge. But he was pragmatic — though he probably didn't know that word — and he figured that fighting a poor shmuck over his wounded pride wasn't profitable.

Recently, however, Severyanov had been doing pretty well for himself: expensive cars, flashy girls... And so Sullen decided to shake him down, ambushing Severyanov as his chick was dropping him off. But Andrew fought back and everything turned out worse than before.

Sullen couldn't forgive such a blow to his reputation, and when the opportunity arose, he struck again. That time, ambushing Andrew as he was waiting for a taxi outside the apartment block. That night, Sullen was ready to kill his old enemy, but he was scared off at the last moment.

A few days later, some guys paid Victor a visit. They picked him up off the street as he was on his way back from the convenience store with a forty in his hand. He was brought before a very important individual.

The importance of this individual was evident in his office, his appearance, and the serious tone in which he spoke to Victor.

"Is that your merchandise?" the important

individual asked.

Severyanov's phone lay on the table. Sullen had picked it up and then immediately sold it to a fence after the ambush.

"Yeah," Sullen instinctively knew there was no point in denying anything. At the moment, he needed to cooperate willingly and diligently. In his mind however, he thought, *"That crooked fence. 'Complete confidentiality,' he told me, 'as secure as a bank...' When I find that bastard I'll thrash his soul out through his nose."*

"Do you know its original owner?" the important individual went on.

"Yes."

The phone had been hacked and the important individual scrolled through it, reading something and grunting occasionally.

"Victor... Your name is Victor, right?" The man waited for Sullen's frantic nod and continued, "Can I count on you, Victor? I have a job for you. But not a word to anyone."

"I'll be as silent as a grave," Sullen nodded eagerly.

* * *

But later on Sullen couldn't resist and started dropping hints that something was afoot to his buddies, distributing generous cash advances in the process.

"I've been called up to the big time," he said. "'We can't manage without you, Mr. Sulenovsky' is what they told me. But no need to worry, oh my brothers, I'll bring you along soon enough."

Sullen's cronies nodded thoughtfully and kept their doubts to themselves. Besides Sullen, no one had seen this "important individual" and their leader never did furnish any proof of his existence. In the end, they discussed their doubts behind Sullen's back but didn't dare voice them aloud.

"Holy shit!" Hammer's eyes suddenly went wide. "Who's this coming our way in a ride like that?"

A sleek, low-set sports car rumbled up to the apartment block along the narrow, snow-swept driveway.

"That's a Ferrari!" proclaimed Zheka.

"Bullshit! Ferraris have a horse emblem!"

"Then what is it?"

"A Lamborghini!"

The cronies began bickering over what was on the hood of a Lamborghini.

The car pulled up to the benches where they were sitting, stopped, and two chicks got out. The guys immediately forgot all about their automotive disagreements. They had only seen women like this in expensive porn vids — just after the opening credits when everyone was still wearing clothes.

The girls walked towards them, stepping disdainfully over snowdrifts and frozen puddles in their high heels. One, a blonde in cream-colored pants so tight that a crease was visible between her legs, wore a short light fur coat that did nothing to obscure the view.

The other was a brunette in a tiny miniskirt and black boots that reached above her knee, where her lace stocking peeked out. Above the waist, she wore a leather jacket with a fluffy collar, open at the chest, revealing her prominent breasts.

Their outfits completely ignored the considerable cold and the filthy apartment block courtyard, giving them the semblance of Martians.

"Which one of you is Sullen?" the brunette asked haughtily.

She gave the group a look full of icy disdain and blew a bubble with her pink chewing gum. The bubble popped in the dead silence that had settled on the place.

"Victor Sullen?" the blonde purred.

At the sound of her voice, muscles the fellas didn't even know existed tensed in their groins.

"Well, that'd be me," Sullen lifted his chin.

"Let's go," the brunette grumbled.

"Where?!"

"Straight to paradise," the blonde laughed brightly. "Where else?"

If an observant and imaginative person had been in the yard, they might have said the pair resembled an angel and a devil. But Sullen's crew was far removed from such artistic generalizations; they just drooled and ogled at the unexpected surprise.

"What?" Sullen was stunned.

"We're going to see the boss," the brunette

explained lazily.

"What boss?!"

"He's also dumb," the brunette turned to her companion.

"Don't insult the boy," the blonde objected. "I like him. He probably has a bright future."

She locked eyes with Sullen, and it felt like her playful whore's eyes were peering right into his soul, turning it inside out. Without breaking eye contact, the blonde ran a nimble pink tongue over her lower lip. Sullen started sweating.

"Like the lady says, we're gonna go have a chat," he said to the gang with a slightly hoarse voice, "Don't worry, fellas, I'll keep you foremost in my mind."

"Get in," the blonde said, opening the car door for him and then getting in the back.

Sullen settled into the car's crimson leather seat. The cabin smelled luxurious, like the office of the "important individual," and Sullen finally relaxed. The brunette shifted gears with a jerk, turned the sports car around in the courtyard and peeled out onto the street.

She drove the car as confidently and brazenly as she looked, ignoring speed limits and overtaking in the oncoming lane. Settled into the luxurious interior, Sullen started to get comfortable.

"What kind of car is this?"

"Maserati," spat the brunette without taking her eyes off the road.

"Expensive?"

"Oh yeah!" The blonde laughed from the back.

"Do as the boss says and you'll have one too."

"Did you blow him to get it?" Sullen joked casually, trying to build rapport.

"Do you think that's what he'll ask of you?" the blonde countered. "Or is that what you hope?"

She leaned forward abruptly, enveloping Sullen in a sweet scent of perfume, and he felt the soft touch of lips on his skin.

Then there was a *click*, and Sullen's body went limp.

"Stop," the blonde said. "We need to move this carcass."

*   *   *

Sullen woke up from the cold. It was dark around him. Somewhere in the distance, water dripped rhythmically, irritatingly. *Drip... drip... drip...*

Victor tried to move but couldn't. His hands and feet were spread apart and tightly fastened.

As his eyes adjusted, Sullen made out the outlines of a stone vaulted ceiling above him. Judging by the feel, he was also lying on a stone slab. And, judging by the ambient air temperature, he was completely naked.

"What the fuck?!" Sullen thought. Actually, there wasn't a single thought in his head at that moment that didn't contain swear words. At first he was going to shout them out but then he became afraid. No matter how bad his current situation was, the possibility that someone might be nearby while he was so helpless scared him even more.

An unseen door creaked on its hinges, light seeped in, and the two chicks came into view. This time they seemed to have swapped roles.

The brunette wore nearly transparent white lace lingerie, with a tight corset and fishnet stockings on garters. The blonde was adorned with a costume of thin black leather straps that clung to her body like a harness, hiding nothing at all.

Her luscious large breasts bounced with each step, and her exposed, rosy nipples jiggled cheerfully. Despite the crazy situation, Sullen's member stirred again. Looking at the girls, he felt both fear and arousal, and this drove him even crazier.

Instead of clothes, the blonde's body was covered in tattoos, among which tiny nimble spiders stood out, tracing a path from her thigh up to her ear, hiding under her blonde curls.

"You ladies into S&M?" Sullen said with a confidence he didn't actually feel.

What the hell was going on?! Did he screw up in front of the boss?! Had he bungled the job somehow? Leaked information at some point? Sullen's mind raced, unable to come up with a single justification for his strange predicament.

Even if he had been sold out... or set up... Why stage this whole show?! Maybe this was just a prank! The new boss decided to reward him for his first successful operation, sent two expensive hookers and they were about to give him a full service. Exotic, but who knows with the rich... Maybe they can't get off any other way. His mind found this comforting explanation so alluring that Sullen even smirked.

"Look at that, he's not afraid of us at all," the blonde said with some surprise. "You were right, he really is dumb."

She ran her nails from Sullen's chest down his body, over his stomach to his groin... evoking a massive erection.

"Come on!" Sullen commanded. "Get on with it!"

"You still don't get it," the blonde laughed. "Look over there."

Sullen turned his head where she pointed and saw another silhouette. The arousal drained from him instantly, as if he had been dunked in a tub of ice water. Instead, he thrashed against his restraints and howled in anger and fear.

"What the fuck are you doing here, asshole?!"

From the darkness, Andrew Severyanov's face looked back at him.

"And now," the blonde leaned close to Sullen and whispered directly into his ear, "it's gonna hurt just a little."

CHAPTER 26

AT THAT MOMENT, SULLEN FINALLY understood. There would be no meeting with the "big man." And there would be no fun sexual adventure with the two hot chicks either. The presence of that asshole, Severyanov, didn't fit at all into the thug's fantasies.

The blonde bitch ran her finger down Vic's body, from his neck to his groin, lightly scratching his skin with her sharp nail. Her nipples were hard, either from the cold or from arousal. She looked at Sullen like a piece of cake after a long diet, and her completely mad gaze made him feel especially terrified.

"Get the hell away from me, you bitch!" he yelled. "Go fuck yourself! I'll find you... My boys and I will find all of you! We'll make you crawl before us, bitch! We'll make you aaa-a-a-a-a-A-A-A!"

Sharp nails dug into his balls sending Sullen

screaming. He no longer saw anyone — neither the dark-haired chick nor the bastard of a neighbor who'd set him up. There was only cold, darkness, and the crazy blonde.

But along with the pain came rage. Sullen had earned the little authority he had among his pathetic buddies for a reason. He was cunning, slippery and very angry.

"What are you gonna do, whore?!" he yelled now. "Trying to scare me, you losers?! You won't do shit! You don't have the guts to kill me. I'll get out of here! And you bitches will regret being born! You'll all end up begging to blow me, all three of you!"

"What a smart boy," commented the blonde, unfazed. "He's thinking... Drawing conclusions... He's not even afraid of me..." She pouted. "But Vics, it's not because you're smart... It's because you lack imagination. That's okay though," she giggled, "I have enough imagination for both of us."

The blonde stepped back and stood nearby. If he tilted his head and squinted, Victor could see her almost entirely. This crazy woman's body was covered in tattoos. The narrow black strap of the leather "harness" between her legs didn't hide anything, but it didn't arouse him anymore either.

The only thing Sullen wanted now was to strangle this bitch. To feel her struggling in his hands, hear her begging for mercy, see her eyes widen in terror, and her tongue loll out...

His fantasies were interrupted by a barely noticeable touch. Something was tickling his right leg. Sullen looked at the blonde again, but she was too far to reach him.

Something invisible was crawling up Victor's leg, pressing into his skin with tiny claws. This light touch filled Sullen with such primal horror that he screamed at an almost ultrasonic pitch:

"Get THAT THING off me! Get it off... Get it off, you bitch!"

"Why you two haven't even met yet," the blonde said with a smile.

The soft touches moved to his stomach and Victor finally SAW it! A spider — huge, black, with stiff green fuzz — was crawling up his body. It reached his chest and paused, lifting its front legs as if greeting him.

"Eeee!" The thug arched and thrashed against his bonds, trying to shake the spider off.

But the arachnid clung on with its hooked furry legs, like a cowboy on a wild bull.

"Who tipped you off, Victor?" The blonde's voice was silky smooth and it still sent shivers down his spine, although of sheer terror now. "You're a dumb fucker, Vics... A stupid thug... A basic scumbag... Trash..." She savored each word. "You wouldn't have thought of extorting Severyanov's mom on your own. Who tipped you off?!"

Sullen was torn between his fear of and revulsion at the spider and his fear of the "important individual." Here, he was just terrified, but the boss could easily have him buried in the woods outside town. Victor pictured the boss's cold, dead eyes and hissed through his teeth:

"Go fuck yourself!"

"The guerrillas caught a girl... Stripped her and started torturing her..." the blonde sang out of tune. "But her girlish lips whispered..." she trailed off, evidently forgetting the rest. "Go on... resist, Victor... It's more fun for me that way... You still don't get it? You're mine, Victor..."

The tickling became stronger, appearing at his heels, then under his armpits, then, horrifyingly, right between his legs. Another spider climbed onto his stomach, followed by a third. They scurried over Sullen's spread-eagled body, their furry abdomens rasping against his skin.

"Talk, Victor... Who? Who got to you? Who tipped you off, you little shit?"

The blonde smelled of something sweet and spicy. She enveloped him with this scent, completely unnatural in the cold, damp cellar.

One of the spiders shook itself, lifted its abdomen, and suddenly burrowed under Sullen's skin. Just a moment ago, it had been sitting on top, rubbing its furry legs contentedly, and now it was the large lump under his skin.

Victor felt the disgusting creature wriggling inside him, its legs pushing through his flesh. The lump slowly moved upwards along his chest. The other spiders repeated its action; one of them slowly, as if for show, burrowed inside... then the second...

Something snapped inside Victor, and he howled... low and plaintive... like an animal.

* * *

"Arachnophobia is one of the most common fears among people," Anna quoted. "It affects one in ten men and half of all women. That's what my dad told me," she explained. "I was afraid of spiders as a child too."

"Will he lose his mind?" I asked just in case. Not that I felt sorry for Sullen. That bastard deserved everything coming his way for messing with my family. But he still hadn't told us what we needed to know.

"I hope Fike can keep herself under control," Anna replied doubtfully. "Though she's always been a bit crazy. But she is sweet."

"Fike?" I was puzzled by the unfamiliar name.

"That's what they called Sofia in Austria," Anna explained. "A nickname, like Soph or Sonya. We met in an Austrian boarding school. Two Russian girls among two hundred Germans. Her parents were divorcing... splitting yachts and factories... They had no time for her. And you know about my parents."

When Anna suggested involving Sofia Pars, I was skeptical, but she assured me she trusted the "Spider Queen" completely. So I agreed. There were no better ideas anyway.

Go beat up Sullen? Thrash him so he couldn't get up? Sure, I could do that. Maybe even take down his gang if things went well. And then what? Everyone liked to act tough out in the streets with the rest of the hood watching, but he'd go to the cops later and file a report, and then I'd end up in jail just like my dad.

"Like father, like son," they'd say in court. Heredity. Genes. It would be the outcome everyone expected and wanted.

Sullen would never have thought of such a complex scheme. Fabricating evidence, pressuring my mom, knowing it would provoke me... It was too complicated for him. Someone tipped him off. Who? And more importantly, why?

I had two options left. Solve the problem with my fists, which would surely get me kicked out of the game. Or negotiate, hoping Sullen would offer something decent. Either way, I was facing a total loss.

Anna's idea initially sounded crazy, but at least it gave us a chance.

Sofia was thrilled about the upcoming operation. It wasn't so much that she wanted to help us, but her artistic nature demanded an outlet, and this was a perfect opportunity to shine.

The blogger, model, and aspiring singer dumped out the contents of two wardrobes and, running around the apartment in nothing but transparent panties, began crafting looks for herself and her friend.

She immediately put on a frivolous blonde wig: "For contrast — the yin and the yang — cool, right?"

Anna found her clothes a bit tight. I was pleased to discover that the champion, with her athletic body, had a rather large and beautifully shaped chest. Shameless in cyberspace, Anna was a bit shy here in real life, which only added to her charm.

Meanwhile, after making sure Charlotte was securely locked in her terrarium, I settled into a chair with a cup of coffee, admiring their graceful figures. As the girls flitted past me, my anger slowly faded, giving way to pure sportsmanship.

I had to wait out Sullen's kidnapping two blocks away in a nearly always deserted courtyard. Fifteen minutes later, the Maserati pulled into the archway and we moved the unconscious figure to the back seat.

Sophia gently sat down beside me and placed Sullen's head on her lap. If we were stopped, we could say he was just tired and resting. But our precaution turned out to be unnecessary. The cops didn't even glance our way, and we reached our destination without incident.

"There are only two fully functional VR pods," Anna warned. "The other two interfaces I have are locked in spectator mode. The most they can do is create an avatar of the spectator, like a hologram. Physical interaction isn't possible with them."

"Can I do the interrogating? Annchen, please?" Sophia clasped her hands to her chest and widened her eyes pleadingly. "I'll be careful... Really... Just tell me what to ask... He'll tell me everything... Even what he's long forgotten."

The "spectator" interfaces looked like ordinary VR headsets. Anna and I sat on the couch in the living room, simultaneously moving through the virtual space like silent ghosts, using gloves to input the controls.

We stayed "silent" so we could communicate in the real world. Soon, we became invisible too. Our avatars looked rather pathetic, so after making our presence known and giving Sullen something to think about, we let Sophia take over completely.

When the lump on Sullen's chest opened, spurting a thin stream of blood, and curious spider legs emerged, the jerk broke down.

He spoke for a long time, eagerly interrupting himself, as if hoping that all the new details of his hideous existence would stop what was happening.

Sullen confessed to five cases of mugging ("only a sucker flashes his wallet like that"), two rapes ("she was the one reaching for our beer, then she started playing hard to get") and even one murder ("he felt warm, so we covered him with leaves so the janitor would find him").

He also admitted to ambushing me with the brass knuckles the night I was waiting for a taxi, which didn't surprise me at all. His entire confession was meticulously recorded by a 3D camera in the game, just in case. The most interesting part was something else. Just the day before yesterday, an "important individual" had met with Sullen and began asking whether Victor knew me and had any connections to my family.

And then today, Sullen received a phone with

fake screenshots and instructions to use them to extort my parents (who had lived through the 1990s and remembered the mob chaos that reigned in Russia back then) and to thereby force me to negotiate.

He had even assumed that the two girls' surprise appearance was a reward for a job well done.

"Who's your boss, you bastard?" Sophia hissed in his ear. "Tell me his name!"

The spider on Sullen's chest angrily waggled its legs, as if affirming the blonde's words.

"Sloinsky... or Slonimsky... Modest Slonimsky... He owns a nightclub downtown... And half the city's hookers work for him... Him — it was all him!"

Shiloh! So, it was that sleazeball after all. I had figured the trail would lead me to the MosTech execs or perhaps a mystery player, but it turned out to be much simpler.

Shiloh decided to hedge his bets. Or maybe he was just offended by my audacity and wanted me to crawl back to him on my knees begging for his patronage. After all, he could easily solve any real-world problems that he had created in the first place.

Sophia also realized that the conversation ended here. Whereas she had played the role of a determined girl from a horror movie prior to Sullen's confession, now her face just looked serious.

My conscience was clear too. I had known that my classmate Victor had grown up to be a bad person, and now I was convinced that for someone like him, anything went.

"Did you like the spiders?" Sophia taunted, not waiting for a reply. "Then allow me to introduce you to their mother!"

A new sound appeared in the room. Whereas earlier it had been the rustling of dozens of tiny legs — somewhat like the rustle of leaves — now it was more like the confident creaking of a powerful chitinous shell.

A spider leg appeared above the slab to which Sullen was tied. It was black, hairy, and very large — about the thickness of my arm. Sullen saw it too and froze; it seemed he even stopped breathing from fear.

A smaller copy of Lolf, laboriously dragging her massive abdomen, crawled onto Sullen's body. She curiously prodded the thug with her front appendages, which looked like short legs.

"It seems she likes you," Sophia laughed. "But remember, spiders have a completely different physiology. Even though she's a girl, her ovipositor... It looks more like... Well, you'll see it... Hell, you'll even be able to *feel* it..."

The ovipositor emerged as a tentacle from the plump abdomen of the giant spider. It wavered in the air, then started probing Sullen's body. And that's when he began to howl again.

I didn't watch the rest. What was happening in the room now resembled twisted porn — not even zoophilia, but more like arachnophilia. If Sullen retained even a shred of sanity after this, he certainly wouldn't tell anyone about it.

After the procedure, we took the trembling, drooling Sullen to a small but very serious-looking mental clinic.

Anna knew the address. When I asked how, she replied, "I've spent half my life in places like this," which killed my curiosity.

A young, respectable doctor wearing fashionable glasses with a Prada frame listened to us carefully and said that "insect crawling syndrome" is characteristic of schizophrenia or paranoia.

At first, he talked about some "guardianship rights," but when he saw three thousand euros, he immediately changed his mind. It turned out that Sullen urgently needed a thorough examination, which would last at least two months. And yes, any contact with the outside world was strictly not recommended.

At the last moment, I left the doctor the phone number of Sullen's grandmother, asking him to warn the elderly woman but under no circumstances return her grandson, under penalty of a full refund.

As we were leaving, I glanced at the neat windows with tightly drawn white curtains and thick steel bars. It was a real private prison, and to end up here, you didn't need a prosecutor or a court. Getting out was almost impossible.

After that, I looked at Anna differently. To go through all that and retain sanity and faith in herself and her righteousness... that deserved, at the very least, respect.

"What are you going to do?" Anna asked.

She noticed my look but interpreted it her own way.

"With Shiloh?"

"Who else?"

"First, I'm going to get a good night's sleep," I said, and that was the absolute truth.

I had hardly slept the previous night. I had run all day on pure adrenaline, and now my energy was draining away like air from a punctured balloon.

"Then I'll take you home," she offered unexpectedly.

The girls dropped me off on the other side of the building to avoid attracting unnecessary attention from the other neighborhood thugs. As I approached the entrance, Sullen's gang was still sitting on the benches. Not more than an hour and a half had passed. But without their leader, they didn't dare make a move.

As soon as I entered the building, my phone vibrated in my pocket.

"I know who it is!" Marina declared as soon as I answered.

She was apparently driving somewhere; I could hear her preferred lounge EDM playing on the car speakers.

"Who?" My mind was still occupied with the Sullen and Shiloh business, so I didn't immediately remember the assignment I'd given her.

"You won't believe it!" Marina was so excited that she didn't notice my confusion. "I got the video recordings... Aren't I amazing?!.. And I've already watched them... You would never guess... WHERE THE HELL ARE YOU GOING, DUM-BASS?!"

I smiled, imagining the blonde behind the wheel and recalling her driving style.

"Marina, come over to my place, I'm at my parents' house. You can tell me everything here!"

I realized that the mystery was almost solved, and I was fully awake with anticipation.

"Wait a sec... This imbecile... He's trying to overtake..." I heard a thump and rustling, as if the phone had been thrown onto the passenger seat.

"Marina, be careful!" An acute sense of danger washed over me.

"WHAT THE HELL ARE YOU DOING, YOU FREAK?!" Marina screamed.

A dull thud sounded over the phone and then there was silence.

E N D   O F   B O O K   T H R E E

Want to be the first to know about our latest LitRPG, sci fi and fantasy titles from your favorite authors?

Subscribe to our **New Releases** newsletter:
http://eepurl.com/b7niIL

Thank you for reading *Kill or Die!*
If you like what you've read, check out other sci-fi, fantasy and LitRPG novels published by Magic Dome Books:

NEW RELEASES!

Crossroads of Oblivion
a portal progression fantasy adventure series
by Dem Mikhailov

Gakko Academy
a portal progression fantasy adventure series
by Evgeny Alexeev

War Eternal
a military space adventure LitRPG series
by Yuri Vinokuroff

The Hunter's Code
a LitRPG series by Yuri Vinokuroff & Oleg Sapphire

The Order of Architects
a portal progression series
by Yuri Vinokuroff & Oleg Sapphire

I Will Be Emperor
a space adventure progression fantasy series
by Yuri Vinokuroff

An Ideal World for a Sociopath
a LitRPG series by Oleg Sapphire

The Healer's Way
a LitRPG series by Oleg Sapphire & Alexey Kovtunov

A Shelter in Spacetime
a LitRPG series by Dmitry Dornichev

The Village
a LitRPG progression fantasy series
by Dmitry Dornichev & Alexey Kovtunov

The Dark Healer
a historical progression fantasy series
by Alex Toxic & Nadya Lee

Ghost in the System
An apocalypse LitRPG series by Alexey Kovtunov

The Last Portal Jumper
a LitRPG series by Konstantin Zubov

Lord of the System
a LitRPG progression fantasy series by
Alex Toxic and Furious Miki

Kill to Live
a LitRPG progression fantasy adventure series
by George Bor and Yuri Vinokuroff

Kill or Die
a LitRPG series by Alex Toxic

The Strongest Student
a portal progression action fantasy series
by Andrei Tkachev

Living Ice
a portal progression alternative history series
by Dmitry Sheleg

Law of the Jungle
a Wuxia Progression Fantasy Adventure Series
By Vasily Mahanenko

Reality Benders
a LitRPG series by Michael Atamanov

The Dark Herbalist
a LitRPG series by Michael Atamanov

Perimeter Defense
a LitRPG series by Michael Atamanov

League of Losers
a LitRPG series by Michael Atamanov

Chaos' Game
a LitRPG series by Alexey Svadkovsky

The Way of the Shaman
a LitRPG series by Vasily Mahanenko

The Alchemist
a LitRPG series by Vasily Mahanenko

Dark Paladin
a LitRPG series by Vasily Mahanenko

Galactogon
a LitRPG series by Vasily Mahanenko

Invasion
a LitRPG series by Vasily Mahanenko

World of the Changed
a LitRPG series by Vasily Mahanenko

The Bear Clan
a LitRPG series by Vasily Mahanenko

Starting Point
a LitRPG series by Vasily Mahanenko

The Bard from Barliona
a LitRPG series
by Eugenia Dmitrieva and Vasily Mahanenko

Condemned
(Lord Valevsky: Last of The Line)
a Progression Fantasy series
by Vasily Mahanenko

Loner
a LitRPG series by Alex Kosh

A Buccaneer's Due
a LitRPG series by Igor Knox

A Student Wants to Live
a LitRPG series by Boris Romanovsky

The Goldenblood Heir
a LitRPG series by Boris Romanovsky

The One Who Changes the Future
a dystopian portal progression fantasy series
by Boris Romanovsky

Level Up
a LitRPG series by Dan Sugralinov

Respawn Trials
a LitRPG series by Andrei Livadny

The Expansion (The History of the Galaxy)
a Space Exploration Saga by A. Livadny

The Range
a LitRPG series by Yuri Ulengov

Point Apocalypse
a near-future action thriller by Alex Bobl

Moskau
a dystopian thriller by G. Zotov

El Diablo
a supernatural thriller by G.Zotov

Mirror World
a LitRPG series by Alexey Osadchuk

Underdog
a LitRPG series by Alexey Osadchuk

Last Life
a Progression Fantasy series by Alexey Osadchuk

Alpha Rome
a LitRPG series by Ros Per

An NPC's Path
a LitRPG series by Pavel Kornev

Fantasia
a LitRPG series by Simon Vale

The Sublime Electricity
a steampunk series by Pavel Kornev

Small Unit Tactics
a LitRPG series by Alexander Romanov

Black Centurion
a LitRPG standalone by Alexander Romanov

Rorkh
A LitRPG Series by Vova Bo

Thunder Rumbles Twice
A Wuxia Series by V. Kriptonov & M. Bachurova

Citadel World
a sci fi series by Kir Lukovkin

You're in Game!
LitRPG Stories from Our Bestselling Authors

You're in Game-2!
More LitRPG stories set in your favorite worlds

The Fairy Code
a Romantic Fantasy series by Kaitlyn Weiss

***The Charmed* Fjords**
a Romantic Fantasy series by Marina Surzhevskaya

More books and series are coming out soon!

In order to have new books of the series translated faster, we need your help and support! Please consider leaving a review or spread the word by recommending *Kill or Die* to your friends and posting the link on social media. The more people buy the book, the sooner we'll be able to make new translations available.

Thank you!

Till next time!